WE. ARE. FAMILY.

WE. ARE. FAMILY.

PAUL MITCHELL

MidnightSun

First published 2016 by MidnightSun Publishing Pty Ltd
PO Box 3647, Rundle Mall, SA 5000, Australia.
www.midnightsunpublishing.com

Cataloguing-in-Publication entry is available from the
National Library of Australia.
http://catalogue.nla.gov.au

Cover and internal design by Kim Lock

Printed and bound in Australia by Griffin Press. The papers used by MidnightSun
in the manufacture of this book are natural, recyclable products made from wood
grown in sustainable plantation forests.

In memory of my grandmother, Shirley Trotter (nee Millar).
I can still hear your voice.

We. Are. Family.

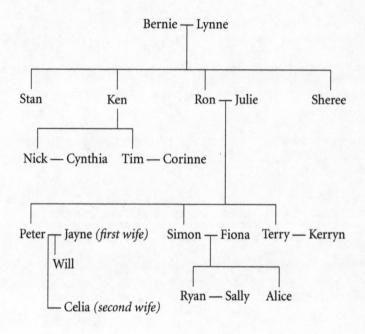

1. The Stevensons

Ron Stevenson drove his family back home to Corumbul from Tonvale in his new yellow Corona station wagon. It had adjustable seating and a push-button FM radio. He pushed a button and the radio changed stations to the one he had preset. A miracle. He wanted to clap his hands but he kept them on the wheel. In the rear-vision mirror he saw his three boys, sitting in the backseat. The eldest, Peter, was staring at the paddocks and the hay bales clumped beside windmills and puddles.

Peter was imagining the paddocks were football grounds. That dark green one, just now, was VFL Park, Waverly. If Ron had known that he'd have turned around and ruffled his son's hair. The paddocks went on for miles and Peter wondered whether Collingwood could beat Carlton in next week's semi-final. He hoped it would rain next Saturday because then the 'Pies would have more chance against the Blues' famous mosquito fleet. They would run the pants off Collingwood unless it was muddy. He saw Ricky 'The Racehorse' Barham dashing along the wing of a paddock, touching the ball in a puddle then kicking long. As the car took a bend, Peter's waterlogged footy rolled on the floor.

Ron wore a short-sleeve business shirt and tie. He'd thought he might be able to duck down to the office after the trip. A stupid idea and he knew it. They wouldn't make it home until after eight because they'd have to stop for fish and chips, or else the kids would be at him and Julie the rest of the way. 'When are we going to get the fish and greasies?' they'd whine. The two younger boys, Simon and Terry, were at each other as it was, fighting over a Darth Vader doll. It had a missing foot, but they still wanted it bad. Ron waited for Julie to turn around and barrel them, but she kept her eyes on the highway as if she were trying to stare a hole into the windscreen. She had a bee in her bonnet, he thought. And this one isn't going to buzz out in a hurry.

It had rained on and off all day. In Tonvale, the grass out front of the white stone building had been smooth like a skating rink. Peter had slipped around, trying to kick his footy. His brothers got amongst it, but they weren't much fun. They were too little to kick properly, and they just rolled around and tackled each other. Then his dad had joined in.

The last few months, Ron had been busy at work learning how to be the transport company's branch manager. He'd always worked for them, but this was his first go at the top job. And he was tired out. But he'd felt light this afternoon as he'd dashed around in the drizzle.

'Good roost,' he'd said, even when the ball had dribbled off Terry's sneaker. Ron would have copped an earful as a kid for kicking as shithouse as that. But his old man had long disappeared. So it didn't matter what he thought. Ron chased Simon and Terry. Just for fun, to keep them on their toes. They laughed and tackled each other all the more.

Peter got sick of his brothers getting all the attention. He walked to the window and looked in. He saw his mum. She was in her white polo neck jumper, talking to a nurse in a chalk blue dress. They were standing next to his Aunty Sheree who was lying in bed. It was the middle of the afternoon and she was asleep already, her scraggy yellow hair spread on her pillow. Next to his aunty were three other beds, grey blankets on them but no one underneath. His mum saw him. She mouthed *Go!* and shooed him away with a swipe of her arm.

Peter copped an elbow from Simon, who was having another go at getting Darth Vader from Terry's grip. In the front seat, Julie turned, her voice like a radio without much signal.

'Stop it you three.'

'I wasn't doing anything.'

'Just shut up. All of you, shut up.'

Ron hadn't said anything for half an hour, but he knew he was included. The apple cart was already upset and he didn't want any more fruit to fly off.

Everyone shut up. Then Terry made a grab for Darth Vader's light sabre. Simon belted him and Terry squealed. Julie swung around and Peter noticed what Ron hadn't: the red rims of her eyes.

'Right...' she said, her voice shaky.

Ron waited, they all did, for her to say, 'Ronald, stop the car, your sons can walk home!' But her voice drifted off and all they could hear was the Corona and its highway whistle.

Soon the sky turned rough charcoal like the barbecue when Ron forgot to clean it. Stars queued up quietly on the horizon and Ron saw his youngest two were asleep, their arms and legs in a tangle. He wanted to reach over and touch them, but that was Julie's job. He kept on with the driving, head down, his mind full of what he didn't want in it: which trucks were going to come back with gear problems next week, and which tractors were causing dramas at whose farms. The trucking world was a bugger, but he was too short for wood chopping, as his old man had told him. Five hundred times.

No matter where they'd moved, Ron had always made sure Sheree could set up house in the same town as his job. Wasn't that enough?

The car vibrated and Peter allowed his head to thrum against the glass. He asked himself the same questions he'd asked his parents all day.

Why couldn't he go into Aunty Sheree's room today? Why did they take her into the white building? Is it a hospital? Is she coming back home to Corumbul?

They'd all got the same answer: 'Good boys should be seen and not heard.'

His aunty was lying in a grey bed in Tonvale tonight instead of her own, but no one would tell him anything.

12

Whenever his mum took him and his brothers to their aunty's house, Peter was happy. Because that's when his mum was happy. She got into her flowery dress and a good mood, and Peter skipped beside her on the footpath. He leapt the steps of his aunty's bricked-in patio and felt a warm buzz when he saw the colours shooting from her glass kookaburra mobile hanging low at her front door.

Ron thought that bloody mobile was a health hazard. His hands were tighter now on the wheel. She's his sister. And he's not bloody made of stone. He's got feelings.

'What was I supposed to do, Julie?'

He said it loud enough to be heard above the car whistle. Which was really pissing Ron off. It was supposed to be a new car. Julie kept her voice low like he was a waste of her breath.

'I'm not discussing it now.'

Bugger her. She always decided when they could talk and when they couldn't. Ron gunned the accelerator. The Corona whooshed and he thought that would be enough to let Julie know he was miffed. But, of course, it was alright for her to talk again, even though she'd just said she wasn't discussing it. And she didn't even look at him when she did, just peered at the hills turning black as her mood.

'Your own sister!'

'What was I supposed to do?'

Simon stirred and Peter shut his eyes quickly.

'The kids!' Julie hissed.

Ron shook his head.

The kids don't care, he thought.

Peter would skip up his aunty's patio and past the rainbow kookaburra. Once he got through the forest of fat-leaved rubber plants in his aunty's corridor, he came to long strings of hanging beads that made a coloured picture of Jesus. He always beat his mum and brothers to Jesus. He smashed both fists into Jesus' stomach and burst into the kitchen, the beads brushing his face.

Sheree's kitchen was a wall of cupboards with mesh holes in the doors. Peter thought they were so the food could breathe. Sheree would always be at her table, poking around in the junk from the op shop that she'd spent her dole money on: porcelain cats, watering cans, huge biscuit tins, dusty vases, and big fluffy toys. When she stuck her head out from behind it all, Peter thought she looked like a canary poking out of a clock.

'Greetings my darlings, my sweet lovelies... Do you want a lolly?'

Peter and Simon always knew better than to take the bait, but Terry didn't.

'Yes please, yes please,' he'd say and Sheree would tell him she didn't have any.

'But I've got something better.'

One day she pulled from her pile of junk a doll that was plain dumb compared to a Chewbacca. It was a soldier, his uniform dyed purple, yellow and red, and where he should have held a rifle she'd stuck a guitar made of balsa wood. As stupid as it was, Peter had kept it and plonked it on his windowsill to watch over him at night.

When Sheree handed out her presents, her eyes were as big

as hubcaps and her bright lipsticked mouth stretched into a smile that didn't show her teeth. Peter thought her smile looked like a skinny red banana stuck to her face. After they'd received their gifts, Peter and his brothers would go outside and play on the wooden swing set she'd made especially for them. Back when she had a job. The set was painted like a rainbow. Peter would swing back and forward, looking through the window and watching his mum and aunty at the kitchen table. Sheree laughed and waved her hands around and Julie giggled.

His aunty's house was like a carnival. Peter wished they could all move down the road and live with her. Aunty Sheree would, he was sure, let everyone sleep on the wonky beds in her spare rooms.

'Why are you only happy at Aunty Sheree's?' he'd asked his mum once on the way home. She'd looked at him with squinty eyes and said nothing for a while. Then she'd said he and his brothers were driving her mad with their questions and couldn't they behave better, more like a yard manager's sons?

Peter watched his mum grip her handbag in the green light from the dashboard. Ron looked at the bag, too, wondering if it was supposed to be his neck and with one more squeeze she'd get the life out of him. Julie turned to the darkness in the back-seat and Peter closed his eyes again.

'Ron—'

'I've got to head to work when we get back.'

'Too busy for anyone! Even your own sister!'

Ron took a slow, deep breath. He turned to Julie and was about to let rip but, as always, he couldn't think of anything to say. He swallowed his anger and it tasted like burnt toast. Julie unwrapped a piece of gum. She chewed so hard on it that Ron thought he could hear her above that damned car whistle.

The sky blackened. Rain splashed Peter's window and he looked at his reflection in the droplets. He was sure now his aunty would be staying in that bed in Tonvale. For good. He remembered the room they'd left her in, the white walls and the grey beds. He couldn't imagine what his bright-coloured aunty would do in there all day. The more he churned it, the more he thought it was some kind of hospital. And his aunty was there because he'd dobbed on her.

She'd done a wee in her backyard, holding her pink and orange skirt in her teeth. She was supposed to be babysitting him and his brothers. Peter had told his mum about it that night and she'd said, 'Don't worry, don't think about it anymore.'

Then Julie had told Ron. And Ron had rung the Tonvale Mental Hospital. What else was he supposed to do? He'd told Julie they couldn't have their kids dealing with that kind of thing. 'She's finally lost her marbles, completely,' he'd added, then turned off their bedside lamp.

After Peter dobbed on her, they didn't visit Sheree much. And she hadn't been at her kitchen table the few times they had. She'd been flopped instead in her beanbag in the lounge, surrounded by her hand-made cushions. Sometimes she'd lifted her skirt up and down like it was annoying her. When she'd done that, Peter's mum had sent him and his brothers out to play on the swings. Another time her church friends were there, praying. A woman in a white dress had made Sheree's dinner and then done her dishes. The last time Peter had seen Sheree at her house she had been sitting on the backyard swing. She had bare feet even though it was winter. She had smiled then cried, over and over. Her red banana lips had gone up and down like a clown trying to learn how to be in the circus.

Today, Sheree had slept all the way in the backseat, even when Ron had turned up the radio. Peter loved that new ELO song. He'd sung along. Something about a woman, sweet-talking.

He felt bad for singing now.

The window vibrated and Peter's head nodded against it. His eyes went heavy. His parents were dark shapes in the front seats. Then his mum's voice.

'The church people said they'd look after her. You knew that... And me. I could have looked after her. But we couldn't have that, could we? What would the town say?'

Her breath came in short gasps.

'And what about when we move next? What happens then?'

Ron went silent for a long time. When he finally answered, the Corona was on the outskirts of Corumbul.

'She'll get looked after.'

Ron turned the car down their street. He and Julie didn't look at Sheree's house as they passed it. But Peter did. Ron turned to Julie, but she wouldn't take her eyes off the windscreen wipers. Peter watched them too, flicking back and forth, trying to touch each other but never making the distance.

2. Ron Stevenson

He only knew what everyone else in Laharum knew: The Butcher was the archenemy's new gun forward. Derrinallum had recruited him from Echuca. Fresh for the '51 season. No one knew what he looked like because no one in Laharum had clapped eyes on him. He was just chatter around the school monkey bars and whispers in the dark at the flicks. A myth Ron's older brothers, Stan and Ken, tossed around as they all climbed the elm behind the farmhouse.

They say The Butcher carries two carcasses from his van to his bloody sawdust counter.

The Butcher's thighs are as thick as a bull's. Two bulls.

Did you know The Butcher was pissed off one Satdee because Echuca lost so he rammed his shoulder into the clubroom wall and he fell through? Right into the Visitors' change room? Right in the middle of when they were singing their theme song!

His brothers went on and on. Ron looked down from his perch to the farmhouse and its peeling tin red roof. He wondered if his father was in there, worrying about The Butcher.

Maybe. But Bernie Stevenson was tough as nails that had been banged into a shed wall, gone rusty, and pulled out again. He'd won his division's boxing title in the war. Ron would hear him puffing as he shadow sparred behind the shed. He'd never seen his father throw a fist in anger, but Ron had copped his belt and the back of his hand. Plenty of times.

His dad was wiry. His arms were better suited to steering cows around paddocks than carrying them dead on his shoulders. So Ron was glad Bernie was Laharum's centre-half-forward. Because that was the position The Butcher played for Derry. His dad and The Butcher wouldn't meet on the field. And that was good. Because Ron had been to the Laharum Butchers. He'd seen the chart on the wall. All the different cuts of beef, marked for chopping up. The Butcher of Derry would have some other poor Laharum Demon on his wall chart, not Ron's dad.

'They say The Butcher carries a carcass on each shoulder and loves the smell of blood,' Joyce McKenzie said as she put the last tin of peaches into a brown paper bag for Ron's mum, Lynne. It was the week before Laharum was set to meet Derry in round one and Ron was with his mum at McKenzie's Mixed Business. Joyce was behind the counter, straw hat on as usual. She'd packed Lynne's apples, pears and bi-carb of soda into paper bags sensibly. But she'd been strangely quiet before her outburst.

'It's just Derrinallum trying to stir us up, Joyce,' said Lynne.

She pulled up the flap pocket on her big floral dress and grabbed out her purse. She gave Joyce her shillings, smiled and rearranged her brown curly updo.

'Well, good luck to Bernie. Glad my Howie's not playing...'

According to Bernie, her Howie couldn't kick over a jam tin. Lynne huffed and didn't say goodbye or thank you. She dragged her bags and Ron to the door. The shop bell rang them out and they chugged back to the farm in the 29th Anniversary Buick. Ron was embarrassed to be seen in that car. It didn't have a roof. Everyone's car had a roof for God's sake.

He asked his mum if she was scared of The Butcher.

'Ronald, sit back in your seat and keep quiet will you?'

He was a church mouse all the way back to the farm.

The Derrinallum Kangaroos had won the 1950 Horsham District Premiership. They'd played Laharum in the Grand Final and beaten them by 62 points. They'd slammed the Demons into the brick-hard oval time after time. And they'd won the punch-up on centre wing in the third quarter.

Ron had stood next to his father all day. Bernie hadn't talked to him. He rarely did. Except to say, *Get out of me bloody road, runt.* Bernie hadn't played in the Grand Final because his wonky knee from the war had given him trouble. He could barely stand. But he'd held his beer bottle so tight Ron had thought he was going to smash it to pieces. When the punch-up started, he wondered if his father would jump the fence. But Bernie had just yelled at the umpy to open his fucking eyes.

After his mates had finished getting their belting, Bernie had limped into the rooms and savaged them.

'Where's your fucken pride in the jumper?'

The Demons had to go one better this year. They had to win the flag. Regardless of The Butcher. Laharum hadn't won a premiership for twenty-two years and Derrinallum couldn't keep having it their own way. That's what the coach, the players, the runners, the boot-studders, and even the juniors said. Ron didn't play in the juniors, he was too little, but he hung around the club all pre-season. The Demons were serious. No sky-larking, lots of sprints, no ball work at training until a month before the first game. Kids weren't even allowed in the rooms when the senior team was in there. It was a new rule to show how fair dinkum they were, Ron's brothers said. And Bernie's knee was finally right to go. He was set to play in the first round, the Grand Final replay against Derrinallum.

And so was The Butcher.

'Couldn't give two hoots about him,' Bernie said when Lynne asked him if The Butcher was as tough as everyone said. It was the night before the game. Mutton dinner in kero light.

'Only asking,' Lynne said, clearing the plates and popping them in the dish bucket.

'And I'm only tellin'.'

It was a Demons home game on a blue, autumn day with streaks of cloud on the horizon. But it was chilly, even at midday. It would be freezing by the final siren, Ron thought. His mum sat first, then everyone joined her on the tartan blanket in front of the Buick. It was the Stevensons' spot: outer wing with the thickest pine trees protecting them from the wind. The Thermos sat with them and next to it a basket full of food: curried egg sandwiches, jelly slice, pickles, cream buns and dry biscuits. They watched the reserves play and Stan and Ken knocked off most of the egg sandwiches. They had their blue and red Laharum jumpers on and it made Ron jealous. His mum hadn't finished knitting his. And she hadn't brought it with her today to work on. His sister Sheree was in her sailor dress, whinging and banging her fists on her knees. Lynne filled the girl's face with cream bun as the Demons ran out. The Stevensons jumped from their blanket as one and roared. Car horns tooted and Bernie ran the edge of the Demon pack. He bent down and pretended to pick up a ball, first one side then the other. The team got warmed up with a few sprints then had a kick together near the goals at the south end.

Derrinallum didn't come out for another five minutes. But the jeering started up as soon as the first blue and white jumper charged from the clubrooms. And it didn't let up until the Kangaroos had gathered in the middle of the ground.

It wasn't hard to spot The Butcher. There were nineteen blokes in blue and white striped jumpers and then there was a tree trunk with arms. The Butcher was six foot or more and the only player on the field with tattoos. Ron could see the dark blue smudges on his skin. Probably skulls with snakes weaving through the eyeholes, he thought. When the Kangaroos took off again, The Butcher didn't run so much as shunt along the clubroom flank. His legs were browner than the rest of his mates' and they pistoned up and down.

Ron got a closer look at The Butcher's head. His face was narrow, like a hawk's. And he had a boofy hairdo like Frankie Laine. The Butcher looked like he could rock and roll in more ways than one.

The teams headed to their positions. Lynne sucked in a sharp breath because Bernie was off to centre-half-forward, as expected, but The Butcher was rumbling to centre-half-back.

'Bloody hell,' Stan groaned. 'He's gunna play on Dad'.

'Language,' Lynne hushed.

Bernie offered his hand for The Butcher to shake and the big man took it. Then he stepped sideways and cannoned his beefy shoulder into Bernie so hard that it rocked Ron's father on his heels. Before he could right himself, The Butcher did it again and Bernie was on the ground rubbing his shoulder. Players ringed them and a scuffle started. Nothing serious, just push and shove. The umpy trotted from the centre to sort it out. Bernie got up. He ignored the scrap going on around him and the umpire's shaking finger. He pulled his leg in a thigh stretch. The umpire finished his warnings and headed back to the football he'd left in the centre circle. The Butcher let loose an elbow into Bernie's ribs that doubled him over.

'Ronald,' his mum said, 'you and Sheree head to The Valley to play.'

The Valley was behind the line of cars their Buick was in. It was a dip sheltered by a row of low-hanging pine tree branches where kids played once they got sick of the footy. But Ron wasn't going down there today, not on your life.

'I'm watching the footy!'

'You'll do what I say.'

'No!'

There were about ten things he shouldn't say to his mum, but 'no' was top of the list. She picked Ron up by his armpit,

Sheree too, and dragged them both to The Valley. She put both her hands on Ron's shoulders and burrowed a stare into him.

'If you so much as poke your head up near the car before I say you can, you'll be on barn duty for a week.'

A few weeks ago he'd done barn duty two days in a row. The worst job, of many, was cleaning the slime out of the horses' stable. His mum trooped up the rise and disappeared. And the siren sounded to start the game that Ron couldn't see.

Shit.

A huge roar went up then some faint booing that got louder. Then some shouting. Horns started tooting like it was New Year's Eve. It sounded as if everyone in the crowd was ready to fight someone. Ron crouched and hung onto Sheree. She'd started crying and wet her pants. He looked at the puddle in the dirt and didn't know what to do.

Lynne came back to The Valley for them at quarter-time and ushered them to the blanket. The scoreboard on the other side of the ground showed the Demons up by sixteen points. But the silence on the Stevensons' blanket made Ron feel like they were down thirty. His mum took off her shoes. She scratched so hard at her toes it was as if she were trying to get them off her feet. When the Demons dashed to a forty-seven-point lead late in the second quarter, Stan and Ken barely raised a cheer. They looked edgy. Ron had seen those looks before. Whenever their father was on the warpath at home and looking for the belt.

Bernie had a new opponent. A motley looking bloke with skinny white arms.

'Where's The Butcher?' Ron asked and his mum put her finger to her lips. Stan shook his head and looked along the wing at the rows of blankets with Derrinallum supporters sitting on them.

'Keep it down will ya?' he whispered.

Bernie took a speccie just before three-quarter time. He was on top of two Derry backmen and still heading skyward when the ball landed on his chest. The Demon crowd in front of the beer stand let rip. Ted 'Lion' Ryan snapped goals from each forward pocket in the last quarter. His second gave the Demons a sixty-three-point lead. The Dees were in front by more than the margin by which Derry had won last year's Grand Final. But instead of roaring, Stan and Ken headed for The Valley.

'Why aren't you watching the footy?' Ron asked as he followed them. Stan made for the pines, but Ken turned around.

'Don't want to.'

'Why not?'

He shook his head like it was the stupidest question he'd ever heard.

The final siren blasted, the Laharum crowd roared, and car horns tooted their songs of revenge into the cold air. The Demons slapped each other's shoulders and Derry trudged off the ground, some refusing to shake hands with their opponents. Once the ground was clear, every kid in the district ran on and kicked footies. Ron played with Stan and Ken and their mates. He picked up the ball, tried to kick it, but it spun pathetically from the end of his shoe. A boy with a crew cut and a long-sleeved Demons' jumper watched him with hands on hips. And cacked himself.

'Shut up, Randall,' Stan said.

'Sheila's kick,' Trevor Randall taunted.

Oh no, Ron thought, that's it. Stan's gunna have him.

Trevor was ox strong but sheep stupid. A smartarse, everyone knew it. And when it came to his family copping a ribbing, Stan never took a backward step.

Usually.

'Just watch your trap, Randall,' Stan said. And he walked towards the boundary line and the blanket. Ron stood amazed until big Syd Henty, still in his footy gear, yelled from the club-room doorway.

'Hey Stan, lads, your old man wants to see you blokes.'

Syd had a beer bottle in his hand. Behind him, men walked around the clubrooms. Some were bare-chested in shorts and socks, others still wore their jumpers above white jockstraps.

Stan didn't move. None of the boys did. They knew the rules.

'It's all right fellas. You can come in. Come and see the legend.'

The brothers crept up the wide concrete steps and the laugh-ter from the rooms got louder. Ron saw hairs on players' legs. Tommy 'Gun' Korth had a white bandage round his knee with a dark patch in the middle. Ron's stomach was light and he wanted to shit. But Syd slapped him on the back and ushered him in.

A cloud of blue smoke drifted above the men's heads. Their voices rose and fell like a car engine getting revved. Players sat on the white bench that ran around the walls. They smoked and tied big ice blocks covered in tea towels to their legs. Men were everywhere, smelling of beer and sweat and liniment, but Ron couldn't spot his father. And he'd lost sight of Syd. A hand fell on his shoulder and he cowered. But it was only Syd again, saying something he couldn't hear because just then the room roared and one voice chirped high above the rest.

'Rat ta tat, ta tatta ta tat...'

It was the Club President, Dicko Thomas, in his suit and standing on a chair. The room joined him and sang the Demons' theme song. Tommy Korth sat with his football boots in his hands, banging the stops to the beat. His redheaded son, Andy, had snuck into the rooms and Andy put his arm around his dad. He was Ron's mate from school. Ron waved at him and he waved back. He didn't have the chance to tell Ron the story then, the one his family wouldn't tell him. He had to wait until playtime on Monday.

'Nah? You're joking?' Andy said, wiping milk from his lips. 'Your mum sent you to The Valley? And you missed it all?'

Yeah, Ron had missed it. Missed his father decide that if he was going to get through the first game of '51 unscathed he'd better be smart. Ron hadn't seen the umpy bounce the ball to start the match. He'd missed the umpy keep his head down long enough for Bernie to splatter The Butcher sideways with a right cross. He hadn't seen, either, Andy run to the fence to see The Butcher carried off on a stretcher with his jaw at right angles.

Through the changeroom's forest of legs and arms, Ron finally caught sight of his father. He was sitting on the floor against a wall. His socks were down and a beer bottle rested between his legs. He waved Ron over and the boy scuttled to him. Dicky Thomas leant down and slapped Bernie on the shoulder.

'Bloody ripper, Bernie Boy!'

'You know little Ronnie, my son?' Bernie asked.

'How are ya mate?' the President said but Ron didn't notice. *Little Ronnie, my son.* He belonged to his father today.

3. Peter and Ron Stevenson

Corumbul in Gippsland had a view of the hills and they were always green. The Stevensons' white weatherboard was on the corner of Blake Court and Simmons Street. A low white brick fence surrounded its front yard where Peter was playing with his football on a warm March afternoon. A car crawled past, and a few streets away swans were honking on the ornamental lake. Peter heard the rise and fall of barracking high school kids in the nearby basketball stadium, the patter of water from a sprinkler against the side fence. Peter's elderly neighbours politely discussed which flowerbeds needed a soaking. Somewhere, way off, a golf club whacked a ball, whooshed, and then faded. His aunty, Sheree, he thought, couldn't hear any of these sounds. Because she was in a hospital bed in Tonvale now, had been there a few weeks.

'Sheree's not the full two bob, never has been,' he'd heard his dad tell someone on the phone. 'But she's getting looked after now. Apparently the voices are dying down.'

But Peter's were starting up.

He didn't know if they were in his head or his dreams, or coming out of his mouth. But he woke every night and his dressing gown hanging from his bedroom door billowed as if it were just about to yell at him. Like his father did, more and more. So Peter would turn on his bedside lamp, hoping he wouldn't wake his sleeping brothers, and the dressing gown would retreat.

Peter was skinny. Tall for his age. He could almost hold his football in one hand. He kicked goals between the small front yard trees carefully; too big a kick and he'd have to chase the ball down the street. He played football daily now because his mum had told the primary school he wouldn't be coming again until next year. Peter had been crying one day at school and the Principal had found him behind an elm tree. 'It's his aunty going into hospital,' Julie had told the Principal on the phone while Peter played patience in the lounge. 'He's taken it hard, for some reason. And the new town. He's having trouble getting used to it.'

Peter bounced his football, up and down, and it made soft thwacks on the couch grass. Later that day, he walked with his father and brothers through a paddock over five miles from town. There was no wind to shake up the long yellow grass. So Ron did it, pushing aside the raspy stalks then marching on.

'Watch for snakes, lad.'

Peter looked out for a black wobble and listened for a hiss. But there was only his father's steady breathing and the push and charge of his pale and hairy calves. Despite the heat and what they had to carry, Peter and his brothers had been told they could only rest when they made it to the dam. It was in the middle of a paddock and the size of a small lake. A farmer had told Ron he could fish there anytime. The farmer knew

Ron was the new truck company manager, but what favour he could possibly want out of him, Ron didn't know. He'd been in town six months, and everyone was still sounding him out. And he hadn't fished for ages. He didn't know where the decent spots were around Corumbul, and he hadn't had a minute to ask anyone. No time to scratch himself or even figure out if he was itchy.

'There's redfin in there, Ron,' the farmer had told him. 'Got big, they have.'

Peter walked and swung the empty plastic bucket his father had asked him to carry. He wouldn't get to watch Disneyland on TV tonight but his father was taking him fishing. His father never took him anywhere. He was always too busy. Peter didn't care about Disneyland now. What was it, anyway? A few singing mice?

His brothers carried their father's nylon fishing bag. Simon and Terry were trudging through the grass, but they wore huge grins. This adventure was so big the three boys thought they might never go home again. This might be their lives now and it would be okay.

'Watch yourselves getting under that fence. There's barbed wire.'

Peter copped a nick on the arm but didn't cry out. He didn't even check to see if there was blood. He picked up his bucket and followed his father, who'd turned into a massive insect. The folding chairs he carried were wings and the rods he held were large feelers. They shook and pointed.

'This way boys.'

It was silent at the dam. Not even a cicada. Then a cow groaned, way off. Peter's brothers were quiet. That was odd. They normally fought with each other, or tried to fight him. But they were motionless in their Stubbie shorts and singlets, waiting for their father to say something. To do something.

The dam was how wide? Peter couldn't kick a football across it. Maybe he could whack a tennis ball over it if he really got onto one. He stared into the distance. Glassy blue water. A gentle hill on the other side of the dam that hid more paddocks and maybe a farmhouse where the farmer was probably eating a dinner of sausages and salad. Wishing, no doubt, he was fishing at the dam.

Their father had brought cheese and gherkin sandwiches. Peter wanted one but he knew he had to wait. And some cordial. That'd be good. He swallowed the spit in his mouth instead.

The edge of the dam was hard brown dirt. Cracks in it. Big ants crawled in and out of them. Terry bent to investigate.

'Ant, Dad? Jar, jar?'

Terry wanted to take a sample of an overgrown crawly. Ron glared at him from under his toweling hat then pulled it further down on his forehead.

'No, Terry. And you lot are going to do exactly what I say or you won't be coming fishing again. No matter what your mum says.'

Ron took the fishing bag from Simon and put it on the ground. The boys fell to their haunches and watched him unzip it. From its guts he pulled a can of insect repellant, two red and white plastic floaters, and a clear plastic box full of sinkers and hooks.

'Will I have a rod of my own, Dad?'

'Shut up Peter. Just wait.'

Ron marched to a gum tree and its exposed roots. He found two large sticks and cracked sections from them so that both had a V at their ends. He tossed them next to his bag. Terry farted and Peter knew not to laugh. But Simon couldn't help himself.

'Remember what I said boys. No buggerising around.'

Ron took the bucket from Peter. He hadn't realised he was still holding it. His father crouched at the edge of the dam and scooped at the murky water with the bucket. He turned and tipped the water onto the dry earth, grabbed one of the sticks and pushed it into the now muddy ground. He picked up his rod and rested it in the V.

'Okay you lot. Let's go.'

There was another gum tree to their right. Ron led the boys towards it through knee-high grass.

'Stay out of the reeds,' he said when they reached the dam's edge.

Ron remembered his wife's words before he left: make sure they don't drown. Not, you've been working hard and it's a worry being the manager for the first time; enjoy taking the boys; you need a break. None of that. Just don't drown the kids. But if they were stupid enough to drown here, they could drown in a bucket of water. He snatched the bucket now and filled it from a spot where the reeds had separated. He doused the hard earth and put the second stick in the ground.

'Right, Peter, Simon: that's where you rest your rod. And you share it, all right? Now come here, both of you, and I'll show you how to fish.'

The lesson was quick. It was over before Peter had a chance to figure out how to hold the rod for casting, how to shut and open the bail arm, how to get the worm on the hook and what to do if you got tangled. Or how to catch a fish.

'Right, you blokes ready to roll?'

Simon nodded. He got it. It was simple for him. It was like he'd seen it all before. In a book or something. But he could barely read at all. Still, he could do Lego without looking at the instructions. And the smug look on his face said he reckoned he could have figured out this fishing business by himself.

'Yep, no worries,' Simon said.

'Good. Now let me be for a bit. And look after Terry.'

Ron sipped from his beer can then placed it on the ground beside his canvas chair. The air was cool enough to warrant putting on his velour track top but he didn't bother. He watched his floater. The sun had started for home and the water was sparkling orange.

Don't drown the kids.

Terry was under the gum tree playing with something shiny. Hooting at it. The other two were pulling their line out too often and casting it too much—and using too many bloody worms—but at least they weren't bothering him. He picked up his can and drank. He watched the line, then the floater, and then the line. Clouds were puffing on the horizon. He studied the backs of his hands. They were muddy from digging in the worm container. Greasy from the reel. He should have dried it after he'd oiled it. Stupid. He couldn't do a bloody thing right. Peter started up some trouble with Simon.

'Don't! It's my turn!'

'Shut up you lot! Let a man have some peace.'

But Ron didn't know if he wanted peace. That was the blessing and curse of fishing: if there were no bites and no fish, then it was quiet for sure. But he'd start to think and he didn't want to. Because it was always the same. If he wasn't at work, if he wasn't playing golf and if the fish weren't biting, it was quiet all right. But it wasn't peaceful. Because memories came at him like some of his bosses did up the chain: smiling, but underneath they wanted whatever they could get out of you. They didn't care if they'd dug your gizzards out by the time they'd finished. They just left you like a caught fish on a slimy cutting board.

Christ, he really couldn't do a bloody thing right.

He could have done more when he was young to help a kid who'd got disabled. All spastic and dumb because of Ron's brother.

He could have done more for his mum.

Could have stopped his dad from doing what he did.

No, he couldn't, he was too young. But he could have at least dobbed on him before, couldn't he? And then there was his sister, in a mental hospital.

Jesus! Years they'd lived together in the orphanage near Horsham. They couldn't protect each other then and he couldn't protect her this time either.

But what the hell else? Let her piss all day in front of his kids? What would be next?

He couldn't fix anything. He worked with trucks, for fuck's sake, and he didn't know anything about an engine, only prices and supply chains. He'd never fixed a single stuff up in any car he'd owned and he hadn't ever told Jules about his father or the orphanage or anything. Because if he did, he thought, he'd somehow end up on the bottom of a lake. In his head, it was like he was already there, in the arse end of a swamp, every day he walked around doing this and that.

He'd be no use to anyone dead as a doornail. If he was any use at all.

Christ, shut yourself up. Fucking sad sacks!

He drank from his can and put it down. Then he picked it up again, gulped and finished it.

Maybe the floater was distracting the fish? They could do that. Fish look up: what's that red and white thing, that plastic rubbish? We're getting out of here!

None of his boys were in sight.

Ron stood and, as if on cue, so did Peter. The boy stepped out of the reeds and back to his rod. Terry came out from behind the tree, carrying a stick and a sandwich. Shit, he'd forgotten to tell them to have dinner. But they were having it anyway. Good. He shouted to Peter, who was twenty yards away and playing with his rod like it was cricket bat.

'Where's Simon?'

His eldest pointed to the reeds on the other side of the dam.

Great. He wasn't fishing properly either. The useless buggers, Ron thought. They're not coming again.

He moved to sit, but before his bum hit the chair his floater ducked under and reappeared. He sat and waited. Nothing. The floater rested. He wound his line in and the hook was empty. He grabbed a new can and cracked it. Peter yelled across the water.

'Simon, where the hell are you?'

Ron shook his head.

'Shut up! You'll scare the fish!'

Peter left his line and headed through the long grass.

Peter had wanted from the get go to hold the rod, but Simon had done all the fishing.

'Give it to me.'

'Come back to school.'

'Give it to me...'

'Come back to school! Chicken! Bruck, bruck.'

'Don't Simon, it's my turn!'

'Shut up you lot,' their dad said. 'Let a man have some peace.'

Peter watched his father pick up his beer can and drink. He wanted to leave his rod and go over and fish with him. He watched his father, motionless in his chair. Hat low on his forehead. All his attention on his line and floater.

Peter wanted another lesson. He wanted his father to stand

behind him, hold his arms and take him through the fishing movements.

This way to cast, that's a boy. That way to tug the line when you get a bite. But he had to keep out of his dad's hair. Maybe that's why Ron always wore the hat.

Peter gave up trying to fish and let Simon take over. He watched him cast, expertly. The floater fell flat on the water and waited. Another cast, a re-bait, another cast, a change of direction, searching for a fish. That didn't come.

'This is borin. I'm garn for an explore,' Simon had said.

'We have to watch Terry.'

'You do it. I'm garn for an explore.'

And Simon had headed off. Through the reeds then the long grass. Peter had taken hold of the rod, but once it was in his hands he didn't want it. He didn't know what to do. He thought about asking his father for help. But Ron's silence and stillness were two languages, both of which meant keep away. Peter had put his rod on the stick and looked around for Terry. His little brother was under the tree playing with something shiny on the ground. Turning it over. Singing at it. Was it singing back? No, it was Simon.

'Peter, hey, Peter, ohhhhh, Peter...'

It was like his brother was next to him. Peter had felt around in the reeds and pulled them back, expecting to see Simon's idiotic, grinning face.

'Peter, hey...'

Simon was sitting in the reeds on the other side of the dam. It was a miracle.

'How can I hear you, idiot?'

'I heard that.' Simon laughed.

'How?'

'I dunno. You just can.'

'What are you doin' over there?'

'Shootin you. I'm a soldja. Bang, bang...'

'Idiot.'

'Piss off.'

'You!'

'Why don't you come to school anymore?'

Because he was scared. Because he woke in the night, every night, and there was a weight on him. And voices. He didn't know where they were coming from. He heard them at school. And when he drew a picture of his new house, time froze. It can't do that. He heard the voices then too, and he didn't know what was happening to him. It must be the UFO aliens from his *Biggest, Fastest, Smallest, Strangest* book. The same ones that flew around the Bermuda Triangle. And they were talking to him. And he wasn't going to school. He wanted to be at home and safe with his mum.

'None of your business, Simon.'

'Why don't you come? You a girl?'

'Shut your face.'

'Make me... Bang, bang.'

Simon had pointed a stick, shot at Peter, and Peter had ducked into the reeds. He'd soldier crawled, found a stick, and shot back. Simon had fallen, Peter had smiled and Simon had got up. Then Peter had shot him again and his brother had fallen once more. Peter had stood and tried to locate his brother in the far reeds. Get him in his sights.

'Peter, where's Simon?' his father had called.

'Over there. Somewhere.'

His brother had groaned and Peter had lowered his voice.

'Simon? You all right?'

Another groan.

'Simon, where the hell are you?'

Ron had shook his head and leant for his can.

'Shut up. You'll scare the fish!'

And Peter had headed for his brother.

He found him motionless on the bank.

'Simon? You all right?' He tugged at him. He was heavy and covered in dust. 'Simon?' He touched his brother's leg, looking for a snakebite. The touch tickled him and Simon giggled. He sprang up and poked Peter in the stomach.

'Ha, tricktcha!'

'You idiot!'

Peter fell on him, punched his chest, but not hard enough to do any damage. He wanted to warn him never to do it again. But Simon didn't get it. He never got anything. Except Lego. And fishing, it seemed.

'Rack off!' Simon shouted and his blows came hard and fast. Peter rolled away and got to his feet. The pair scrapped, but when Peter copped a blow to the temple that made the sight of his marauding brother wobble, he gave up.

On everything.

He fell backwards into the dam and lay in a foot of water. His eyes stung, but he didn't care and he didn't close them. Through the murk he saw his shimmering brother. He was shouting across the dam. Peter could have got up but he lay in the cold water holding his breath. It was so quiet. He heard his heart in his ears. He let his breath out slowly. Time froze. There were bubbles in his face and he choked. He thought he could hear his head breaking up and disappearing into the silt. His brother's muffled shouts were cool on his body, caressing him, sending him to sleep. It was peaceful. Something tore him from the water.

'Jesus, Peter!'

He coughed. It was his father's face. He'd never seen it so close. Each piece of stubble was magnified. Ron pushed his son to arm's length.

'Are you alright?'

Peter nodded.

'You're dripping bloody wet!'

He nodded again.

'What the hell did you do, Simon?'

'Nothing. He fell in.'

'I fell in,' Peter echoed.

'Jesus. You blokes are useless. We're going home. And you're not coming again.'

Terry looked at his brothers and laughed. 'We're not coming again,' he said, and threw the silver thing he'd been playing with into the dam.

'What was that, son?'

'What was that?'

'Jesus, Terry. Are you a parrot?'

'Are you a parrot?'

Ron reeled Simon and Peter's line in. It jammed halfway.

'Christ. It's a mess. It's tangled to shit!'

The two boys looked at their fishing rod then each other. Simon smiled. Peter couldn't tell if that meant, you're a hopeless fisherman or this is a cack. Either way, Peter wanted to run.

'I'm going to have to get in that bloody water now and untangle the line from that log. Did you notice there's a log there, Peter?'

'I didn't cast.'

Ah, Simon, gotcha. Dickhead! Peter gave him two fingers.

'Simon?' his father went on. 'Did you see the log?'

'Yeah, but...'

Ron shook his head.

'That's a decent rig I've got on there for you. You're not coming again.'

Ron waded into the dam. When the water was almost touching his shorts, he plunged his arms into the dam and brought up the bulk of the tangle in one swoop. And a good-sized redfin on the end of it. Terry squealed.

'A fish!'

Simon was ecstatic.

'We caught a fish, Dad! We caught a fish!'

The fish was in Ron's arms. It was dead, wasn't it? Several pounds with the requisite red fins. And something silver stuck in its large mouth along with the hook hanging from its bottom lip. Ron began to edge the hook out. Peter shivered. How much would the fish hurt if it were alive? He watched his dad work at the hook, pull it this way and that, then out. He realised then his dad could probably do anything. If he wanted to. He could fix anything. Stop any sound, tell anything to shut up and leave Peter alone. But when they'd got home that night and Peter's mum had told them all that Sheree had died, his dad had just slunk off to his bedroom. He'd left their mum to hold her boys and they'd cried together until they'd all got tired. But they'd still sat up and talked well past bedtime.

'There's just some things in life that are very hard to explain, boys,' their mum had told them, watching her closed bedroom door.

The dam's silver sheen brightened now and Ron smiled.

'Well, you blokes, you've done a good...'

The redfin gave a sudden wriggle and Ron yelped. The fish dropped headfirst from his hands and into the water. There was nothing Ron could do. He couldn't stop it. He couldn't. That bloody fish. He stood stunned and motionless in the dam with his hands turned out. As if the fish might think twice and launch itself back into his arms.

4. Ron, Stan and Ken Stevenson

Ron wasn't supposed to be there, no way; it was his brother Stan's and his mates' party, outside Laharum at McKenzie Falls. They'd have said piss off, Ron, if he'd asked them if he could go. He wasn't even supposed to know about it.

They all went to the Falls on their bikes. In the dark, just a kero lamp between them to light the way on the dirt road. They dropped their bikes where the valley started and Ron hung back, then dropped his too. He didn't have a light, but he could see theirs, heading down with them as they walked through the scrub. And once they got to the Falls, he could hear them.

God, who couldn't?

They were drinking beer out of big bottles, yelling and laughing as if they were men. The Falls were smashing down and glowing in the light of their bonfire. They were all hanging around the flames, and Ron smelt the gas when they threw in their mums' empty Taft hairspray cans and watched them explode. They were pretending WWII hadn't finished after all, and they were troops getting bombed. They yapped about Crete and the Middle East as if they'd been there and shot blokes, like some of their dads had.

There were six of them: Stan and Ken, Bob McKinnon, Trevor Randall, Willie Thompson, and Willie's younger brother. The freckly one.

And Ron. Hiding in the bush. Watching them.

He heard his brothers in the lounge one night after school talking about the party they were going to have. They were sitting near the fireplace and yapping about how they were going to sneak out the bedroom window, meet their mates at the start of Mt Victory Road and ride the eight miles to the Falls. They'd have a bonfire and chug on some grog then ride back, drunk as skunks they said they'd be, and no one would be the wiser. They'd only get two hours sleep they reckoned. Then they'd be on the school bus the next day as if nothing had happened. But, by Jesus, it'd be a rip snorting night, wouldn't it?

Yeah, sure would. Until macho Trevor Randall started giving them all lip. They should have expected it. The bloke was a mouth, plain and simple.

As one of Ron's teachers used to say: live by the mouth, die by the mouth.

Ron had followed them to the Falls that night, but on the way he did some hunting. He hunted a few times a week. When Stan and Ken were asleep, Ron snuck out the bedroom window and went searching for UFOs in the paddocks above the Grampians, those mountains that looked like witches hats in the moonlight. He usually saw some UFOs, though deep down he knew they were only stars or night birds the moon was shining on. But he went home shivery, telling himself he was one of the few, one of the special ones. Like those army blokes in Sydney.

He'd had the news clipping stuck to his bedroom wall since he was seven. It was yellowing at the edges, but the black and white photo of the bell-shaped UFO was clear. He didn't know it then, but that photo wasn't of the UFOs in the article. It was just one put in the paper to show what the real ones floating over Sydney Harbour on the night of July 9th 1947 might have looked like.

Two army officers had been out for a late night stroll at Elizabeth Bay. They were alone on a strip of sand, with just a few moored boats for company. Silver dishes were suddenly in the sky about 10,000 feet above them, they reckoned. The UFOs flipped on their sides, had a look at the Sydney Harbour Bridge, then exploded off again to wherever they'd come from. There were a few other witnesses, but they weren't as 'reliable' as those two blokes. If they saw something, then there was something there. End of story.

Start of story for Ron. He clipped the article and pinned it right next to his pillow so he could see it before he went to sleep. But UFOs wouldn't come into his dreams so he had to go hunting. And they were there, he'd found them. It proved what Mrs Larson had told them at school, her bum in a grey skirt wiggling and her chalk fierce on the board.

'We may not be alone in the universe.'

But it didn't stop Ron from feeling alone on the farm.

God, what a whinger he was. And there was nothing worse than one of those; that's what his father Bernie told him. Especially when Ron was complaining about helping in the cattle yard.

'Ron, what's a bloody whinger good for?'

Nothing. He knew it. But he still felt lonely.

Once calving season ended and Bernie had finished shoving his hand up cows' arses all night. Instead he was in the paddocks every day. He sorted out the feed. He fixed fences. When that was all done he was in the shed. He tried to get the tractor going. If he couldn't get it going soon, he said, they'd be buggered. He wouldn't call anyone to fix it. And there was more chance of moving the Grampians than changing Bernie's mind.

'We need to bang in some oats this year,' he reckoned. 'If we don't, we won't have enough money to eat mutton, let alone lamb.' So Ron could forget about getting a new Ross Faulkner footy. He'd be lucky to get a pair of socks.

Bernie was too busy to even say hello. And Ron's mum wasn't much better.

She swept and cooked and cleaned and ironed and barely took time out to breathe, let alone talk. No time, really, for Stan or Ken or Sheree, and definitely none for Ron, the second youngest. And the eldest whinger.

Sheree wasn't great company. Stan and Ken didn't talk much to him either. They were both at high school and couldn't have cared less what was going on anywhere else. Definitely not the bed next to them.

Alone at home? For sure. The universe? Who knew.

Trevor Randall had a crew cut. Liked to pretend he was a soldier. He was always on a mission, that was for sure, to give everyone the shits. He put a beer bottle to his fat lips and told them all what a deadset hero he was.

'I can shoot a rabbit from fifty paces...'

Glug glug on the grog he went.

'...'tween the eyes...'

Stan didn't look at him. Talked to the fire instead.

'Goodonya.'

'What can you hit?'

Stan shook his head. He picked up a decent-sized rock and aimed close to where Ron was hiding. He threw it and hit smack in the middle of a tree nearby. A bit of bark flew into Ron's lap.

'Good enough for ya?'

Trevor laughed.

'Yeah. That'd kill a rabbit. If it was a toy one.'

Randall was big and strong, and he always put shit on his mates until they wanted to belt him. Only way he was ever happy. His old man was the same. In fisticuffs at the Lake Wartook Pub every second week.

'Yeah, but we wouldn't want to kill your toy rabbit,' Stan said.

'Why not?' Glug glug on the beer and now a packet of cigarettes from his shirt pocket.

'Why not? Because then you'd have nothin to wank off on at night.'

They all cacked themselves.

'You're a fucking poofter, Stan Stevenson.'

Fucking was a bad enough word, Ron thought, but poofter? Jesus, you didn't call someone that unless you wanted to start a brawl. Which, of course, Trevor did. Get a brawl going and then get all friendly afterwards. He was a maniac, one mad son of a turkey. But he didn't deserve what happened. And for the life of him, Ron didn't know, then or later, why Stan did it.

He could have taken Randall down any other way he wanted. But he called out, 'What was that?' and pointed up. Of course Ron was first to look: Jesus! It must be a UFO! he thought. But there was nothing. If there'd been something, he'd have seen it. Stan's mates all yelled, 'What?' and they must have looked up too. When they lowered their heads, Trevor Randall was on the ground.

'Get up, Randall,' Stan said. He nudged him in the ribs with his boot, but Randall didn't move.

'Come on Trevor, you numbskull,' Ken added. He bent down and shook him. Randall moved, but made a choking sound. Then nothing. Willie Thompson took off his beanie and looked to Stan.

'Shit, is he all right?'

'Who cares?' Stan said. He took a bucket to the crashing falls and came back with it full. He threw water on the fire and it hissed and gave off steam. Two more buckets and it was out. Ken shook Randall again.

'Leave the dickhead. Let's go,' Stan said. The boys looked at each other and then the trees. They were silent and Stan lit the kero lamp.

'You can stay and watch this drongo snooze, but I'm heading off.'

He carried the lamp through the clearing and his mates followed.

Ron could have gone over to see if Randall was all right. But all he could think about was getting home before his brothers did. He took a short cut through the bush, got his legs scratched to buggery, but found his bike and charged for home.

They must have ridden pretty slow. Ron reckoned he'd been in bed quarter of an hour before they got home. The idiots turned on the lamp and he pretended to be asleep. Stan jumped into bed, but Ken sat up on his.

'Shoulda checked.'

Stan was silent. He turned to the window and the dark out there.

Randall had made it to the Bennett farmhouse, lumbered up and knocked on the front door. The Bennetts said he looked like something from another planet. He was days in hospital, but he never said what happened to him. When he got out, he never spoke properly again. Or anything.

Ken sat on his bed for ages like a dummy that night. He saw Ron watching him, but he didn't move or tell his brother to piss off. Ron got sick of watching him and stared at his UFO photo until it faded into sleep.

In the morning, when the news had got round and everyone knew what Stan had done, Ron pulled the photo off the wall. He took it into the lounge where the fire was going. He poked at the kindling, put a small log on, and tossed the news article into the flames. The words crumpled first and then the UFO. Grey then black then charcoal pieces up and out through the chimney.

5. Nick Stevenson

Nick Stevenson butted his cigarette out and watched the skinny bus driver pile his Adidas bag into the guts of the Greyhound. Bus to Victoria's a bastard, Nick thought. He shoved his hands into his ripped jeans and cursed being unable to afford a plane. Plus the trains weren't running on account of the heat and the warped tracks. Truth was he didn't want to go to Westmore at all, by bus or plane or car, but his uncle Ron had kicked on. Cancer. Stevensons were coming from around the country to send off the old spud. Nick's dad Ken was Ron's elder brother. So Ken was going to support his former sister-in-law Jules at the funeral. And he wanted his sons beside him.

'Least you lot can do,' the old boof-nosed one had said over a cup of tea after he'd finished in the garden one afternoon. There were lawn clippings in what was left of his grey hair. 'So get your puny arses sorted out.'

Nick could have got a lift with his mum and dad and brother; they'd decided to head to Westmore as a crew. But after the last few weeks of spending time a bit too close to his brother, the idea of sitting in the backseat with Tim made Nick opt for the bus.

Which, now he was on it, was a sardine can, smell included. Too many passengers had peeled off their shoes and let their socks loose. It was so foul his dead uncle Ron could have smelt them coming by the time they reached Mt Gambier. There wasn't enough room to fart. Nick had to let them go by cupping his hands in his lap and hoping none of those disasters snuck out and got up the nose of the young bloke beside him, who was too polite for Nick's liking.

The bloke wore a shirt and tie, even though he looked a few years off being bothered by facial hair. Excuse me, would you like this, can I move that? He kept asking. Nick couldn't have cared less. The young bloke had glasses that he wore to read, and when Nick saw the book he was flicking through, he checked round for spare seats. A useless idea. The carry-on luggage rack was his best chance for somewhere else to sit.

The bloke was reading the Bible. And he was right into it.

A few weeks before, Nick and Tim had sex with the same woman. At the same time. It was crazy shit and it took him back to when he and Tim were kids. They used to piss in the same bowl, streams clashing like swords. But, thank God, there was no clashing when it was one girl between two. Not if you were careful. And Nick was.

Crazy shit doesn't just happen. Nick put it down to when his dad Ken had said Nick and Tim's wives were in good pastures. That his sons served life up to their women on a platter and all those women had to do was sit back and fan themselves. But Ken hadn't dared let his daughters-in-law hear it; he'd told Nick and Tim on Christmas Day while they'd sat together beside the barbecue, cracking heads off prawns. Nick had been complaining about the double shift he'd worked the week before at the wool classers. He'd had to head straight home after it and make dinner because Cynthia had a hair appointment. It was a Thursday night. Only night for hair, it seemed. Nick could never figure that out. He guessed it had to do with all the hairies being busy on the weekends going to the Moresworth Hotel nightclub. Getting down and boogieing with a busload of boys on a footy trip. But whatever the reason for Cynthia's cut and style, Nick had had to look after the kids while he was trying to cook fried rice. He shouldn't have bothered having a go at fried rice because he never knew how much soy sauce and how many peas. But he gave it a shot because Cynthia was always onto him about not being able to cook anything but spag bol or snags. Ken listened to him complain and ran a hand through his sweaty grey hair. Then he shook his head slowly and added some oil to the barbecue hotplates. Tim piped up.

'Same thing happened to me last Friday,' he said.

He was in a singlet. Tatts of Hawaiian girls dancing on his muscles.

'I picked the kids up from school and kinder. Knocked off early from the trout farm...'

Then he'd cooked up a storm of spaghetti, but Corinne had complained that she didn't like cream in pasta sauce, he knew that, so why did he put it in?

'Jesus, I didn't know she didn't like cream.'

No, apparently she only liked tomatoes. And not too much pepper, not as much as he'd stuck in.

'I told her, well, you know, I'm sorry. I'll try and remember that for next time.'

Ken stared at him. Then Nick.

'Women today don't know how good they've got it.'

Their dad's remark stopped them in their prawn-shelling tracks. Hadn't they just been saying in the lounge over a stubby that they weren't getting any sex? Well, you know, maybe once every couple of weeks. And even then they had to have dinner cooked and the baby's nappies on before their wives would even look at them. Plus, no matter what sort of thing they wanted to get up to once the gear came off, it was just a case of get your prod out, do your investigations, and then piss off out of there.

'Different in my day,' Ken said. He flicked the prawns onto the hotplate and they juiced and sizzled.

Not long after Christmas, Tim hooked up with a girl after work. She was down from Flinders Uni, doing a placement at the trout farm. She was a rezzie there, she'd told him.

'As long as you're not what rhymes with it,' Tim had laughed and she'd shaken her black hair and poked her tits out, he said. Like one of those beauties from Erandale. Tim was twenty-nine, but he looked younger and he surfed. He'd given Nick the gory details of how he'd got her ankles at her ears in the wagon part of his Commodore. Then Tim had dropped her at the station with a thank you from him and a tongue kiss from her.

A month later, they picked up a girl each at the War and Tooth Hotel. It was a Thursday night; all the hairies had finished scissoring, and it was open mike night. Nick and Tim sang 'Brothers in Arms' with some hippie bloke on guitar. They'd sung a lot as kids. Nick had even learnt guitar for a bit. And their rendition of the Dire Straits song had brought a Vietnam vet to glassy eyes, along with the two girls they'd got friendly with afterwards. They took them back to Tim's mate Raisin's place. He was away in Adelaide for work. Tim got the bedroom and Nick the lounge. The telly whispered now and then and the lights went on and off: Raisin had the house set to a timer to keep burglars away. The brothers showered with no soap or deodorant and were back to their wives by ten.

The bus made it out of the suburbs and onto the highway proper. The bloke with glasses flipped through the Bible, stopping every now and then to close his eyes.

Nick hadn't copped a look at the Bible since RE in Grade Five. He'd told his teacher Mrs Wilkins that 'Jesus' was a swear word and she should watch her mouth. It got him a few a laughs—and a trip to the Principal.

'Don't tell me to watch my mouth, Nick Stevenson.'

He'd been a bit confused about getting in trouble. According to Mrs Wilkins he hadn't sworn, so why had he still ended up outside the Principal's den? Nick had his Bible for Juniors on his lap for the wait. There was a cartoon picture of Mary on the cover. But there was nothing on the Bible beside him now. It was black leather. The bloke held out his hand for Nick to shake.

'Leigh Forsyth,' he said, like it was a name Nick should know.

He thought there should be a law against these blokes talking to you about their religion, when all you wanted to do was whack Nirvana in your headphones and remember back before you got married. Slabs of West End and Holdens with flames down the sides. Women like the ones Tim had organised for them a few weeks back. But he shook the bloke's hand anyway.

'Nick Stevenson.'

'Are you going to Melbourne for work?'

'Uncle carked it.'

'Oh, sorry to hear it.'

'Don't be.'

'Why do you say that?'

Christ, this bloke wouldn't budge. It was going to take something stronger.

'Because he was a cunt,' said Nick.

Tim's wife Corinne took the kids and nicked off to Queensland for a couple of weeks. She had to help put her mum in a nursing home. With Corinne gone it was on for young and old. Mainly old, but Nick and Tim did manage the occasional young girl. There was one called Fizz. That was the best Nick could make of her name; she was all fluttery eyelashes for Tim while they were at the pub. But her even younger friend Lil couldn't have given two shits for Nick on account of him being too old for her. She went home, had to work—who didn't?—and they were left with Fizz at the War and Tooth. Nick was the third wheel. He was ready to rock home, it was getting onto nine thirty, but Fizz wouldn't have it.

'Nah, nah, stay,' she said, and he watched the silver stud on her tongue roll.

She smiled and slapped Tim on the knee. Leading him by

the dick. But she'd drop it soon and head home. As soon as she could do it without making Tim feel like too much of a twat. Not that Tim would have given a shit.

'I feel woozy,' she said, and all but fell off her barstool.

'You drug her?' Nick whispered.

'You fucking kidding?'

They didn't know what to do. Hospital wouldn't have been a good look. Their wives knew too many nurses. So they helped Fizz into the Commodore. She was slurring. They headed back to Tim's man cave and Fizz fell asleep.

'Don't you get any ideas,' Nick said.

Tim looked crushed. 'What do you think I am?'

'Randy.'

Nick thought Fizz would be skates on and out of there once she woke up. But she flipped her tits out. Both nipples were curled with tatts.

It all happened too quick, before Nick had time to think.

Or maybe he didn't want to think.

He propped in from behind while she sorted Tim out. They swapped halfway, and when they finished, Fizz fell asleep on Tim's biscuit-crumbed couch. When she woke, she didn't want to leave. She wanted to move in with Tim. She wanted to talk about her father and her uncles. And her brothers. The bad shit they'd done. She started slurring again and Tim got her into a cab. Nick had his shower and washed himself over and over, with soap this time, a lot of it. So much that when he got home, Cynthia said he smelt nice and tried to kiss him. He told her he felt shithouse and he went and threw up in the ensuite loo.

Nick thought the c-bomb would be enough to bury the bloke's head back in his Good Book. But no such luck.

'What did your uncle do?'

Normally Nick would have given this bloke nothing. But there were six hours of bus ride to come, and he could choose to either shut up or motor mouth. He chose to motor. Because he still held hope that if he shocked the bloke enough he'd leave him alone.

'He had a crack at his sister when she was a girl.'

'He hit her?'

'Nah mate. He did the dirty with her. And then stuck her in the loony bin when she went mental years later.'

The bloke went still. Shut the Bible. He nodded like a toy dog stuck on a car dash.

'Oh...'

'Yep and the granddad did the dirty with my uncle apparently. Granddad died of natural causes, apparently, right after my grandma died. That's what everyone says. But someone should have shot the cunt.'

Nick wasn't sure if any of those stories were true. The only part of any of them he knew was true was that his dad and his siblings had been in and out of orphanages after their parents had died. They'd got passed around, like the stories when Ken caught up with his brother Stan.

The pair of them got pissed in front of the Vulcan heater while the footy blared on TV. Nick wasn't sure the two old buggers even believed their own stories, but it was like they had to keep telling them. Like the stories were sharks that couldn't stop swimming from here to there or they'd cark it.

But they never talked about Nick's grandmother. No talk of natural causes or any causes at all.

Whatever had really gone on in his family didn't really matter to Nick now. Because he'd decided they were all nutjobs. Sometimes he wished the whole family line had gone down in Ash Wednesday when the fires had threatened Stevenson houses in three states. And missed them all. But an Ash Wednesday bake would have taken Nick out too. And he was just now starting to live a bit, wasn't he?

He'd thrown up heaps after that night with Fizz.

'My Aunty Jules is a bit of a stress head because of it all,' he went on. 'And she's tough enough to take on lightning in a sword fight.'

Nick wanted to shut up. He would. Soon.

'Right,' Bible boy said. 'It's pretty honourable your family's going to the funeral...'

Nick laughed.

'Nah, mate. It's not that. They just don't admit anything. They all act like they're happy families when they're a mob of pricks to each other. But once they get on the sauce, Christ, do the feathers fly...'

Nick sucked on the chocolate bar he'd brought; it had melted in his bag before he'd got onto the bus and the air con.

'Sounds like you've had a rough life.'

Uh, oh, here we go. And Jesus will put me back together.

Nick thought the night with Fizz would be the end of it. Corinne was due back from Queensland late on the next Sunday. But when Tim got an orgy sorted for the Saturday night, Nick knew he had to go. It was one of those once in a lifetime, bucket-list things.

Eight blokes and six girls in Tim's man cave listening to Michael Jackson's *Thriller*. The girls were in lace undies and stupid masks. The blokes, except for one who had a leather g-string on, were in jeans and t-shirts. All looking at g-string boy and what he carried in it.

Which was a lot.

When it was over, Nick didn't want to do anything like it again. It was too risky having fourteen people in Tim's man cave. What if Cynthia had decided, oh, stuff it, I'll get a babysitter and go and watch the bloody State of Origin with the boys? Plus, in the weeks after the orgy, he felt flat as two-week old lemonade. It got so that booze and smokes and, Christ, even Cynthia's hands on him, when she finally did go for an explore, made him feel nothing.

But while the orgy was on, and there were moans and shrieks and chomps and chunks and sweet smells rising, it was bloody fantastic. He'd felt something that night he'd only heard on TV shows about India and yoga. He was connected, somehow. In a way he'd never felt. Not when he was a boy, when he'd got married, or when he'd had his kids. It was embarrassing, but in the orgy he'd felt like a warm piece of a body that loved itself, over and over. And it didn't seem like it would ever stop. Until it did. And they all whacked their pants back on and went home.

And then he felt worse than shit.

Nick had been outside the War and Tooth too many times on a Friday night, munted full of beer and kebabs. That's when dim-witted Bible bashers from Happy Valley or whatever church got in your face, closer than garlic sauce. Told you what a sinner you were, which sounded a bit like they were calling you a shithead, but it didn't matter because Jesus could save you. Nick would say thanks buddy, but no thanks, and hail a taxi before he gave in to his desire to pop the bastard on his arse.

There was no taxi rank on the bus so Nick needed to hail some smarts.

He told Bible boy that, no, he hadn't had a rough life; his life had been fine, thanks. He told him about giving it to Fizz with his brother and then the orgy. And not only the orgy, but how much he'd liked it. He skipped the bit about feeling as numb later as after a morning at the dentist.

The bloke sat back for a while. He shifted the Bible here and there on his lap. He might have been trying to hide a hard on. But then he turned and looked at Nick. His eyes were marsh-mallows. Hot ones. Full of goo.

'There's a search for goodness in everything we do.'

The bloke was surely a full-blown nutjob.

'Deep down, you just want to belong.'

Nick felt squeamish. No, much worse. He felt genuinely sick.

Like he was getting smashed around the head with something. He couldn't shake the bloke off. He wanted to belt him. A punch would shock the crap out of him. He'd squeal and his eyes would water. But he let the bastard yabber on. Hallelujah, yabber, yabber. 'Hallelujah', the Jeff Buckley version. As Bible Boy spoke, Nick pictured for one crazy second all the blokes and chicks in the orgy singing it.

He was going out of his scone.

He was sweating. There were pools of it under his knees. But the air con was making everything icy.

'You want to hit me, don't you?'

And now he had a mind reader sitting next to him.

'No,' Nick lied and plunged his hand into his seat pocket, hunting for his Zoo mag. Where the hell was it?

'Even that means you want to be close to people.'

Nick felt like he was in primary school and this younger bloke was the teacher. And Nick was the naughty dickhead in class. Again.

He couldn't sit there for the next five hours. He raced to the front and told the bus driver he had to get off. Now.

'Are you sick?' The skinny driver had pen ink tatts on his hand.

'I just want to get off.'

'It desert round here bloke, hey? Nothin for miles.'

'I want to fucken' get out.'

The driver yapped on about spirits in those parts, but he eventually gave up and stopped the bus. Before Nick got off, he looked at the road ahead and the bitumen snaking to the horizon. All shimmery.

'Neck town eighty kay. You be right bloke?' the driver asked as he led Nick off the bus in the screaming wind. He pulled Nick's gear from the baggage compartment and Nick waved that he was okay. The driver hopped back on and the doors whooshed shut.

The bus engine revved and it got ready to go. Nick's forehead was dripping and his case's handle was slippery. He found himself wanting Bible bloke to get off as well. Maybe so he could belt him. Extra hard. But it was going to be a big-arsed walk. If Bible bloke got off, Nick wouldn't say anything to him. He could just walk beside him. They'd be quiet together. They'd listen to whatever message the wind was shouting. It was a message, surely.

But the bus took off. And Nick couldn't see Bible boy in the window seat where he'd been. Had he moved? There was no room in there.

6. Peter and Ron Stevenson

Peter doesn't know exactly when it happens, but he must be a very naughty young boy. How naughty he is. He must stop being so naughty.

'I said now, Peter!'

Was it ten seconds later? Thirty-five years? Sometime later. He must stop. Peter must be so incredibly naughty because here he comes; it's his father. Look at him: he's wearing his work tie and short-sleeved shirt. He's going to work at the truck yard office in Corumbul. He's the manager, his mother has told him, and he's got pressures. He's putting his briefcase on the kitchen's black and white checkered lino and, look now, he's picking up the knife from the middle of the breakfast table.

Or is it from the drawer?

It's in his father's hands, his shaking hands, and look how the blade shakes too. Look at his father: his eyes are shiny.

His father is raising the knife and he's telling Peter now, ten seconds later, thirty-five years afterwards, that he is a very bad boy. So bad his father's saying he's going to kill him with the knife if he doesn't shut up.

He's going to kill him and his brothers.

Look at his eyes.

Peter is sure his father is going to kill him.

They're very shiny eyes.

But it's okay. If they die it's okay, because the boys have shrunk.

Peter and his brothers have melted into their seats, through the floor and under the house. They're never coming out. They're safe down there. Under the house where they can't be killed.

Then Peter's back. And his father's standing in front of him, his jaw shaking. Peter's there and beneath the ground. He's heading to the earth's hot core, it's getting hotter, and his dad and the knife are shaking.

Do you hear me, son? Never again!

He must know how naughty he is. So naughty he's still at the table, ten seconds later, thirty-five years ago.

And his father has gone to work.

Peter's family had moved to Corumbul from Ballarat. But Peter had liked Ballarat. Until he'd started school. It'd been a nice place before that: spider webs grew in the back garden, all across the azaleas and pom-pom flowers, blue and white. He'd got a t-shirt with Mickey Mouse on it. A prize in a Tip Top bread competition. He'd wanted to win and go to Disneyland. But he'd got a consolation prize. He'd worn his t-shirt, proud and smiling at his nice neighbour and her curly hair, and he'd still thought he was going to Disneyland. Instead, he started school at Ballarat's Lake Worth Primary School. He'd cried at the gate the first day, but his mum had left him because she couldn't come in, mothers weren't allowed in, and it was so hot in the classroom he sweated up his thighs and shorts. Little ponds formed on his plastic seat. So thirsty, he went for the iced drink bottle his mum had given him.

'You don't drink til recess, Peter! Leave it alone!'

How did the teacher see him? How did she know his name? She was so far away. At the blackboard. And everyone looked at him. And his drink bottle. He put it back and cried and someone laughed. This was school.

He doesn't go to school for months in Corumbul. His mum pulls him out because he's crying all the time at school and not adjusting. But when he does go he learns that footy cards are what he needs to make friends.

Before school each morning, his mum sends him on his bike to buy bread at the milk bar, and she lets him use the change to buy a packet of footy cards. The more swaps he makes the more friends he'll have, so at the counter he holds two footy card packs close together, and pays for only one. Because of this, it must be, he scores two Leigh Matthews. Lethal Leigh is the hardest card to get. Boys mob Peter at recess under the old elm and he swaps a Matthews for a Rene Kink, a Billy Picken and two Peter Moores. He doesn't need both Peter Moores, but he takes them anyway because Darren is nice, he doesn't tread on Peter's toes in the crush, and he believes in UFOs.

Corumbul is his father's first post as a yard manager. He'd been an assistant in Ballarat, but now he is an important person. Peter's mother leaves him at the yard office a few times after school while she goes shopping. His father shows him to the workers behind their desks and they ask who he barracks for. He tells them Collingwood, the mighty Magpies, and they boo with smiles on their faces. Later, he gets to play in his father's office. He mucks around with what looks like a black Scrabble tile holder. It says Ronald Stevenson—Manager. Peter turns it in his hands, taps it like a drumstick on his father's rubber desk mat, uses it as a mouth organ, then places it in front of him and pretends he is the Manager.

He is his father.

His mum is so happy. Peter has finished adjusting, he is going to school, and he has a friend! The first time Peter asks if Darren can come over and play she says yes, even though she has to prepare for a dinner party while his father is at golf. But she keeps an eye on Peter and Darren, smiling as she stacks cream and diced fruit into parfait glasses. She asks what Peter and Darren want to do together, you two friends? Peter says he wants to get all the liquids he can find in the kitchen—milk, cordial, chocolate topping, water, tomato sauce, orange juice—and mix them into a glass. And drink them. And his mum says yes! But be careful.

'You go first,' Darren says when it comes time for the taste test. His eyes are bright beneath bushy eyebrows. He has a bowl haircut. Peter knows this is what it is called because his father has told him he has one, too. Peter takes the glass, raises it and gulps.

'Not too much!' his mum cries. Darren drinks two glasses —and almost throws up. Later, Peter puts him to another test, but he knows he'll pass: he loves Peter's *Biggest, Smallest, Fastest, Strangest* book. It has a red cover with dusky drawings and black and white photos of giant crabs, ostrich eggs, huge pies, the Mary Celeste and, on page 72, UFOs! The main photo of the flying saucer above shadowy power lines and the wire fence is, the book says, a fake. But that's stupid. Why would they have it in the book if it were a fake?

UFOs are everywhere. There's one behind every star that hangs above the Corumbul paddocks at night. They fly around the graveyard on the hill. They are maybe even the voices Peter hears at night, sometimes, when he can't sleep and he's thinking of his dead aunty Sheree, still wearing her colourful clothes in her coffin, waiting to wake up on the last day like her church friends said.

Of course the photo is real.

And Darren can stay the night.

The dinner party clangs and glitters in the formal dining room, the one Peter is never allowed into. It's for the Queen and for people who work for his dad's company in Melbourne. He and Darren hunt the front garden and then the nearby footpaths for UFOs. He always sees them when he's by himself, just last week he saw two, but tonight, nothing. None above the darkening tile roofs, none in the distant hills.

They talk about times they've seen UFOs out car windows on long trips, or walks just like this one—damn it, last week!— but Peter doesn't care. He and Darren run up and down the footpath, laughing at how long the moon makes their shadows, until his dad calls from the porch for them to stop their racket. The boys stand still and their shadows retreat.

They launch then they fly, those angry thoughts and angry feelings, up and down at night in Peter's stomach and his head. And the feelings talk. They come at him with blades in his dreams and they tell him they are taking him, there's nothing he can do. He feels the blades pierce him and when he wakes his stomach is aching and he tells his mum he can't go to school. But she says, 'Peter, you've been doing well. Come on, buck up, be brave.' And he goes. But the blade people come in the night again and his father, who hasn't again said he wants to kill Peter, goes to work in the morning, and Peter goes to school.

His father whacks and thumps him for being a bad boy but the hits don't hurt. It's like his father's hands and belts are banging on one of the used oil drums in the truck yard. When his father seethes towards him, belt raised and ready, Peter doesn't care. There's no knife. Peter's still under the house and huddled with his brothers. Where he can't be killed.

The voices follow him to the classroom. Where he's not sure if his father wants him alive, and he's sick of his aunty being dead, and the voices won't leave him alone. When he gets home, he stays in his room as much as he can. With his UFO book. And the fake UFO that is as real as the hand he uses to turn the pages.

Is there a place UFOs go when it's cold at night? he wonders.

When is it too cold for UFOs to fly? Do they go under their houses?

One strange day in Corumbul, it snows. His mum takes photos; she's in a coat with red trim and her dark hair dances on the collar. She could be Santa's wife. There could be UFOs in the snow, maybe they brought the snow. His father doesn't get home in time to see it before it melts.

That night, Peter decides to make friends with the voices. Come and talk to me. Come and take me wherever you are! But they don't talk or come. Peter's brothers are asleep when he turns the lamp on and opens his book. He laughs as he draws onto the photo of the UFO a picture of an alien holding a football.

Peter's just become a teenager when his family moves to Westmore, a satellite city of Melbourne. They'd had another move before that, from Corumbul to Tarmit, but they'd made it now to Westmore's redbrick suburb of Hillton. One of the neighboring families is from Vietnam. Peter's never seen anyone from Vietnam, and now he lives next to people from Vietnam. Westmore is strange, but he'll get used to it, his mother says, and his father's gone. Working at a new yard. A bigger one. Peter listens to David Bowie all the time now because Bowie has a red lightning bolt on his face and he sings about stars and men waiting in the sky. Peter climbs naked onto the roof one night when everyone's asleep. There are fewer stars in Westmore than anywhere he has lived. He hums 'Starman' to the sky until his bum's freezing and he can't remember why he's naked or on the roof.

The Stevensons have a barbecue dinner with the chemist, David Crane, and his family: The Cranes. They've just moved to Westmore from Romville, a little town near Tarmit, the town Peter and his family have just left behind, that he didn't want to leave behind. He liked Tarmit, like he liked Corumbul, like he'd liked Ballarat. He doesn't think about Disneyland anymore. He'd had a girlfriend in Tarmit who hadn't known she was Peter's girlfriend. She'd sat at the desk in front of him, and half her bum had hung over the side of her plastic seat. It made Peter think of nectarines. He likes them, with ice-cream. But now he's in Westmore, having a barbecue. Sausages. And the Cranes have only boys to play with.

The families share broad accents and community mindedness. Both are struggling, they say, in their new hometown. This Westmore, city slick one minute—traffic lights, a Village Cinema—and a country town the next. If you've got red hair you go to school at St James School. If you've got a tattoo you live in Corton or East Blemton. If you've got a posh accent, a plum in your mouth, darling, his mum and Mrs Crane laugh, you must live in Weeeeeling!

David's son, Andrew, he's got something more like a date in his mouth. His speech is so wide and slow Peter can see cows walking behind him on their way to their evening milking. He tries Andrew on posters and music, but his new friend can't make sense of David Bowie. He takes him for a kick of football in the front yard instead. The chemist's balloon-biceped son lands thumping drop punts on Peter's skinny chest. Only Peter finds out later that Andrew and Cal aren't David's sons. The boys' real father drowned in a fishing accident, in Lake Romville. Their mother, Wendy, so the gossip went, married David before her late husband's bed was cold.

There aren't enough spaces at the dining table. Everyone gathers as best they can at the round one near the kitchen bench. The daylight saving sun through the glass sliding doors turns everyone's faces orange. The chemist has to make sick people laugh, every day, that's what he says. That's why he's a great storyteller! He's got wrinklier cheeks than Peter's dad's but they rise as he tells of his hypochondriac customers. Everyone lowers their sausages in bread, laughing about Westmore people who are city slick but country slow.

Peter's never heard of hypochondriacs, and that night he learns another term: Chinese bladder. It's how Peter's mum describes David's need to empty himself every hour after he's added beer. On one of his returns from the bathroom, he stops and points at the sliding doors.

'What's that?'

None of the Cranes look. And the Stevensons know the chemist's joking ways by now. But David keeps on.

'What the bloody hell was that?'

There's ivy on the trellis, an empty outdoor setting, and a bin lid-style barbecue, black from frying sausages.

'What?' Wendy asks, her thin smoker's lips drawn tight.

'It came down over there...'

David's at the doors and opening them, stepping onto the porch and saying something to the backyard.

'...it had red lights, and green, and it was glowing,' he adds on his way back to the table. Wendy has a look on her face like a teacher watching a brilliant but problematic student. Is her David using an old trick or a new one? Peter can't tell, then or later. But Wendy joins in when everyone else starts asking questions.

Could you see aliens? Did they have lightsabers? How close was it?

UFOs are the talk for half an hour. Peter says he used to believe in them. David says he should, because one just landed in his backyard! Ron brings discussion of the first cricket Test to the rescue. David doesn't joke anymore that night. He glances now and then at the sliding doors, and disappears through them for a smoke as often as he goes to the toilet.

The Stevensons become close friends with the Cranes. Peter plays football with Andrew, and David joins Ron's tennis team as a fill-in. The chemist never sees another UFO and he dies of lung cancer in his early 50s, leaving Wendy a widow for the second time.

David is the only dad Peter sees die. That's one more than he wanted to see, and two more than the Crane boys wanted to see. He visits David with his mum in the sick room at the chemist's house and David manages to joke. As Peter leaves, he takes a last look at the suddenly old man's bulbous head and wafer skin. It's stale pickle grey, and flaky enough to float from his bones.

Peter's father says he should never have visited him.

'Your father is under a lot of pressure,' his mum says, and Peter wonders, if UFOs exist, can they see in windows? Can they see when sons become teenagers who don't know what's happening to their bodies? Can they see when their fathers are screaming at them, like engines roaring, that their drug-taking behaviour has lost them, lost them like a picture of a stumpy alien in a secret army filing cabinet?

And still when his father's fists land on him, Peter senses nothing but an echo rising from somewhere inside.

Peter will become a poet and then a painter.

Ron won't see that coming.

Because he always thought his son would play footy.

Peter was a brilliant junior. Starred. Kicked nine goals from centre-half-forward one day. Ironed out one of the red-haired St James' boys. A fair hip and shoulder.

Ron told his mates his son would play at the top level, it was just a matter of when. But in his late teens, Peter got into drugs and girls and never lined up in the big league. Ron said it was a waste of talent.

Christ, I'd have been a premiership player.

On the dais, medal around his neck.

Ron didn't talk to his kids much when they're were little. He didn't know what to say to them. Kids were for wives. They sorted them out.

I was at work all day, and then I had the lawns and the bins and the dishes, chucked the papers in the incinerator, played footy, golf and tennis, went fishing. The boys came fishing. And I got them into sport.

He wasn't hard on his boys.

I was a bit of a stress-head when they were teenagers. I was doing million-dollar deals then, in Westmore. But I did what I could at home.

Ron never forgot coming home and going to town on his boys; belts, whacks and punches, throwing pens and plates, yelling, saying they were no sons of his.

They drank a heap, you see, got into that bloody drug nonsense, too. Terry? He even planted the frigging things on my roof...

He whacked Peter and Simon, both of them with a shovel on the arse in the front yard. Ron never forgot that, either.

Didn't get any clues from my old man. Well, I did. The wrong ones. And I couldn't ever figure out how to put the right ones in my head.

Ron got his boys through to their late teens. Through and off his hands.

Not because I didn't like them.

It was different at work. His staff liked him; he managed the yard well, even the first stint in Corumbul. But, by Jesus, it took it out of him. Sales were down for a long time and wasn't he copping it from Head Office?

'What are you running, Stevenson? A fucking charity?'

But he kept the yards running, with his bare hands and his late night typewriter. Kept his chin up for the staff. And when he got home and the kids were acting up and bickering and fighting—and his wife rode him about it all—well, he wanted to disappear.

You know, I never blamed Jules for leaving me. By the time we got to Westmore, I was sick of myself. Fairly obvious she was as well.

It's a rainy day in central New South Wales. The Parkes radio telescope looks like it's drowning in dishwater. Peter's there with his mum and brothers. His dad has moved out and his mum works full-time now. But she's taken the boys away for school holidays. He's fourteen, on holidays and listening to a murky science talk. The lab-coated man drones on and Peter sees a poster: the giant telescope and its smaller sibling at dusk, two ears listening to the universe. If anyone or anything is whispering beyond those photographed orange and purple clouds, the telescopes will hear. Peter buys the poster with the money he's saved from mowing his mum's lawn and sticks it on a large pinboard above his bedhead.

Somewhere in his weightlifting, wet dream teens, after his dad has left and he only sees him on weekends, Peter replaces the telescope with Sylvester Stallone. Machine gun at his waist, red headband keeping fake sweat from his sharp blue eyes. In his early twenties, he consigns Rambo to the same case that holds his footy cards and early attempts at poetry and sketches. He's now Mulder's biggest fan, searching with him for hidden truths, werewolves, shapeshifters and Scully's kiss.

At a dinner party at his rental house in the nineties, Peter's friends laugh at him and say there's no such thing as a UFO.

Notwithstanding the popularity of *The X-Files*, despite UFOs occupying the front cover of *Time* magazine and being the subject of numerous documentaries. He knows he should let the subject rest and go back to talking about the *Three Colours* film series, but fuck them. Peter works part-time at a magazine and he does research and he knows things.

'What's going on is similar to what happened at the turn of the last millennium. There were mass hallucinations and people seeing crosses in the sky. But, of course, there was nothing there...'

'Just like UFOs,' says Walt, a man-child with a black goatee beard and parents with too much money.

'Yes. And no. Yes, because most sightings are hot air balloons, weather probes, planes, searchlights on clouds, helicopters—and even flocks of birds caught at certain angles in the moonlight...'

Walt's getting bored. And so are the others, in their black polos and ripped jeans, sipping their cheap wine.

'But some sightings can't be explained.'

'Little green what-the-fucks?'

'Real unidentified flying objects.'

'Can you hear yourself, Stevenson? Real unidentified flying objects? I'm going for a smoke...'

Fuck him. And his parents' money.

'Yes, real UFOs, Walt! They get hearts racing. They root people's feet to the ground. They shake up the earth. They grab it by the collar and shout that we might not be as lonely as all the empty caves and canyons say we are!'

'You're fucking nuts.'

'Whatever. Despite all the bloody skepticism, we can, I'm telling you, look into the skies in wonder.'

'I wonder about you, mate.'

And Walt goes for his smoke. And Peter's girlfriend Jayne looks at Peter like maybe her hope that this man might one day father her child is not such a great plan after all.

In the night Peter leaves Jayne to her worried dreams and gets up and goes to their dining room that doubles as their lounge. He smells the wretched aftermath of the dinner party, the carpet stained with squashed sundried tomatoes. He sits in an armchair and writes verse after verse of poetry about invisible men.

He sees a psychologist regularly in his thirties.

What did the voices say? And when did they stop? Have they stopped?

The portly man with varicose-veined calves tells him that if an adult remembers an incident from early childhood, if a pea bobs its head out of the bubbling soup of memory, chances are the event happened only once.

Before primary school one morning in Corumbul, Peter's father appears on the porch where his mum should be. Ron wears a pale blue shirt, a patterned tie, dark blue shorts and knee-length cream walk socks. He holds a black briefcase and smiles. Peter doesn't smile back.

Where's his mum?

She normally drives him to school.

What if he's been naughty?

Where is she? Is she sick?

Peter watches how his father holds his briefcase and he grips his own smaller, white school case firmly. Does his father say anything? Is he saying anything? Listen: Ron's feet, Peter's feet, together on the gravel and then the bitumen.

Is his father going to reach for a knife? Is this what it's all about, this walking to school?

He's walking with Peter, but he's not talking. What should Peter say? What should he do? Keep walking?

They reach the end of the court and the laneway entrance and his father holds his hand. He's never done it before and he'll never do it again. But his father's hand is on his. The laneway and the blossoms that hang from the fences on both sides spiral, loop and form a tunnel that seems to have no end.

His father's hand in his carries Peter all the way to the dirt car park behind the truck yard. Then he lets go. Ron's still smiling and he says Peter can walk the rest of the way to school.

But his mum always drops him off at the gate.

Peter stands and scuffs his school shoes. But his father says go on, son, you go. You can make it the rest of the way down the lane.

The next ten seconds and however many years, he can do it, because his father will be watching him.

Peter walks; he crunches gravel, spots the school gate across the road, but turns around. His father's briefcase is on the ground and his hands are behind his back. Is he walking towards him now? Is he angry?

Peter runs to school, he runs and doesn't turn around again.

7. Terry Stevenson

On the Saturday morning, the phone rang in Terry's one-bedroom flat and he knew it would be his mum, Jules. And he knew exactly what she'd have to say about his father. Terry put the spliff he'd just rolled onto the phone table. Jules was crying and he heard himself say, *It's all right, Mum,* and they made arrangements to get together later in the morning. He hadn't showered, he was still in his jocks, but he'd have time to see her before he had to work in the Mitre 10 nursery.

After he hung up, Terry went to the back porch and sat on his stained deckchair. He tried to prepare himself. The spliff useless in his hands, he watched clouds shitting around above the bare plum tree.

His mum had been showing up at the hospital for weeks, sitting all day in the plastic chair next to Ron's bed. She said it wasn't just about doing the right thing, but her voice was always flat. Like the shirts she'd ironed for him when they were married and he worked at the truck yards. She'd stare at Ron in his hospital bed and ask if he needed anything. The remains of Ron's grey hair were always sweaty and stuck to his forehead. He'd half open his eyes and say, 'Nah, nah, I'm right Jules... I'll be right.'

Most days, Ron looked like shit sliding down the side of a dunny bowl. Terry would watch the old man wriggle in his bedclothes. What a mess. But there was nothing Terry could do about it.

'Heading off now, Ron,' he'd tell him. Terry had never called him dad.

Ron's eyes would brighten for a second as if Terry had turned into something that sparkled. Sure enough, he had.

'No worries son. You're a gem for comin in.'

One dreary afternoon in the hospital, Terry stuck in his Walkman earphones and was about to say goodbye when Ron chirped, 'Tez, did ya hear Gazza's comin in to see me?'

Terry pulled one earphone out.

'No, I haven't heard that...'

Ron had played at the same football club Gary Ablett Senior had played when he was a kid. But it would take a miracle for Ablett—or 'God' as they called him—to come and visit Ron Stevenson. And, anyway, God was busy getting ready to strike the Eagles dead in that weekend's second semi-final.

'Yep, Spider Thompson gave me a tinkle and said Gazza'd be in later in the week. Maybe early next... Best player to ever pull on the boots, don't you worry...'

Bloody Gary Ablett. The way Ron carried on about him you'd think he was the saviour of the world. And with all that religion Ablett went on about, thanking Jesus left, right and centre, maybe Ron believed it. But if you had to have that God bothering stuff, Terry would rather his mum's take on it. Sitting there, turning rosary beads over in her fingers without anyone noticing. He wasn't sure if she believed in any of it, but spinning the beads calmed her down.

'Yeah, that'll be great, Ron,' Terry said, watching Jules fiddle around in Ron's bedside drawers. 'And seeya Mum, thanks for comin in.'

The first few times he'd said that she'd taken the bait. She'd given Terry a spiel about Ron being her ex-husband so of course she was going to come in, what else was she going to do? But she had a new tactic now.

'No worries, Terry. Thank you.'

She rearranged the Get Well cards on Ron's dresser, though they were already in perfectly good order, and Terry left for the nursery. It was empty that afternoon, except for an old couple wandering the Australian Natives aisle. Terry sat on a plastic milk crate, hidden behind a bunch of rubber plants. He stuck his Nirvana tape into his Walkman. AC/DC had always been his thing, always would be, but he'd seen Nirvana at the Big Day Out with Scotty Collins the year before. Scotty had taped their new CD for him. He loved their train engine guitar sound and mad lyrics about getting contagious and denied while polly got a cracker.

He and Scotty had formed a band. Scotty could play three chords and Terry yelled. Ron had got wind of it before he'd ended up in hospital. He'd let loose with his usual crap: 'Stick with what you know, son'. Christ, how many times had he heard that? There was a recession on that goose Keating reckoned they had to have, and that seemed to have given Ron extra license to badger him: 'You can't pay the bills with that music bullshit. And what about if you get a woman?'

So Terry stuck with what he knew. Which wasn't a hell of a lot. About the only thing Ron had ever taught him to do was kick a footy, and he hadn't even done that well because Terry had played Under 16 Cs and had hardly ever got a touch. He'd run around the backline with his jumper hanging out, watching other boys pounce on the ball like cats looking for a feed. He was bloody useless. And, as far as he could find out, Ron hadn't been much better. A little rover, he was. Jules said he used to get in and under the packs. But Terry didn't think Ron would have done more than shirk a few issues while the hard men got their hands dirty. His folks were the same like that. Jules endlessly rearranging the bloody Get Well cards, and Ron who'd once loaned Terry his car—a fucking Mazda—on the proviso he put some air in the tyres because Ron didn't know how to do it.

All this from a bloke who'd worked around truckies! No wonder he pushed paper.

And now he couldn't even die properly.

The thick chords of 'In Bloom' thundered in Terry's earphones and Scotty pushed a double-decker trolley under the rubber plants. He had his Yankees baseball cap on backwards. He stopped in front of Terry.

'How's ya old man?'

Terry pulled off his headphones

'Same.'

Scotty leant on the trolley handle. The herbs and

seedlings wobbled.

'Same? Shit, he's been the same for weeks.'

'Yeah.'

Scotty looked at him. All crinkly eyes.

'Gotta get these herbs to their brothers and sisters,' he said, fingering the leaves on a basil bush. 'Are yours right for tonight?'

Terry put his headphones on, but didn't turn on the tape.

'When are they not?'

The way Terry saw it mull was from the earth so it had to be good. Forget all the other drugs. Smack might come from a poppy, but bikies wrecked it. You didn't get nature's best. If a drug was made in a lab, it cooked your grey matter and left you feeling like a cockatoo without any feathers.

Terry knew how to turn nature's herb into cash. As long as he didn't dig too far into his supply. He was down to a choof a week, and that was usually only three cones. Daily bucket bongs, hash pipes and massive spliffs? Things of the past. Like 'The End' by The Doors. He'd listened to that song so many times that when he and Scotty had driven around the factories, their own big spliffs throwing smoke into the night, Terry reckoned he could hear it with the stereo off. He even heard the rotor blades from Apocalypse Now above that ugly bastard's guitar picking. Jim Morrison's voice felt like it was coming out of Terry's mouth.

Too much dope. One night he saw Jesus in the sky and the son of God pulled every nail out of the cross he was hanging on. Terry didn't know how he managed that because he was well and truly stuck there. But those nails came out, one by one. Truth be told, Terry shouldn't have been getting hallucinations on grass. Unless it was laced and how could it be when he was the freakin dealer?

He really wished he could've told his mum about his trip with Jesus. It didn't exactly make Terry religious, but he looked at the crosses in her house differently, and he stopped getting pissed off when she played with her rosary.

And he didn't want as much green.

Jules had called Terry on the Friday as well.

'You better come to the hospital.'

It was the fourth time in two weeks she'd got panicked. And every time it was the same: Ron was sleeping more than usual and his heart rate was down. Then a few hours later he was up and not dying at all.

Bloody useless.

'He'll be right,' Terry said.

'The doctor isn't so sure, Terrance.'

She used his full name when something was important. But she reckoned a lot of things were important. His mother had a tendency to work herself up. And that was lucky, in one way, or she might never have got up the guts to leave Ron.

'He'll be right. You can't get rid of the old bastard that quick.'

She didn't say anything. For too long.

'You all right, Jules?'

She still didn't say anything. Terry didn't know where to

look. There was nothing to look at, really. Just his *Back in Black* album poster. It was coming loose at one end. The Blu Tack had lost its stick and he was pretty sure his mum had started crying.

'Come on Jules...'

'He's your father.'

'Don't remind me.'

Another silence he didn't get to end.

'And he's going to die.'

'Not at this rate.'

Terry had to get to work. The digital clock on his kitchen bench said nine thirty-seven and he started at ten. Jules said something he couldn't catch.

She whispered like she was blowing out birthday candles.

He did the right thing and turned up at the hospital with her later that day. And Ron did look crap. Terry put his hands in his overall pockets then took them out. He looked at the walls, the blue curtains that hung on one side of Ron's bed. He checked out his mum's back as she smoothed his blankets. He looked at the flowers in their vases, anywhere he could. Until he couldn't avoid it any longer.

His father was a skeleton with skin on it.

The old man hadn't exactly been firing the last couple of weeks, but he couldn't have turned to shit so badly in a couple of days, could he? He was just a lump under a sheet.

At the nurse's station, women in pale blue uniforms hung around with their hair in buns. They laughed about some episode of *Sylvania Waters*. Terry watched them until he couldn't ignore the bags under Ron's eyes anymore. Bugger this: he couldn't stand around and do nothing for the bloke. He was in pain. Heaps of it. And he knew he could give him a bit of relief.

'Ron, I reckon I—'

'—he came in mate...'

His father's eyes lost their bags. They were wide open and white. And the old bugger grinned. Sudden and scary.

'Who?'

'Gazza. The great man.'

Jules looked up from Ron's blood pressure chart.

'What are you talking about? I've been here all week...'

'He was in last night, Jules.'

Ron's eyes were still bright. Like a campfire had lit up behind them. Terry didn't know what to say to him.

'He came in and he was wearing a big long coat.'

Oh yeah, Terry thought. White, no doubt, with a halo above him.

Ron slapped his sheet.

'He came right up here and sat down. He said, 'Ron, we're lookin' after ya.'

The Geelong Cats?

'You sure you weren't dreaming, Ron?' Jules asked.

'Nah. I had me eyes open the whole time.'

Gary Ablett: the ghost of Christmases yet to come! Terry wanted to ask Ron to find out if Ablett thought Geelong would get over West Coast. He could put a few bucks on them. But Ron's eyes narrowed. His face looked shithouse again. Terry wasn't sure if the old man was breathing, and Jules had the tears on. Even if it was just for her, which he wasn't sure about anymore, Terry had to do something.

'Ron, I reckon I can make things a bit easier...'

He said it loud enough that his father at least turned his head. Ron let out a whistle that was probably him trying to say, 'She'll be right, get back to work.'

Terry went to the nurse's station. He bailed up a doctor in glasses who was built like a centre-half-back. He said he wasn't in charge of Ron. Terry asked for the bloke who was, and the centre-half-back said he was a she.

'Well, where is she?'

'She's a specialist. Not here all the time.'

'Got to see her.'

'I'll do what I can.'

Terry wanted to grab the bloke by the scruff. Burly or not.

'Mate, listen. I have to see her. The old man's dying. Or giving it a go.'

'All right,' the doctor said, quiet to his chart. 'She's in tomorrow.'

Kurt Cobain was on the cross. Blood pissing out from his side. He was mumbling lyrics Terry couldn't understand so he went up closer. 'Stick with what you know' was the song and Ron was singing it loud and proud. Terry could've sworn it was Kurt, but Ron was staring down from that cross now. He had thick hair again and his muscles were round and strong. No wrinkles.

Blood was pissing out of him. Ron's feet and hands. His dick hanging there, too.

'Sallright,' he smiled, but the blood was still gushing. Terry thought, No, it's not alright, and he tried to say it, but his mouth was like a cold engine.

'I'm free as a bird, happy as a lark...'

Terry couldn't remember if it was in the dream or later, but he thought 'happy' was not a word you'd use to describe Ron. He'd barely seen him after he and Jules had split, but Ron had sometimes picked Terry up from parties when Terry was drunk and stoned. And said nothing to him. Didn't tell him off or even ask if he was okay. But at least he wasn't around to whack Terry and his brothers and yell like a clapped out rockstar.

It must have been in the dream. Because even though Terry wasn't saying it, he was definitely thinking it, that little word.

Dad.

The dream went on and Ron hung there, bleeding. He talked Terry through a heap of stuff, but Terry couldn't remember much of it later. He did remember the soldier. He came in and gave Ron a belting. With the butt end of a rifle. Terry tried to drag his dad away, but Ron said: 'Let him keep at it!' That soldier had a young body but an old bloke's motley face. Terry had never met his dead grandfather, but he wondered if that was him. Then the old bloke was a farmer in overalls trying to punch Terry, but Terry thumped him. His dad laughed, his hands still nailed down. So Terry didn't know how they ended up around him, and he couldn't tell what was on his face, blood or tears.

His or Ron's.

When Terry woke, it was Saturday morning. He wasn't crying or sweating, instead he felt like he'd been swimming in a river. Out his window the day was blue and shiny. There were power lines against the sky instead of trees, but he didn't mind. He got out of bed nice and casual. No rush. Smoothing his doona and opening the false drawer in his dresser, he took out the driest, best batch of head he could find. He put it on the lounge coffee table and swept it into a sweet pile. It would make a spliff fit for a king. He didn't consider how he would keep the smoke from getting out from under Ron's hospital door and alerting the whole hospital.

He picked up his dad's joint. It was a perfect piece of engineering. He almost wanted to smoke it himself. Maybe they could share it, he thought, when the phone rang.

8. Peter Stevenson

The first door was pale blue and thin. Peter didn't knock too hard in case he split it. A glassy-eyed woman answered.

'Hello?'

Her hair matched the door and the hallway was full of bleating budgies in cages.

'Hi, I'm collecting for the Salvation Army today. I was wondering if you could make a small donation?' Peter shouted.

He shouldn't have said small. Just donation.

'Oh,' the woman said. Her face was excessively made-up. Lipstick smudges on her chin. If she had a dollar it would be as lonely as her. Peter looked at his embarrassing Salvo's bib. The budgies hushed and checked it out too. How many budgies made up for a guard dog?

'You're a gem,' the old woman said finally. 'You've restored my faith in young people.'

Peter had just turned 32. He puffed his chest out and stood straighter in the doorway. The old woman sang herself along the corridor to her battered bureau. She returned to Peter with a dollar eighty in ten- and five-cent pieces and the bonus offer of a cup of tea.

'I'm sorry, I can't. I've got quite a few houses to visit yet...'

The budgies amped up.

'You're an angel, good luck to you.'

One down and one-hundred-and-forty-seven to go. Peter should have sat for the rest of the day on that old woman's wicker chair. Had that cuppa. It might have saved his marriage.

The Red Shield Appeal was his wife Jayne's latest social justice campaign. Our way, she said, of giving something back. Peter had stopped suggesting that the campaigns were to stop her feeling guilty about working in finance and having a skyscraper wage. It wasn't worth the hours of silence between them. Or the sharp turn of her head on the pillow.

The last campaign had involved looking after disabled kids as respite for their parents. They'd stayed the night in their spare room. Peter's studio, actually. His easel, canvases and paints had to be moved aside and covered with a white sheet. Maybe the kids thought it was a ghost because they roared all night and Jayne got sick of it. She'd just got pregnant and her friends had told her of the upcoming sleep deprivation. So it was bye bye disabled kids.

But hello Salvos.

Peter agreed to enlist. Under sufferance. Only a few days before, he'd finally got ready to start a new work. The sketches were finished and he'd even circled a Saturday on the calendar. It was the day he'd stand in front of his stretched and primed canvas, set out his oils, in their colors, in a neat row, and get down to it. But he was marching the footpaths instead, collecting. After the old lady and her budgies, he'd gathered a kilo of coins, some notes, a geranium from a cross-eyed Italian grandmother, and three blunt pencils from a pigtailed toddler. Plus a dozen doors slammed in his face. The hardest of those slams had come at house one-hundred-and-forty-two on his list. A ferret of a teenager in a white Guns 'N' Roses singlet. He didn't look like he'd seen light since he'd farted from his mother.

Peter was still pissed off as he strode to house number one-four-three. It wasn't the biggest he'd seen that day, but it spoke wealth like no other. The iron gate was heavy, the brickwork smooth and sleek, and the path that led to the verandah wound through rows of bullet-shrubs. Two shiny steel sculptures—a winged bull and a nude woman with a bow and arrow—were chained to a bright green lawn.

Peter gathered himself on the verandah. This campaign would soon be over. He could rip off his vest and pour a glass of red. At least start work on his canvas. He gave his buckets a quick rattle and got ready to ring the bell. Got ready for who-ever was inside to appear and look at him like he was vermin. He'd learnt to keep his receipt book in his pocket on verandahs like these. Owners would fish around in antique vases for a tax-deductible two dollars in silver. Just like he did whenever the collectors knocked. In future, he'd give nothing less than a ten-dollar note. Like the Westco-wearing mum had earlier. Two kids snorting around her plastic anklets, she'd declined a receipt because she thought the Tax Department would track her down. Peter warmed to her. Until her kids started scream-ing. He'd thought, No child of mine's going to be a screamer, and then he'd had to dodge the sudden memory of his late father. Ron calling him a screamer when he was a kid. Peter had always, even despite his father's recent death, tried as hard as he could not to think of Ron. Or his childhood. Because whinging about Ron or anything that happened was useless. And so were whingers. Which was what his father had told him. And the irony that he tried not think about his childhood because of something his father had said during his childhood was more than Peter could handle. So he tried not to think about that, either.

The walls looked slate yet could have been thick glass hiding security cameras. He rang the bell, but there was silence behind the dark wood door. He touched it. Probably mahogany. It was the only expensive wood Peter knew. He caught his reflection in the bronze doorknocker and saw the mole on the left side of his neck. Like Ron's. Peter gave the knocker three quick raps. There was a rustling in the house but no steps came down the corridor. He reached for the knocker again but the door opened and revealed a wiry man in socks and a slick charcoal tracksuit. His tanned face was covered in light stubble. And tears.

'Sorry,' Peter said to the man's shiny floorboards. He turned to leave but the man grunted. Peter looked back and the man raised his hand for him to stay. Then he slipped in his socks to a steel cabinet and came back with a white cotton bag. He gave it to Peter and he had to stop himself from rummaging through the loose fifty-dollar notes inside.

'Thanks, that's really...' he wanted to say unnecessary but settled on generous. He turned again to leave but the man wouldn't allow it. He grabbed Peter's arm and sobbed.

Those puffy red eyes and that tear-sloshed face. Whatever

had happened to get his waterworks going had broken a dam built strong over decades.

Peter tried to stop himself but he remembered his own tantrums as a kid. How he'd sit in the car on his own and scream.

His mother had cried for weeks when she and Ron had finally broke up. She'd leant on Peter. And he'd held her up. Even though he'd wanted to fall in a heap himself.

The man disappeared into one of his rooms. He returned this time with a black briefcase and opened it. There were fifties and hundreds clipped to the lining. He tossed them at Peter and the man's desperation rang Peter's alarm bells. Real ones might have gone off at a bank recently. Or a mob leader's mansion. He imagined a hit being organised through cigar-smoke.

The notes kept floating to the floorboards and the crying man bent to pick them up.

'Hang on,' Peter said. 'Could you write me a cheque?'

'It's all legit,' the man said and his voice was clear for the first time. 'Every dollar.' He swallowed a sob. He's not the Mother Teresa-type, Peter thought. But if it was dirty money, wouldn't it have been in Port Philip Bay by now?

'Wait!' the man yelled, and Peter watched him slide the length of his corridor and open French doors onto a gymnasium-sized back room. There was a home bar and the man disappeared behind it. Peter heard what sounded like a hatch open, presumably into a cellar. Then there was silence. Peter was left with the sound of sparrows and the occasional car crawling past. The man was gone so long Peter was about to leave, but then he caught sobs echoing out from wherever the man was hidden.

Peter ground the heel of his runner firmly onto the doormat. Too many tears, fella, he heard Ron say. Pull yourself together, boy.

Another reason Peter hated tears. He couldn't get any of his own out. His father had dried them up.

Cut out the bawling, son. Or there'll be bloody hell to pay.

A sliding door thumped shut like someone thrown against a wall. Peter shivered. For a moment he saw Ron bolting down the corridor towards him, ready to let Peter have it, then the crying man dropped two black garbage bags at Peter's feet.

He'd never seen so much cash. There were enough hundreds in those bags to allow him and Jayne to renovate their house twice over and still not have to go to the ATM for months. He wanted to plunge his hands in, hold a single note up to the sun like an old-time crime boss. Whisper something like: 'Pleasure doing business with you.' Instead, he accidentally shook one of his coin buckets. The man wiped some tears on his sleeve then sank to his knees and collapsed. Sniffling on the floorboards.

'Can I call someone for you?'

He didn't seem to hear. He mumbled at the hall ceiling and its ornate light fitting. Peter decided to leave the bags. He didn't have a ruling from the Salvo squad leader about massive donations. But it wasn't right that someone had so much cash in their house, and surely it was a worse idea to collect it? He wasn't even sure if he'd be able to carry the bags to the checkpoint, so he took what the man had already given him and left the bags on the verandah. He hadn't got far down the path when the man tapped him on the shoulder.

'The money,' he whispered. His breath smelt of garlic and

shellfish. He whipped back to the porch, picked up the bags, easily, and brought them to Peter. Peter took them, brushing the man's cold hands as he did. He pulled out his receipt book but the man ran for his verandah, clicked his door open then slammed it behind him. Peter stood shocked for a few seconds, vacantly staring at the sculptures. A tinny voice came through speakers somewhere.

'You can take the sculptures! I've got bolt-cutters.'

'Jesus,' Peter said. He waved in the direction of the house, a gesture he hoped would say enough was enough.

There were more houses on his list but Peter figured he'd finished for the day. He puffed along with the bags until he saw Jayne sitting under an elm on a median strip. Her pregnant belly pulsed above the waist of her sleek track pants in a way Peter found suddenly exciting.

'What are you doing with rubbish bags?' she moaned. 'You could have at least pretended to be a Salvo...'

She crossed the road to where he'd dropped the bags by the kerb.

'I'm king of the Salvos.'

Jayne looked in the bags and blinked.

'What did you do?'

'My job. I collected,' he said in a Mafia voice.

'Who gave it to you?'

'A guy... He was upset.'

'Upset? As in vulnerable?'

She pulled a bag open again and took a long look. Then grabbed his hand.

'He mustn't have been thinking straight...'

They shut up. Behind them a woman in high-heels clicked down her patio's stone steps. Two immaculately dressed kids followed her into a silver Mercedes.

'Should we return the bags, Jayne? Money-back Salvos guarantee?'

The Merc dribbled down the street and Jayne let go of his hand.

'Do you think it's, you know?'

'He'd have dumped it,' Peter said. 'Or laundered it. Or something.'

'Do you think so?'

'I know so.'

'What would you know? You're an artist.'

She stepped from foot to foot.

'Look, Jayne, he was legit—'

Peter clammed up, surprised he'd used the man's words. He scanned the street. Two dog walkers on one side, three kids on bikes further up. They seemed important. Everything did.

'Let's go meet the rest of the team. Is there a prize for biggest collection?'

He picked up the bags but Jayne grabbed his wrists tight.

'We can't.'

'Why?'

'It's too much... They'll think we're criminals...or something. We should take it home first.'

Now Jayne looked up and down the street. A battered blue Commodore appeared. Inside it a man and woman both had dreadlocks. Peter watched them closely until they passed.

'Let's get out of here,' Jayne said. 'Get this home, then go meet the others. With just our buckets, okay?'

Get out of here? Where were they? Belfast?

'You want to keep it?'

She shook her head quickly.

'We've got to take it somewhere safe and figure out what to do.'

'We'll take it to the Salvos. They're safe. And they'll know what to do.'

'Not those volunteers. We don't know who they are.'

She had a point. Their battalion didn't have a genuine Salvo in it. They were all Reservists like them.

Peter dropped the bags on their white lounge carpet. He'd always thought it was plush but now it looked stringy. It needed a vacuum. Their silver cat Max brushed against the bags as if they were his and where the hell had they been all day? Peter felt the same buzz he got whenever he was about to start painting. A heightened awareness, a brightness in his senses. Like his hands, eyes and even his sense of smell were functioning without his body.

Jayne's perfume, a fruity burst with a dry finish.

She smelt so good he wanted to munch through the air around her then start on her neck and lips.

She sat on her favourite chair. White leather with footrests but she didn't relax. She leant forward, her mug of tea between her knees. Peter found in his jacket some of the crying man's money and threw it at the bags. Max mewled and scampered.

'More?' Jayne whispered.

He threw another handful of fifties at the bags. Her face glowed and Peter wanted to lay her on the carpet, grimy bits and all. Give her attention he hadn't shown her in weeks. Maybe even touch her bare stomach with his.

Although that could be going too far. He still wished with all his heart that she hadn't got pregnant. That he wasn't going to be a father.

Jayne sipped her tea.

'We should take it back to him.'

'He won't let us.'

'But he might have come to his senses.'

'He was a mess. And he wanted it gone.'

Jayne brought her mug to her lips again but put it down.

'What if he's changed his mind? Maybe he's thinking, What have I done? And he'll ring the Salvos...'

Peter shook his head. They stared at the bags splattered with fresh cash.

'How much do you think?'

He shrugged and Jayne winked.

'You want to count it?'

There was more than seven hundred thousand dollars on their lounge room floor. Jayne picked at a thread hanging from the ankle of her track pants.

'It's a lot.'

Peter sat on the carpet against the couch, grabbed a pile of hundreds and squeezed it. Jayne sprang from the carpet and into her chair. Peter was shocked to realise her sudden leap had made him worry for a second about her unborn child.

Jayne sat with her chin in her hands and Peter drifted. Counting the cash, he'd been unable to stop himself from thinking about his old man. His investment in Rockmelon Building Society, or whatever it was, before it collapsed. So much of his and Jules' money down the plughole. That stuff-up alone could have broken up his parents, let alone the screaming and flailing madman Ron became.

'Your father won't tell me what's wrong,' was all Peter's mum would say when he asked if his dad was ever going to stop going nuts. And then his parents had broken up and, instead of feeling relieved, Peter had been angry for years. The voices came back, stronger than ever. He didn't tell his mum, but it didn't matter because painting took them away, most of the time.

Jayne folded her hands behind her head, looked out the window and Peter followed her gaze. The sun was yellowing the white blossoms on their Pyrus trees.

'We need to take it back to him. Just to be sure.'

Peter caught another waft of her perfume. The bags were flat as used party balloons.

'Okay.'

'I'll work from home tomorrow,' she said. 'We'll go together.'

They went to bed naked for the first time in weeks. Peter

gently maneuvered Jayne onto her back but she turned and lay on her swollen belly. She looked back at him with a smile and a raised eyebrow. He didn't need any more encouragement. He tried to get some rhythm going, but Jayne worked against him. Her backward thrusting almost flung him from the bed.

Morning sickness kept Jayne under the covers until after lunch. Peter fed her dry biscuits, when she could stomach them. Between waiting on her, he got started on his new painting. But the idea he'd had before the Salvos mission, an abstract city landscape with light towers, seemed stupid. The shapes, the texture, even the colours, the reds that were supposed to be emotionally rich, looked like a child's attempt at a fire engine. He tried some layering and blending but the whole thing got worse.

He went to the kitchen for a sandwich and paced up and down. He stopped and stared through the window at the piles of building materials in the backyard. All that junk made the ponds, bonsais, hanging plants and orchids look ugly.

The backyard was a disaster. Worse than his canvas. And the house was no better. Their second bathroom was half finished and they hadn't even started on the kitchen. Jayne said it needed a complete overhaul: a new industrial oven, a triple sink and wall-to-wall shelving. The window had to be replaced with one double the size. Then dinner party guests would get the best view of their Japanese garden.

Because Peter worked at home every day it was his job to

manage the project. He'd thought about stopping painting for a while. Become the full-time project manager-cum-builder. But Jayne wouldn't have that. Her assessment of their situation made her well up.

'You can't stop your work. It's finally selling.'

Peter had agreed with her, if only to stop her tears. And now the backyard was a pile of wood, steel casings, pipes and ducts. He didn't know what any of it did and Jayne didn't have a clue either. But she knew it was no use to them cluttering the lawn.

'Worksite chic is not part of the Japanese garden aesthetic.'

Still, the renovation was largely on hold due to an unhappy relationship between budget and design. Jayne returned to social justice in the interim, but, according to Peter's agent, it wouldn't be for long.

'That will change when you have the little thing,' said Wessel. They were at an opening. Wessel had an hors d'oeuvre in one hand and a champagne flute in the other. 'She'll have someone to care about. And the starving Africans and everyone will have to go stick their puny hands in someone else's face.'

Peter sculled a glass of water now and Jayne appeared in the kitchen. She looked mousy in her white dressing gown. She moved to fling her arms around him, but checked herself and reached for the cereal cupboard.

'You been busy?'

'Trying...Will you be alright to go and sort out the money thing with me?'

Jayne took a bowl of muesli and a tub of yoghurt to the table.

'I'll see how I am.'

She put yoghurt on the cereal. After two mouthfuls she clanked the spoon on the edge of her bowl.

'I'm going to lie down.'

She stretched on the white couch in the adjoining lounge and snuggled cushions under her head.

'You go. You know him.'

Peter wouldn't have said that. Still, he nodded and went to the safe he'd thought useless when they'd bought the house.

Never look a gift horse in the mouth. Or he'll bite you on the arse.

'Can you carry it all?' Jayne asked.

'I'll take the car.'

'I want to get some stuff for dinner later when I'm feeling better. Can you ride?'

Not a bad idea. He needed fresh air. And a good bike ride always reminded him of when he lived in the country before Westmore. When they had some good times.

He couldn't carry the money on the bike.

'Well...don't take it,' Jayne said. 'Just go and see him. Make sure he doesn't want his money back guarantee,' she laughed.

He locked his bike to a street sign and made for the heavy gate. He didn't want to see the bloke's crying face again or talk to him. He wanted to go straight back home and make a better fist of his work. Or, if that proved pointless, maybe have a closer look at those building materials out back. But he was in the bloke's yard now. And he wasn't home. Nothing was home.

The sculptures had gone from the lawn and just their chains

near bare patches showed where they'd stood. The plants had disappeared from the verandah and the front door was wide open. The corridor furniture was gone. Peter stared along the floorboards to the empty back room.

'Hello?'

The echo surprised him. He didn't know what he'd expected. The man to come running, full of tears? He'd expected anything, really, but not an empty house and garden. Which, now he thought of it, was stupid. Of course the guy was leaving town! Peter left the verandah, embarrassed at his naivety, and met a fat guy in bike shorts and tight singlet at the gate.

'You a mate of his?' the guy asked, scratching at his balloon of a gut.

'Sort of,' Peter lied.

'He's gone.'

Don't have to be Sherlock.

'Know him well?' Bike Shorts asked.

'No. You?'

'I'm his neighbour and I didn't even know the bastard's name. He never said hello or goodbye or anything. Dodgy.'

With that, he marched up his driveway. Peter hoped it was to find a bike and use those shorts. He looked at his own stomach, pressed a bit too tight to his new Sonic Youth t-shirt. And rode hard for home.

The garage was empty. Jayne had taken the car. Peter clacked his bike against the wall and puffed inside. He took a bottle of red from the wine rack and poured half a glass. He flopped on the couch and turned on the TV. The man's empty house had unnerved him. It had reminded him of when he'd been obsessed with UFOs as a kid. When he'd learnt that UFOs took people from their houses in the night, that they singled out people for probes and tests then sent them back into the world and they didn't remember a thing.

Peter couldn't think about painting let alone do any.

You wouldn't work in an iron lung, son.

He held fast against the urge to check the safe and the money. He flicked the channels and came across a kids' quiz show. He loved quizzes, but told himself he'd turn it off as soon as Jayne pulled into the driveway.

He should have offered to cook tonight. But he thought he'd just wait and see what she brought home. Hopefully it would be something he wouldn't know what to do with. Then he could make his offer and she'd say, 'Don't worry, I'll cook.'

The kids on the quiz show were in school uniforms.

He was going to have a kid. Soon!

That he didn't want. He wanted a kid about as much as Ron had wanted the cancer that had killed him a few weeks ago.

Never had much of a chance to win that battle, did I? But you've gotta have a go...

Peter thought of the phone calls he hadn't made. About his mother, dedicated to Ron regardless of their divorce. She'd stayed single, despite offers. Ron had too, minus the offers.

The TV kids tried to answer questions and memories came at Peter like burglars. Searching for a weak spot where they could break in. They found a couple, too.

Peter was the new kid in class, again. Laughed at for wearing the wrong shoes. A girl called him an ugly turd when the teacher left the room.

Ron, standing at the breakfast table in Corumbul.

Reaching for the kitchen drawer and that fucking knife. The knife in his hands. Ron's face contorted.

Peter shaking inside but totally still, his hand tight on his spoon. His brother Simon, sitting across the table, his face frozen. Peter feeling something inside, something he didn't even know was in there, drain out of him fast. Like the last curl of bath water that picks up speed at the edge of the plughole then races for oblivion.

Ah, forgive and forget, son. You don't complain about the beltings, why worry about a silly threat, kid?

'What's the capital city of the USA?' the quiz host asked.

'New York?' came a short boy's reply.

'No, sorry Jason. It's Washington.'

Jesus, fucking hell! He was going to be a dad!

And his baby would grow into a kid.

Who had better know the capital of the USA. Or at least Australia.

He sculled his glass of wine and poured another to the brim. A tall girl with braces fluffed an easy question. But she got another chance.

'In which country are you most likely to find a lemur?'

'Thailand,' Peter answered confidently. Jayne had involved him in a campaign to save the hairy things.

'Peru?' the girl answered.

'That's right Brianna, Peru.'

He switched off the TV and flicked through a newspaper on the coffee table. The urge to check the money came again and he gulped more wine. He checked the clock on the kitchen bench: 6:14. Late for Jayne to still be at the supermarket. She hated them at the best of times, and recovering from morning sickness was the worst.

Though none of their friends had them, Jayne had insisted they buy mobile phones. Peter didn't think they'd be much use. Although he was these days using his computer more. Maybe it would all change. He picked up the home phone and rang her mobile.

The thing buzzed in its black leather pouch on the kitchen bench.

He couldn't hold out any longer: time to check the safe.

Just to make sure everything was in order.

Hold the cash up to the light.

He pushed the stone vase away from the wall, slid the panel and punched in the code. He closed his eyes. The safe buzzed open and he pulled out a few elastic-wrapped wads. He held them in his fists and felt disgusted at the thrill.

It's serious clams, son. Good onya.

He threw a bundle on the carpet and stared at it. It was like a kid's fallen domino. He reached into the safe and pulled out a few more bundles. He wasn't sure if there was as much there now as they'd shoved away last night. He filled his wine glass again.

6:31.

Where in the hell was she?

He decided he would count the cash in one of the piles, make sure the others were the same height, and then count all the piles. Quick and easy. But he sat frozen. He gulped wine, went back to the couch. He couldn't ignore that damn money.

Jayne would be back soon.

He had to count it.

It couldn't be more than a 10-minute job.

He handled a couple of piles. The trim looked uneven. How had they stacked it last night? They'd been tired but strangely energised and full of jokes. Who knows how they'd done it? Maybe they didn't have as much money as they thought. Or maybe they had more.

6:36.

She might be at her mum's. But she only went there, really, when she was pissed off with him. And that had been fairly often lately. Because she was pregnant and he didn't care. Her words, not his. His would have been worse.

Women's business. Keep out of it. If you're smart.

He'd looked after her like a princess today so she couldn't be at her mum's. Maybe she'd run into a friend at the shops and they'd gone for a drink? But she wasn't drinking. He pushed the couch onto an angle and flicked through the notes. Fifteen hundred in one pile; he put it to his left. A thousand in that stack; he put it to his right. He was onto his third when the front door opened and Jayne tumbled in. Her keys jangled and his scalp prickled. He stuffed cash into the safe but she was in the lounge in a flash.

'What are you doing?' she asked, her face beside a breadstick poking from a shopping bag.

'What?'

'Does the guy want it back?'

'He's gone.'

'So where are you going with our money?'

'Nowhere... I'm...counting it.'

'Why?'

'To make sure it's all there.'

'Why wouldn't it be?'

He went silent. For too long.

'We could have been robbed.'

She put the bags on the couch and sat next to them.

'Have we been robbed?'

'I didn't hear the car.'

'I ran out of petrol. I had to walk, with these bags. And now you're...'

Her eyes misted.

'Why didn't you call me?' he whispered, then remembered her phone on the bench.

'Why are you asking me these questions?!'

'Because you are.'

'You had our money on the carpet...'

'I was only counting it.'

'Why?'

Her lips wobbled. She ran her hands up and down her track pants.

'Have we been robbed?'

'I don't think so.'

Peter got his act together. He stood and put his arms around her and she dropped her head on his shoulder. Then took it off quickly. He let her go and piled cash into the safe. Jayne watched, then knelt to help.

She stopped scooping money. And went silent for a long time.

'What are we going to do with it?'

He was the expert now?

'Take it to the Salvos, I suppose. Where's their head office?'

'Wyanirna,' she answered, picking up a bundle. She sat quietly and all he could do was stare at her belly.

'I'll take it tomorrow,' she said at last.

'I'll come too.'

The idea seemed to bother her.

'Are you sure? You didn't get much work done today... did you?'

'It won't take us long,' he said, knowing it would. Bloody Wyanirna. Jayne looked at her knees as if they were a fresh discovery.

'Okay,' she whispered at last, then flitted too quickly, Peter thought, to the wine rack. He wondered for a second why she was suddenly having a drink, then got busy sliding the safe door closed.

He woke and pulled out his greasy earplugs. They hadn't blocked much of Jayne's clanking in and out of the en-suite in the night. He flopped his arm to touch her but it made a cool slap on an empty sheet.

Ahhh, she was up. He could stretch out on his own for a while. Diagonal if he wanted.

He fluffed the doona. They didn't have to be at the Salvos any particular time. Another half-hour's sleep would make up for Jayne's nocturnal ruckus. And he'd work tonight.

He listened to the suburb. Kids chirped on their way to school and cars purred on newly upgraded bitumen. Not exactly the sounds of paradise. But when they finished the renovation and if Peter's work kept selling, they'd be, she said, in a position soon enough to put a deposit on that beach house they'd looked at. The one in Airey's Inlet, not too far from the famous one that stretched out from the cliff. They'd get down there most week-ends with their little one, she said, let the surf wake them up, eat toasted rye bread from the bakery. With marmalade, which Jayne loved. They'd watch from their balcony as clouds puffed on the horizon and they'd taste salt on their lips.

Peter preferred the bush. But he'd fit in with Jayne's plan. So long as he didn't have to mind the kid too much. At all. He might take up coastal scenes. Use more blue than reds. Unlikely, but he'd do what he could.

Happy wife, happy life.

Like yours, Ron?

He shifted the pillow beneath his head and turned on the clock radio. It was fixed on some classic pop station. A guy he couldn't name from a decade he hadn't lived through. Something about a ferry crossing to a land that someone loved.

He wondered if Jayne was alright. Maybe she was down there on the couch again, sick? He'd have to go to the Salvos alone.

He got out of bed and pulled on his white dressing gown and matching slippers. Jayne had insisted he buy the ensemble to remind her of their honeymoon in Port Douglas.

'I'll never forget it now, baby,' she'd purred as they'd left the David Jones' change rooms. She'd told him to try the gown on over his naked body because that's how he'd wear it at home. She'd pulled beneath her skirt and shifted her underwear aside. They'd watched each other in the mirror, faces reddening as they'd tried not to laugh or moan.

That was when she was on the pill.

He couldn't father. He had no idea how to do it. He didn't hate kids, for Christ's sake! He was just terrified of one needing him to be anything or anyone.

He slippered down the stairs. The house was quiet. The kitchen was empty except for Max. The cat pressed against the fridge then Peter's ankles. The lounge was empty too.

'Jayne?'

The only place she could be was the downstairs loo. He knocked on the door. Nothing. He went to the safe, reached in and swished air. His face flushed and he told himself to calm down.

A fool and his money...

There had to be a rational explanation.

...are soon parted.

He looked out the window as if the trees would tell him what to do. He sat on the edge of the couch. Tried slowing his breathing.

Okay. She's decided he needed a sleep in because it would

help get his creative juices flowing. She'd done it before. This morning she'd taken it upon herself to make the long drive to the Salvos on her own. For his sake. To keep him happy. He went to the kitchen for a reason he couldn't figure until he found it. A scrap of paper next to Jayne's mobile.

Peter

Hope you had a good sleep in. You needed it. I've taken the money out to the Salvos. I'll be back for lunch if you're here, otherwise I'll see you tonight. Give me a buzz if you want.

He put the note on the bench.

Her usual 'love you' was missing. And her name. How could he buzz her if she didn't have her phone with her? He stuffed his wallet full of Jayne's cab charges and ran for the door.

In the taxi, he banged away on his phone, trying to remember the Salvos' number. All those ads and now he couldn't remember. He fluked it in the end.

'Salvation Army, good morning, you're speaking to Karen, how can I help?'

'Umm, donations. Could I speak to the donations department?'

'Our fundraising division?'

He nodded, uselessly. The receptionist said the team was in a meeting, could she take a message? He gave his wife's company, said he worked for it. Gulp.

'It's about a donation.'

The receptionist's voice wobbled.

'I can definitely take your number and have David return your call. I'm sure he'll get straight back to you. You've got a mobile phone, haven't you, that's right?'

Peter wanted to say that doesn't mean I'm a millionaire. Then he thought of the cash.

'Yes, that's right. I've got a mobile phone.'

You gotta show 'em who's boss, son.

The taxi driver was quiet. Highway noise barriers blurred and Peter made snap decisions. One of which was to call his mother-in-law, Jennifer.

'Has Jayne been in touch?'

'I haven't heard from her for a couple of weeks.'

Jennifer's strained voice. Like there was a pineapple stuck in her throat and she was trying to talk it out. She'd be standing this morning in her aircraft hangar-sized kitchen, playing with her earrings.

'How are you both?'

'We're fine. How are your cats?'

'Oh, you know. Porsha was at the vet yesterday. Again. How's the renovation coming along?'

'Beautifully.'

'You were wondering if Jayne had been in touch?'

'Yeah, we were thinking of having you and Henry over. I thought Jayne might have made it for this weekend but I'm going away ..'

Now he'd done it.

'Oh, what a pity! We'd have loved to have come! But we'd be fine to come next weekend. Anytime next week, really...'

He opened the window. He could barely hear Jennifer above the traffic. As planned.

'Sorry Jennifer, I've got another call coming in... Hello?'

David Robson. Salvos.

'Hello Peter? You wanted to discuss making a donation?'

'I'd like to meet this morning, yes.'

'Great. I'll be here.'

'Have you had any big donations today?'

Peter heard the Salvo's pen clicking.

'Umm, well... I can't really disclose...'

Peter sighed.

'I'll be there soon.'

A man in a yellow safety vest smoking a cigarette held up a Stop sign and Peter's taxi driver followed orders. At last the man turned his sign to Slow and the taxi edged along in a single lane. Peter thought of the Stop signs Jayne had stuck up for him. That he hadn't seen. Or had refused to see.

All those good works. The caring for lemurs, rainforests in Brazil, the Tassie Devils, kids with disabilities, and now the Salvos. She hadn't been trying to get over her guilt. She'd been telling him it was over. She'd been trying to put something else in her life before she ripped him out.

He hadn't cared enough. Of course he bloody hadn't. They were having a baby and he'd acted like she had a pillow stuffed up her shirt. The last straw for her and the last sign for him. Road in desperate need of works. Maybe even road closed. And he hadn't even slowed down. Now she had more than a little extra cash with which to hit the road.

The taxi turned into the Salvos' car park and the big red shield on the building made Peter angry.

You never know what's on the next horizon.

Fuck off, Ron. That's why it's a horizon. You can't see it because it doesn't exist so nothing can be on it. He fixed up the cab charge and got out. The same Salvo shield was stenciled on the glass front doors. He took off at speed towards them, but pulled up when he heard a familiar car horn.

Their new black Range Rover Classic. Parked with Jayne behind the wheel. She flashed the lights and he blinked. He shuffled towards her, eyes to the bitumen like a lazy dog. She buzzed the driver window down.

'What are you doing here, Peter?'

He couldn't see her eyes behind her sunglasses. Didn't want to anyway.

I've come, Jayne, to make sure you were handing over the money. No, actually, I assumed you weren't handing over the money. I assumed you'd disappeared. To the far north where you've secretly planted fifty acres of Japanese Gardens. You've got a new business selling trinket things at the local market. Good cover for your mad arse plans. I've come to meet David Robson to let him know you've robbed the Salvos. They should call the cops. Start tracking a black Range Rover, licence plate number Jaynee.

'Nothing,' he replied.

'Nothing?'

He shook his head.

'Go,' she waved and Peter got the same taxi home.

The marriage counsellor went on about the importance of trust in a relationship.

'It's the glue, isn't it, that holds the whole thing together?'

The counselor wore a tan shirt and a bright look. Like a man who'd just given up smoking.

'Without trust, it all falls apart. Doesn't it?'

Peter realised they were rhetorical questions. He should only answer the real ones. And then be very careful which. It was asking for trouble to answer everything. And he was in enough of it already.

Session after session, Jayne fumed next to him on the black leather couch. It smelt new. She had decided it was not appropriate to reveal to the counsellor the exact reason for their trust breakdown. The counsellor didn't push them on it.

Trust was trust, wasn't it?

Jayne was like a diver picking through a rusted hull. She brought up problems he didn't even know existed.

'He never, ever lets me achieve my goals. And he crushes my emotions.'

After one session, she tearfully drew up a goal chart on butcher's paper. And Peter agreed to do everything she needed. Work from home, handle the renovations, not get shitty if he struggled to open the corks on his wine bottles. Go back to drinking beer if he had to. But he may as well have talked to the counsellor's sunrise posters.

'He doesn't *listen*... We were supposed to be renovating but all he wanted to do was paint... I thought he was open to who I wanted to become. But then he wanted me to be someone else...'

Rubbish, he thought, but didn't say. It would have opened up another line of attack.

You're a bloody wimp lad, get up.

In the counselling sessions, he swatted away her words as they buzzed in his face. He managed once to say he wanted to change, but it was hard because he couldn't figure out exactly what Jayne wanted. He thought he was doing all he could.

But finally she pointed the counselor to the ticking bomb that he could not possibly defuse. Not quickly enough to save his marriage, anyway.

'I'm pregnant. And he doesn't want to be a father. It's hopeless.'

He couldn't say a thing. The counselor spoke but Peter couldn't take his words in. The truth was in the room, holding a shovel and swinging dirt all over him. He'd be buried in seconds.

'You're a coward, Peter,' Jayne said, crying.

You're chickenshit, son. I had you three blokes!

Great job you did, Ron.

No trust, no love for his child to be. No marriage for Peter and Jayne.

Mr Bright-Eyed No Smokes counselor switched to the importance of positive post-marriage relationships.

To save money, Peter helped the two removalists.

'Nice set of clubs,' the bloke in grey overalls said as he dragged Peter's golf bag into the truck. It had been a long time since he'd had a hit.

It took three of them to get Peter's final item, the mattress from the spare room, into the truck. He had a last look at his double-storey home; the trees tickled by a slight breeze and the flowers in full bloom. The sun was glinting on every window. It was a crisp morning, worthy of a counselling room poster. But his lungs were somehow filled with dirty air and his throat was tight.

He wasn't going to cry, and especially not in front of these rough nuts.

He slid into the passenger seat. The trip was smooth until they hit bumper-to-bumper traffic near Victoria Market.

'Plenty of get-out clauses from a marriage these days,' the driving removalist said. Something about his silver moustache made Peter listen to him. 'My missus said I didn't give a rats about her feelings. Now I'm paying for whoever wants to give her a feel!'

The removalists laughed and the storyteller offered Peter a cigarette. He declined, but it was tempting. The moustached removalist blew his smoke out the window and into the morning traffic.

'How much you comin out with?'

'Just what's in the back.'

'Nah, mate, nah, the property settlement. Your percentage.'

'Oh, 30.'

'Sheesh, you've done alright! Some buggers get nothin'. I got 20. The missus had worked hard and put a fair bit away and, you know, she'd done most of the housework and kids stuff and that. All counts.'

He thought of Jayne's, and his, unborn child. He could hardly breathe.

'You gotta be happy with 30 per cent mate,' Moustache added, as if the number was from a fairytale. He parked the van in a loading zone out the front of Peter's white block of 1960s apartments. The front lawn was mown. Too short. There was an empty stubby on the deck of letterboxes. The removalists told their jokes and shuffled his belongings into their new home. But Peter sat in the cabin. He didn't move until Moustache man put his head in the passenger window to see if he was okay.

You're not hearing voices, son. Don't be bloody stupid. And you can go back to school far as I'm concerned.

The removalists smoked up the apartment and left. Peter tried to throw off the dark mist that had followed him for weeks after the break up. He should count his blessings.

Okay, here goes.

It was good to have somewhere clean and bright to live. First-floor, light-filled. Balcony with a view to the courtyard. With grass and seats in it. Only a short walk to the tram. He had space to paint. If he ever found time again. Child support bills would soon arrive. He'd be teaching more than painting for a long time.

He took from a box some crockery wrapped in newspaper. He'd helped his family move so many times as a kid he knew how to wrap better than paint. He could do it in his sleep. Which was all he wanted to do. But he pushed through his tiredness, and put cups and plates one-by-one into the cupboard beside the kitchen drawers.

He went to the balcony, the cool air. He could see one of the MCG's light towers. If he stood on his toes. He might do a series.

He was at RMIT teaching a few weeks later when he got a fax from his ex-mother-in-law. He had a son.

It was ten days before Peter saw him. Jayne wouldn't answer his calls. Neither would her family. He should have expected that. But now the kid had arrived, a boy, it was all Peter could do from banging the door off his old house. Six days in a row he knocked but no one answered. He called friends, but choked up before he could tell them what had happened. He thought about calling his brother, Simon. He had kids. He'd know what to think. But they hadn't spoken for months. Not since Simon had threatened to bash Peter in front of some lout mates at a pub in Westmore. Just jokin', can't you take a joke? Simon had laughed. He couldn't call his brother when he was on the brink of falling to bits, but Peter kept thinking about it.

To stop himself, he rang Wessel. His agent was helpful. Sort of.

'You must take good care of yourself, Peter. Do not, do not paint.'

Then Wessel started psychobabbling about blockages and delusions. Peter should have seen that coming. Wessel was Austrian. He hung up when his agent was mid-sentence about Peter's 'father issues'.

He thought about calling Poster Boy Counsellor. What did his ex-wife's unwillingness to talk to him or let him see their son say about positive post-marriage relations?

It was a bit shit wasn't it?

But he sat on his balcony instead. He stared at the glow from an MCG light, all the little lights that made one big light. Then the little lights seemed to come loose of each other and fly. He had a half bottle of whisky in his hands. What a bloody cliché I am, he thought. He wanted to smash the bottle but that would be an even worse one. So he just gripped it tight.

It's no good whinging lad. Get on with life.

He met an intensive care nurse a couple of years later who loved cycling. And he learnt to like riding a bike more than he ever had. Just the way that you never have to bear your own weight. You get out of it what you put in. The open air, the sound of your own breathing, in and out, the click and grind of gears, the burn in your thighs that rips every dark thought out of your mind and into the pain your body's feeling. Then, when you're finished, the flow and rush of healthy blood through you when you're enjoying the view from some restaurant or other.

Celia took him on long riding tours, even as far as Hepburn Springs for a spa retreat. That's when he went into detail about his marriage break-up. But he didn't talk about trust. He just rubbed sandalwood oil onto her smooth, pale back, and she rubbed the same sweet smelling goo into his chest.

Celia moved into his apartment after a year together and

they had a party to celebrate. A drunk brunette called Lilly, one of Jayne's old friends, more hers than his, who Peter couldn't even remember inviting, bailed him up in the corridor. Her hair was still wet. It was pissing down outside. Like her monologue.

She wouldn't stop telling him about his ex-wife. Peter knew Jayne had a new partner, but he hadn't met him. And he didn't want to. As long as she delivered his son every second weekend as arranged, she could do whatever the hell else she liked.

'Peter, listen to me. You'll want to hear this.'

Her breath was Sauvignon Blanc and cold prawns. She had a wet hand on his arm.

'Her new house, you've never seen anything like it! Views of Fairhaven Beach from the top of the hill. There's a pool in the house...in the house...and a Japanese garden...'

'Wow, that's great,' he seethed. He knew Jayne had a house down there. So shut up, Lilly.

Peter looked around for Celia. She was at the kitchen bench pouring wine and laughing. He tried to catch her eye, but no luck. She looked gorgeous in her black dress.

'Jesus, Peter!' Lilly said, swaying. 'I didn't know you had that much money between you...'

It was no business of Lilly's, but he gave her the rough figure Jayne had received. He'd had more than a few cabernets.

'Must be her new man,' he told her.

Peter pictured a muscly marketing exec doing laps of the indoor pool. Because he'd be too shit-scared to try the mountainous surf.

'No, Peter. He's a scraggy looking poet guy. Can't even sell a book. Not a dollar to his name... Well, he's got a few now! And do you know Jayne's stopped working at the top end of town? She's started an Aboriginal art business. Sells the paintings... Some people think they're fake but I just think they're jealous of her...'

Whatever else she said he didn't know. Her hold on his arm got stronger and he pulled away. Lilly's wine glass wobbled in her other hand. He wanted to rip it off her and throw it at the wall. He excused himself, said he needed to go to the bathroom, but he headed to the balcony.

The party was rocking inside and it was too wet for anyone to brave the outdoor furniture. Peter sat on a sloppy wooden chair. He remembered the sunglasses on Jayne's face in the Salvo's car park and her blank expression. How he'd been too embarrassed to do anything but catch his taxi and get the hell out of there.

The MCG light tower lit up sheets of rain. It got heavier but Peter didn't notice it or Celia shaking him until the rain was in his eyes and down his face.

9. Trevor Randall

Trevor Randall had been unsteady on his feet since his early teens when he was king hit at a bonfire. He stood now on his Westmore nature strip, tensing his decaying muscles in the winter chill. He put a blue plastic lunch bag into his adult son Anthony's cold hand. Anthony smiled back through his shaggy beard and motioned for his father to hug him. In their heavy coats, Trevor and Anthony embraced. Anthony was a mute and intellectually disabled, but Trevor always knew what he was saying.

Don't watch me, Dad. You know I can do it.

Anthony began to cross Fryall Road. He waved back at his father as he went. Trevor was a lollipop man. Out of habit, he squinted up and down the foggy road. No traffic, he thought, Anthony'll be fine.

But the Holden Calais that turned quickly from a side street onto Fryall hadn't had its lights on. Trevor had turned his back and he was about to open his low iron gate when he heard tyres screech and metal thump on flesh.

The Calais' door flung open. The driver sat shaking on the edge of his car seat. Anthony was face down on the nature strip across the road, the blue plastic lunch bag beside him. Trevor hobbled across the road to Anthony and found his son was still breathing.

A few weeks later, Trevor pushed his breakfast bowl away and opened one of the envelopes on his kitchen table. It was a card with a picture of flowers in a vase and the words *Thinking of You* on the front. A primary school kid had scrawled, *I hope your son will be ok. And come bak to the schol crossing SOON* in red pencil on the inside. Trevor took the card to the lounge room and placed it with the others arranged on the tile mantelpiece. They were lined up next to the framed black and white photo of Pamela, sitting on the beach at Ocean Grove, cuddling Anthony when he was a boy. She'd died nine years ago.

At the kitchen bench, Trevor spread margarine—not too much—on four pieces of white bread. Then he cut the crusts off. Outside, trucks rumbled and horns blasted, long and threatening.

Trevor had worked for twelve years as a lollipop man at Westmore Primary School, a few streets from his house. Children would always say hello to him where he stood in the middle of the road in white pants and overcoat, a beardless Santa blowing a whistle. He'd say *G'day* to the kids, but when parents greeted him, Trevor felt like a boy making sandcastles at the beach and watching waves knock them over. He nodded or sometimes offered a muffled 'hi'. He had to concentrate on the cars.

The kettle bubbled and Trevor poured hot water onto a teabag. He gathered lettuce, cheese and tomatoes and put them on the bench with the buttered bread. He couldn't break the habit of making lunch for Anthony. Beside the hospital bed in which Anthony lay in an induced coma, a nurse had explained why Anthony didn't need food.

'You see those, Mr Randall?'

Trevor had nodded at the thin tubes in his son's nose and mouth.

'They're feeding him. He can't eat any real food because he's in a very deep sleep.'

But Trevor still made the lunch. In the early days after Anthony's accident, before the school decided he needed to take a holiday, Trevor took the lunch to the crossing in his coat pocket. When he got home from the afternoon shift, he stored each lunch in a cardboard box in the garden shed. The smell was terrible. He hoped it wouldn't waft across the fence and into his neighbour's yard.

When Anthony was little, doctors and other experts had offered all kinds of advice.

'If we can just keep working on Anthony's ability to recognise and react to facial expressions, it will really help...' one specialist had told Trevor's wife.

'Yeah, I know,' Pamela had said. 'I've been trying. But it's hard, it's just...'

The specialist had glanced at Trevor. Pamela had looked at her husband too. 'I'm doing me best,' she'd said, and the specialist had nodded.

Anthony's communication didn't improve. But after Pamela died, he at least got better at crossing the road. Eventually, Trevor didn't need to hold his hand or arm. He wondered whether Anthony might eventually help him cross the road.

A man from the City Mission, another man from Human Services and a nurse had sat in Trevor's lounge room. They had decided Anthony could live on his own. So he had been moved to 27 Forrest Street, just around the corner from Trevor, with three other men. The house was clean, and the longhaired man from the City Mission and the nurse in her white Corolla had both visited Anthony regularly. They sometimes visited Trevor too, and told him Anthony was going well.

On Tuesdays and Thursdays, Anthony was picked up in a bus and taken to work at the Brotherhood of St Laurence Warehouse. But before the bus arrived, Anthony walked to Trevor's place to collect the lunch his father had made.

Trevor put slices of cheese on top of the processed chicken meat, which already sat on top of the lettuce. The phone rang, shrill, like a hungry seagull. Trevor held the sauce bottle above the two sandwiches and listened to the phone screech. He dripped the sauce carefully across the cheese slices—just how Anthony liked it—then shook pepper on top.

The phone stopped ringing. Trevor cut the sandwiches in half and parceled them in cling wrap. He found a banana in the fruit bowl that had just enough black and yellow, and an orange, a firm one. The phone screeched again, but Trevor watched it until it stopped. He went to the drawer, pulled out a blue plastic bag and wrapped the sandwich.

News about Anthony's accident had got around Westmore Primary School quickly. Some parents had stopped in the road and asked Trevor how he was going. Others had ignored him and rushed their kids over the crossing. At a school council meeting, Trevor's employment future was Safety Agenda Item 4 (a). After the meeting, the principal told Trevor he might be asked to take a break from work for a while. A couple of weeks later a vote narrowly favoured Trevor keeping his job. But Trevor decided to take a break anyway. Now he wasn't sure how long he'd been away or whether he would go back. He might be able to find work at another school. But he wasn't sure.

The lunch made, he sat at his kitchen table and looked at the other envelopes. He picked one up, felt it. Another card. He didn't touch the two letters near it with the Westmore Primary School emblem stamped on them.

When the phone squawked again, Trevor got up, took it from the hook and looked at the receiver. He slowly brought it to his ear.

'Mr Randall, hello, are you there?'

Trevor grunted.

'I'm sorry, Mr Randall, but, as you recall, yesterday we told you that you'd have to come to the hospital and sign the forms... I'm really sorry to have to remind you of this...'

Trevor was silent.

'Are you there Mr Randall?'

He grunted again.

'So we'll see you at eleven?'

Trevor didn't reply. The caller paused, waiting for Trevor. 'Mr Randall? Are you there?'

'Yes,' Trevor said.

'See you at eleven?'

Trevor hung up. He took his coat from the hook, put it on, walked to the front door, and then turned around. He went back to the bench, picked up the lunch and carried it outside. His wheelie bin was open on the nature strip from the morning rubbish collection. Trevor dropped the lunch into it.

10. Simon and Terry Stevenson

They were with their mates outside the Westmore Hotel night-club. Lining up to get in. A bloke in the front bar window with a yellow surf top accidentally caught Simon's eye.

'What're you lookin at, fuckwit?' Simon asked by way of introduction.

The bloke inside was wiry with blonde hair. He was probably a tradie from one of the beach towns outside Westmore. The bloke lifted the window.

'What was that?'

'You heard me.'

Simon slurred his words and almost lost his balance. The surfie wasn't impressed. Or worried.

'Go home mate.'

The surfie's crew, hair gel and rainbow shirts, were all laughing. Even the girlfriends. With sunnies stuck to their foreheads, as if it was going to brighten up tonight. Simon steadied himself against the wall, pulling his cigarettes from his pocket. His black shirt lifted up so everyone in the line got a view of his chubby, white gut. Simon rounded on Terry.

'That bloke's fucked,' Simon told his brother.

'If we get in.'

Simon dragged on his cigarette.

'We'll get in,' he nodded. 'Don't you worry.'

They'd been standing in the line for half an hour and there were still twenty bodies in front of them. Terry knew that, down at the Eureka Hotel on the river, Harmsy would be on the door. He'd let them in there. Didn't matter how pissed they were, or what they were wearing, he always let them in. But now they were outside the Westmore, with every other trendy who'd come into town. So Terry gave Simon the third degree.

'Told you we should have gone to the Eureka!'

Simon sent his cigarette flying to the concrete.

'Get fucked,' he laughed. 'I told Pete to meet us here.'

Their big brother who'd moved to Melbourne. Years ago and now he was married, too, to a sexy chick called Jayne.

Simon gave Terry a smack on the shoulder and he accidentally bumped into Brooksey behind him. He said, *Sorry Brooksey*, and stupid Brooksey laughed, flicked his thin hair and said, *Don't do it again, wanker.* Simon called Brooksey a wanker too. A major wanker, without a dick.

It was all fun and games. Until someone got hurt. That's what their father always told them. And if they kept fighting he'd belt them himself.

Despite the surfie having a go at him, Simon was pretty chirpy. It was his bucks' night and he was full of grog. He reckoned he was going to dance when they got in, so he must have been more drunk than he looked. They didn't play Metallica in there. All you could hear for miles around was *doof doof doof.*

There were only four of them left on the crawl. Terry, Simon, Brooksey and Thommo, Simon's footy coach when he was in under eighteens. Ron had gone home but his mate Thommo was still there and he'd said, 'I'll look after your lads,' before Ron had headed home. The big bloke was high up in the trucking company, higher than Ron ever got. Thommo was CEO of the whole Westmore business arm and Ron was one of his managers. Thommo looked like a wrestler, but wouldn't hurt a fly. Unless the fly was a pain in the arse that wouldn't leave you alone. He always said he had a black belt, then he'd lift up his shirt and show you the leather one round his pale blue jeans.

Simon pointed down the line at a group of Bell Park Hill footballers. Terry knew one of them, Stringy. He waved and Stringy waved back. Simon summed up the situation. Like he always did. Because, as Peter had always told him when they were teenagers, *For someone who knows nothing, you know everything.*

'They're letting those bastards in, so we'll get in.'

Stringy was in a pair of stretch jeans. And he was staggering. Terry wasn't as confident as Simon that Stringy, or anyone in the line, would get in. And he was even less confident that Peter would be in there already, having one of what Simon called his 'poof beers'. But he couldn't tell Simon that. Because when Simon got on a roll there was no telling him anything. Especially when it came to Peter. Their elder brother was either the devil or Jesus incarnate, and Simon decided which, no one else.

Peter had finished doing his Fine Arts degree at university in Melbourne. Simon never knew what his paintings were supposed to be. Just colours splashed every which way with stuff sticking out of them. So you could have knocked him over with a feather and tickled him while he was down when Peter sold a few. His brother lived the life. With that curvy Jayne and a big house. Only because she made good money. And she didn't like Peter getting loose with his brothers, no way.

The other two couldn't work it out: Peter would come to Westmore and hang around with them, even go out and have a beer, but Simon and Terry thought he never looked like he was having a good time. Still, Simon had invited him to the bucks' night and, according to Simon, Peter had said he'd be there.

Ron's theory was that Peter only ever came back to see if his brothers had changed. No luck there, he told his younger sons. But Terry and Simon told him, what would you know, old man, you only saw us on weekends when we were teenagers, if you saw us at all. Probably scared we'd be belt you back for all the times when we were kids. And Ron would lie and say I can't remember that.

Terry hardly spoke to Peter. Even when they were little. Not because he didn't like him, just because Peter was older. Always off doing his own thing. But Simon, no. Whenever Peter came to town, he was with him as much as possible, hanging shit on him, calling him a poof, saying he dyed his hair, having a go at him about his dick size. Peter ignored him, usually, or said, 'That's big coming from you, Simon. You can't even tell the time.' And he was right. Simon couldn't do it unless it was on a digital watch. After Peter had shaken their hands and gone back to Melbourne, Simon would huddle in a pub corner with Terry and whoever else would listen, dripping on and on about how much he loved his brothers. Especially Peter.

'He's got it all, that bastard.'

They were nearly at the front of the line. Almost in the face of the slinky woman in her black catsuit and her two beefy mates in black singlets. They both looked like Arnie Schwarzenegger after a workout. Simon told Terry and the boys to clam up. He grinned and stuck a finger over his mouth and whispered, *Shhh.* Funny thing was, it worked. If they shut their mouths long enough bouncers let them in, no matter how pissed they were.

In the foyer between the bar and the dance floor, it was *doof doof doof* no matter which way they turned. Simon didn't know what to do first: go to the back bar and have a look for Peter, or head to the front bar and see what was going on with the surfie and his mates.

Terry had known since they'd had their steak and chips at the Cremorne Hotel that night the bucks' party would end up in a fight. And he was worried because when Simon was skunk pissed he could only handle one bloke himself. If that. So it meant Terry would have to cover at least two. Then hope Simon's stupid mate Brooksey was up for a tangle. And he could never tell. It depended on whether the boss had been on Brooksey's case at work during the week. Then he'd fight a grizzly bear. Thommo was good for a bit of push and shove. He'd drag a few blokes out of the box-ons.

Terry moved from foot to foot. Edgy. His father had told him it was alright, it was a good thing to be nervous before a fight. If you were going to get in one. Because Bernie, Ron's old man, had said that before the bombs hit in World War II, blokes shat themselves in the trenches.

Why did I ever tell them a thing about their grandfather? Probably trying to make them proud of me or something stupid like that.

Simon yelled at Thommo over the *doof doof* and pointed to the dance floor.

'Go and see if Pete's in there, will ya?'

'Go bone yourself!' Thommo grinned. 'I've gotta take a leak.'

'Well, when you've finished looking for ya dick then.'

Thommo laughed, reached over and rubbed Simon's spiky hair.

'Righto,' he said and made a beeline for the loo. Simon looked to Terry and Brooksey.

'You bastards right then?'

When the surfie saw Simon had got in after all, his smile faded. Terry got Simon a pot and he toasted the surfie and his crew from a distance. The surfie looked away. Real quick.

'I'll just go over and see if he's having a good night,' Simon nodded and he took off. That was the moment, right there, to say, *Hold on, lad, let's just have a nice beer or two.* But Thommo missed the boat. He got back from the dunny and Simon was already gone.

'Peter here?' Terry asked and Thommo shook his head.

'Fuck it. What are we doin here then?'

Terry took a sip of his pot. He watched Simon, holding his beer in the air and pushing through the crowd. His brother made it to the window, to the surfie and his mates, and started yapping at them. Terry knew what he was saying without even trying to lip read.

You havin' a good night?

The surfie nodded, on cue.

I'm not havin much of a night.

Now the surfie acted innocent. And tried not to look scared in front of the girls or his mates. Terry felt for him. Because it was going to start soon. And it always seemed like slow motion; girls screaming, waving bags all over the place, beers going over. Simon's first punch, always straight into the bridge of a bloke's nose when the poor bugger was in the middle of saying something. They'd all got that advice from Ron. And he'd got it from Bernie.

Shit, why couldn't I shut up about that crap? They were Bernie's bloody ideas, not mine.

Everyone near that window would soon be up and about like a bomb had gone off. The surfie's eyes would be watering from Simon's first punch, and Simon would be giving the board rider another few quick ones to get his teeth wobbly. That was always the plan.

Ron's bloody bickering kids.

Terry usually got in there pretty quick too, straight at the ones just standing around. More advice from the family.

Terry never worried too much about the first bloke who would try to get at Simon. He was usually the drag 'em apart, settle 'em down type. No real problem. The ones standing around were the worry. They sized everything up. One of them might come in with a wild swing. A bloke who'd been thinking the whole time, *Will I get in there?* Those standing arounders weren't keen to cop a pounding and then have to explain it to their wives or girlfriends. So Terry made up their minds for them. He usually went for the biggest one, gave him an upper-cut to the chin. It was a bastard of a punch if it copped you when you weren't looking. Ron had copped one playing footy and the rattle it gave him was enough, let alone the headache for a week. But Terry knew when to hold up and take it easy. Simon? No such luck.

Once Terry had to pull Simon back from booting a bloke in the head who'd copped one and was just lying on the ground. And then there was the night they all went home and watched music videos till late and Simon found a bloke's tooth stuck in his knuckle. It had been there all night.

Terry fumbled now in his pocket for coins for another pot. When he looked up, Simon had two Arnie bouncers in his face. Thommo had seen it all and was on his way and Terry followed him.

'What's goin on?' Terry asked an Arnie.

'This bloke's threatening one of the patrons.'

'*Threatening* him?'

Arnie nodded.

'You can't kick him out for that,' Terry said. And he thought, *Show up, Pete! Make it worth being here.*

'We'll kick out whoever we want,' the other Arnie said.

'Fuck off,' Simon told him, and he gave the bouncer a shove.

That wasn't clever. Both Arnies got him in a headlock. Terry,

Brooksey and Thommo kept their cool. They talked to the bouncers, tried to settle them. And they did. They settled. Good thing for Simon's crew, because now there were six bouncers in the room. Thommo had a quiet word with a couple of them. The surfie and his crew were long gone. But the Arnies stayed on the case.

'Come with me, mate,' one said. The two of them grabbed Simon, and his arms were quick smart round his back as they dragged him through the bar.

'I'm not goin anywhere, I'm fucken stayin' 'ere. Me brother's comin and I'm fucken stayin 'ere.'

Terry followed, yelling stuff just for the hell of it, while Brooksey and Thommo stayed and argued with the other bouncers.

Simon was thrown on the concrete out the front. He banged his head. Terry had a word to the boys in black.

'There's no need for that shit. He was going.'

An Arnie piped up.

'Look mate, the Bandidos have been around the last few nights...'

Which meant the Arnies were hot on idiots and weren't taking any crap. Terry had a chat with them. He thought that for gorillas they were quite reasonable. He yacked about some trouble a mate of his had had with the Bandidos. All the time he was watching Simon on the ground and thinking his brother should just get up, it was embarrassing.

Terry couldn't see Simon's face, just the back of his moaning head. Simon lifted himself, finally, looked along the street at the cars and taxis. Girls in the line laughed at him. *Pete's not comin,*

Terry thought and he botted a cigarette from one of the girls.
And we're going to the Eureka...

You bet they were.

Simon was on his feet and it was *Eureka!* all right. The punch
he gave the Arnie's called a king hit, but that's bringing down a
king's good name.

11. Jules and Fiona Stevenson

In the years after she and Ron divorced, Jules had plenty of time to read more novels that she borrowed from the library. *In dreams begin responsibilities.* That was the quote at the start of the one she'd read just last December. She couldn't for the life of her remember the name of the book, but she remembered that quote.

But maybe it should have said, *In dreams begin bloody madness.*

After Christmas, she could hardly sleep. There were night road works. And the *heat*, God, it was ridiculous. She even thought of taking off her nightie and sleeping in the raw. When she did snooze, she kept dreaming she was doing something she'd never do in real life: dancing with a woman. Her dead sister-in-law, Sheree. They were twirling down the Tonvale loony bin's bluestone hallway. She shouldn't think of it as the 'loony bin', but it's what everyone called it when it was open. The place was shut now. For good.

In the dream, Jules was the same age as she was now, sixty-four. But Sheree's high cheekbones and fluttery eyelashes were in perfect working order. She was still thirty-three, or however old she'd been when they'd put her in Tonvale

When Ron put her in Tonvale.

It wasn't Jules who'd signed the forms.

Sheree danced and spun in that tie-dye dress she always wore, and the hallway went on and on. Down the end of it was a light like a train coming out of a tunnel. But it was changing from white to red and green. And there was a buzzing. There must have been music somewhere—they were dancing after all—but Jules couldn't hear a tune.

Sheree could; she snaked her hips, her brown hair golden in the sunlight shining through a row of arch windows. None of those had been there when they'd dropped her off. It was all drab stonewalls and darkness. But through the windows now were acres of flowers; bright and cheery things, waving madly. As if Sheree and Jules's dance was what they'd grown all their lives to see. Jules was frightened. She couldn't feel her body, just her hands. One was on Sheree's shoulder, the other on the small of her back. And Sheree wouldn't stop smiling. Grinning like a baboon. There was no sign of those sudden tears of hers that used to come on, or the cloud that used to sit on her head like a black swan looking for something to peck. And, of course, there was none of that squatting and pissing in front of Jules's boys.

There must have been an orchestra somewhere because Sheree tilted her head gracefully as if violins had started up. She pulled Jules close and hugged her tenderly. It made Jules's skin prickle. With fear or excitement, she couldn't tell. She felt a heaviness in her chest. Then the corridor was gone and the loony bin with it.

The first time she had that dream it took two cups of tea to shake it off. That green stuff her daughter-in-law Fiona brought over whenever she dropped in. Jules still thought of Fiona as her daughter-in-law even though Simon had disappeared up north. And no one knew if he was coming back.

'It's good for you, Jules,' Fiona said the first time they drank the tea.

Maybe, but Fiona didn't know what was good for her. Jules was more worried about her now than she'd been when Simon first left. She was putting too many sugars in her tea, stacking on a few pounds again, around the girdle. And what about that paint-splattered t-shirt that she wouldn't ever seem to put in the wash?!

Fiona came over more often now her kids were high schoolers. She was one of those empty nesters, like Jules. And neither of them had a husband to stuff up their nests. But at least her ex was alive. Not that Jules had ever wanted Ron back. But she'd like to see her son every now and then. He wouldn't come down south and visit her, let alone Fiona or his kids. Fiona had flown up to the Daintree at one point, wasted a heap of money. And she'd only caught up with him for an hour.

'What? He said he had to go back to work?'

'Yep, Jules, on a croc boat.'

'A *croc boat*? Is he being careful?'

'Didn't ask.'

Now whenever Simon rang, Jules didn't bother to go on at him about what he'd done to his family. She could only waste so much breath. What he did was pathetic if you asked her. But nobody did. Her friends asked more about her work, actually, than her kids. Which was nice of them. It was good not to be asked about her bloody kids all the time. Because the three boys could all have done with a bit more sorting out from their father if you asked her.

But, again, nobody did.

She'd started working at Davison House in Westmore. A mental institution. It brought everything back for her. The nights her mother drifted around the kitchen in Horsham, her apron stained with tomato and whatever else she'd made a hash job of cooking for dinner, when she was really whispering to aliens she could see in amongst the darkening apple trees outside. You could see the footy oval, too, from the kitchen, and Jules's mother thought aliens were landing their spaceships there every night. It was just the new pole lights the footy club had bought for training, but her mother didn't believe that for a second.

Of course, some doctors or someone should have come and put her away but they never did. Jules's father, an ex-army captain, he was all stiff upper lip, like the British. We'll battle on manfully, it'll come up roses, won't it kids? And the children in their tattered school uniforms nodded. Your mother's fine, she just gets distracted, Jules's father said as he followed in his wife's wake. As he patched up her cooking and took away the clothes she'd burnt with the iron. And when she threw herself into the Wimmera River, he said she hadn't been careful swimming. She'd never been a strong swimmer, he said. You kids be careful too, won't you? They hadn't been allowed to the funeral because their father didn't want to upset them.

Davison House, where Jules worked now, was a lot better

than Tonvale had ever been. Not that she'd know, really. She was only there that one afternoon to drop Sheree off. But her sister-in-law wouldn't have died so quickly if it had been a nice place, surely?

Jules had given up thinking she could have saved Sheree. That she could have saved her mother. She couldn't save anyone. She spun her rosary now because, well, she always had. Our Father, who art somewhere, hello? She never heard a word back. But she spun and chanted anyway.

Fiona came over on one of Jules's mornings off. Brought her a box of tea bags. And started spouting off about this and that as always. Fiona was worried about her eldest, Ryan. How he would turn out without a father.

'How did my boys turn out *with* a father?'

Neither of them bothered to answer that one.

'Ryan'll be all right,' Jules told her.

'He wants to get a trade...'

'That's not bad, Fiona. That's good! More money in trades than anything else.'

No money in throwing it into a building society that collapses, hey Ron? But that was another matter. What really mattered was that Fiona should have stuck with nursing. She was still doing it part-time, but she thought she was an artist, like Peter.

All this bloody family! From that Nick Stevenson who walked across the desert, to those other Stevensons who, she'd heard, apparently moved from one train station to another. Homeless wrecks. And then there was her own Simon, heading off to fight crocodiles. You can't choose your family, you don't even like them, do you, sometimes?

But you love them.

You try.

And Jules wouldn't have had it any other way. She knew that sounded stupid, like she was a pair of tangled pants in the washing machine. And she was glad she didn't say it to Fiona. Or anyone. They'd have put her in Davison House.

She worked there just about every other day as it was. Part-time casual was pretty soon near full-time if you happened to know what you were doing. Too many kids that didn't want to work these days, and wouldn't know how. There she was, in her sixties, and she had the psych nurses telling her she was the best Mental Health Social Worker they'd ever had! She just wished they could have given her a better title. Not that she needed it to be important or anything. It'd just have been easier to explain.

'Why don't you have a rest, Jules? God, you raised those boys, pretty well on your own. You nursed Ron to his grave, even though he was only your ex. You've worked with the disabled since wheelchairs were invented... God, put your feet up! You don't need to slave away down at Davison.'

Fiona put three sugars in her cup of green tea. Stirred the little granules around. Jules didn't understand it: weren't green teas supposed to be healthy? Why stuff it up with all that sugar? Behind her, the cuckoo clock's canary shot out for five on the dot. Didn't Fiona have to be at home for the kids, making them dinner? And, anyway, wheelchairs had been around since before Jules was born.

'Don't need a rest. It's good to be busy.'

She put the milk back in the fridge. The Lite Milk she'd bought for Fiona. That was a useless idea.

'So, with the art you're doing, the painting—'

'—yeah, it's going really well thanks, Jules. I'm working three days a week on it now...'

She yapped about the colours and the paint itself. What she put the paint on, what she did to the paint once it was on the canvas. And then all about her latest *raison d'etre*. That's what she called it. Jules didn't understand every word she said, but Fiona used plenty of them for someone who liked pictures. But there wasn't a single word about her kids wearing tatty clothes, one of her cats getting put down because she reckoned she couldn't afford to give it tablets, or the fact that the front passenger window of her old Subaru was gone and covered with a green plastic garbage bin liner.

Next thing she'd be talking to aliens in the backyard. It wouldn't be the first time, either, as far as Jules understood it.

'I'm really getting somewhere now, Jules.'

Jules was in Sheree's loony bin corridor and she could still hear the buzzing. She opened a glass-paneled door into a big, empty room. Sheree was sitting at a table with a pile of junk on it. It was all the old stuff she'd kept on her kitchen table: teddy bears with no eyes, old cake tins from the '50s, springs, jack-in-the-boxes that wouldn't jump—even coloured rolling pins stacked in a pile. God knows how they weren't falling over. Sheree was working away behind it all. Whistling like a sparrow that can't keep quiet once the rain's gone and the worms are out. Same huge windows in this room as the corridor. Plenty of light getting in, but no flowers outside. Out there was barren. Like someone had picked up the Tonvale loony bin and stuck it in the Little Desert.

She said Jules's name. And Jules started laughing. She wouldn't stop. It was ridiculous. There wasn't anything funny. Just Sheree working away furiously, and all Jules could see was her fringe and her eyes. She went in behind the junk and, God, it was all Sheree had! Just eyes and a forehead! No nose, no mouth. So how the hell was she whistling or saying her name?

When Jules woke from those dreams she was shivering. Every time. But she wasn't cold. She went straight to her rosary and said the Our Father times ten.

In the end there was nothing else for it. Well, there were probably a hundred things for it, but she decided she'd take some photos of Fiona's paintings. Then she could send them to Peter. The *ar-teest*, as Ron had always called him. Peter would be able to tell her if Fiona was doing what Jules thought she was.

Wasting her life. And taking her kids down the drain with her. Simon had lost the plot and now Fiona had as well. Jules wasn't going to turn her grandkids into freaks and hobos.

She went to Fiona's for a cuppa. She had on some weird music that honked and fizzed. Her corridor had those prints down the walls of Tahitian women, big and nude. Her studio was a corner of the lounge room that was part of the kitchen. There was an easel with a canvas on it. A painting of a red hibiscus.

The same flower she'd stared at the night Simon and Peter had fought in the driveway of her house.

Jules looked away from the painting, didn't want to remember the mess of that night, with her kids fighting like that, in their thirties, when they should have been having fun with their kids together.

When Fiona had started out painting, she'd done pot plants and fruit bowls. But now, as Jules looked around the lounge, she saw it was red hibiscuses or bust. Canvases leant on chairs and against the walls, and they all featured hibiscuses in various states. Some were just sketched outlines, some already red, some in gardens, and others driving cars. Mad. Every flower had a mouthful of fangs and a fierce grin on its face.

Jules took a sip of tea and nearly gagged. Fiona had stuck sugar in it. She knew Jules hated it in tea. And it wasn't just one teaspoon. She reckoned Fiona had thrown in six!

'This one, I think, is really one of my best,' Fiona said.

Jules slurped uneasily on her tea and followed Fiona's gaze to a red hibiscus riding a bike and giving the reverse V-for-Victory sign.

What was she going to call it? Jules wondered. *I'm a flower on a bike, up yours?* Jules should probably ring Davison House. Right now. There was dirty laundry all over the floor and the other cat had pus in its eye.

'Yeah,' Jules said and she flattened her cotton skirt. It was fresh-pleated. No need for flattening. She figured now was as good a time as any. She wasn't going to ask Fiona if she could take some photos of the paintings. It would only encourage her.

'Have you got those tongs I loaned you?'

'Oh, yeah, thanks for those. You know how it is, no man around to flip the vegie sausages.'

She winked at Jules like they were in on some secret, but Jules didn't have a clue what she could be talking about. She knew she had only women friends now and that she'd gone vegetarian. As far as Jules could figure out, Fiona was having a dig at her son. He was her son, after all, and Fiona had better remember it. He might be a rough nut, but he had a warm heart and Fiona had never saw him when he was a kid, softly crying when he'd been told his Auntie Sheree was dead.

Fiona padded across her back decking to the shed to retrieve the tongs. Jules only had time to take photos of two paintings. But that was enough.

'They're terrible,' Peter told her over the phone.

'Tell me what you really think.'

He laughed.

'They're god-awful.'

'Peter, she's going to have an exhibition. You know I've never understood what you do. But people come along and *buy* yours.'

'I think she's trying to work with symbolism.'

'Yeah?'

Jules couldn't have cared less what she was trying to do Fiona was going to embarrass herself. Not to mention go broke. But she was surprised Peter had even bothered to figure out what

Fiona was or wasn't doing with her painting. He'd never taken much of an interest in her at all. But that probably had to do with Simon and the night of the punch-up. All Jules had tried to do was get the family together for a nice anniversary of Ron's death. Just try to help them do what they needed to do for each other. Just put bad blood behind them and care for each other. At least give each other the time of day. But it had ended in a punch-up in Simon's driveway, Peter taking his son and hot tailing it back to Melbourne, Simon with scratch marks on his arms, and Jules ashamed and blubbing.

And Fiona? She'd stood on the porch like the proverbial rabbit in the headlights, staring over the side fence at a bunch of bloody red hibiscus.

'The red hibiscus has got meaning in Polynesian culture,' Peter said over the phone. 'You know, all those Gauguins she's got?'

Jules nodded.

'Yeah, I think. So what?'

'The red hibiscus means a woman's ready to be married. But those fangs and the poses, well, it's crap work,' he laughed. 'But so was Ken Done's.'

'Right,' Jules said.

'It's like McDonald's. Or KFC.'

What the hell was he on about?

'Mum, she's just out-working the end of her marriage.'

Out-working? Yep, that's what she should be doing all right.

A black dream. Not black as in sad or angry, just dark. Voices in the darkness. Someone hovering over her. Like he or she or it was operating on her. But it couldn't be because Jules was fit as a fiddle. Had been for years. Nothing wrong with her. No time to get sick if you keep working and helping people out.

One of the voices was Sheree's. Or her mother's. A high-pitched giggle. And one of the voices was Fiona's; her sing-song that went breathy when she got excited. And another was Jules's. She was talking. They were all talking, the three of them. But not to each other. It was just gabble, gabble, about bloody nothing, to bloody no one. Jules was angry because no one was listening to anyone. All the boys were amongst it too. And none of them were listening to anyone, either.

In the last of those dark dreams the buzzing was gone. There were just coloured lights. And Ron.

Let her go, Jules.

She didn't want the rosary or Our Fathers when she woke. She just wanted to collapse. She wanted time off. A few weeks, months. She thought of the Wimmera River and her mother, flailing and splashing. She thought of her kids and wanted to hold them tight, regardless that they were all in their thirties. She'd been a good mum, hadn't she? She'd done her best. One off the rails wasn't so bad. Maybe she'd get on a plane, though they made her sick, and go and find Simon. Bring him home, pluck him away from the crocodiles and that river. God, that river.

But she got up and went to work at Davison. She listened to the patients. They were all nicely showered and dressed, mumbling at each other in the meals room. Sunlight was beautiful and warm through the windows and splashing on their poached eggs and buttered corn. But the more beautiful it was, the angrier Jules became. One patient, Menzel, picked up his plate and threw it at the wall. It landed yards away, but she'd wished it had flown at her. Knocked her out of her misery.

Bloody Ron in her dreams! Flashing like a traffic light!

She left work right on five. She'd told Fiona she'd be at her first exhibition, come hell or high water. The devil hadn't been in the papers, there'd been a bit of rain, but no flooding. Nothing to stop her Camry from getting there and parking across the road.

The exhibition was in a café called Motoro. Fiona had conned them into putting her hibiscuses on the walls, surely? Seemed not. Because the place was cleared; they'd pushed tables against the brick walls. And there were more people in there than Jules had seen in any café before. Close and sticky in black jeans and motley shirts. Sunglasses on, some of them, and the crowd was almost pressed against the paintings. A lot of them were drinking champagne, far too early in the day for Jules's liking. She couldn't get near the register to buy a cup of tea. Turned out she didn't need to, they were free. A girl in a dress like she'd worn in her twenties, a floral number, walked around with trays of cuppas.

'Do you want sugar, love?'

'No. And I'm not your love.'

That didn't darken the waitress. Off she went, *loving* and *darling*. Then it was quiet. A hobo in a brown skirt, grey hair gone wild like Sarah from the Bible, that woman who'd got pregnant even though she was three-hundred years old or something, got up on a chair in the corner.

'Hello everyone and welcome. We're here today because Fiona Stevenson has given us all a chance to perceive and understand what we've been missing. In so much contemporary art that features and gives precedence to women's experience, there has been a lack of simplicity...'

There were happy women everywhere. In fact, there was barely a man in the place. Tahitian women, some of them, and a bunch of other girls in those floral dresses; big girls with flabby arms like Jules's mother's. Girls were flipping credit cards here and there, and the café owner in her tie-dye was plonking red dots next to all the red hibiscuses. Jules wanted more than anything to join in and God's sake be happy and laugh and have a good old time. But she was bloody furious. All she could think was, *He's still my son. Simon's still my boy.* She thought about calling Peter, right then, on the spot, but he'd probably have gone on about fast food or something stupid.

Fiona waved from a corner. She raised her champagne glass. There was a strawberry in it. Probably a few spoons of sugar too! The music was too loud and it swayed people here and there on its own.

Two women were dancing. Together. Their arms were around each other like it was midnight. Fiona waved at her then moved her head to and fro. She mouthed that she couldn't get through to Jules. She'd have to stay where she was.

Good, Jules thought, good. You stay right where you are. And

I'll stay right here. Jules couldn't stand it another second. She dropped her cup on the stone floor, deliberately. It smashed and threw tea everywhere, but the room carried on as if nothing had happened.

12. Terry Stevenson

Terry whispered 'Thank Christ' when a gang of dark clouds finally surrounded the late afternoon sun. He flipped up his new Monaro VZ's sun visor and took a bend at speed as he cruised the highway from Bairnsdale to Melbourne.

The move back to Gippsland had done him good, but it meant it was a long way to get to gigs. Decent ones, anyway. Tonight he was off to the AC/DC concert, singing along to one of their CDs. One night stands and rock 'n' roll bands. Bon Scott let rip with a bagpipe solo and Terry turned up the volume, too far. His ears stung, but he didn't care. Just for fun, he tooted the horn. Magpies flew off a fence in fear and he gave them another toot for their trouble.

He'd been out at Bengweeran for the last few days, planning and building a burn off. It was rough work and his knees ached. Even after Kerryn had washed his Parks Victoria shirt, a grease stain hadn't budged from near the logo. *Healthy Parks, Healthy People.* But Terry was brand spanking now, in a clean 'Highway to Hell' t-shirt. He grabbed a sneaky stubby from the travel esky. He was about to crack it when his boss, Nifty, called.

'Hey numb nuts, guess what? It's out of control!'

'What is?'

'My dick... Waddaya reckon, Terry? The burn off!'

'Jesus.'

'Yep, and all his fucking apostles.'

Terry didn't bother asking how it had happened. He knew it would be the CFA. The Country Fire Authority—the Chook Fuckers' Association. If the chookies weren't stirring up flames to piss their hoses on, they weren't happy. They'd done it tough on Black Saturday, like everyone had, so why couldn't they just let a burn off be a burn off?

'Nifty, you know I'm not comin' back.'

He'd had a newborn way back in '96 so he'd missed AC/DC. Kerryn had had the flu so Terry had looked after the kids. But tonight he was going to rock out. And no two-bit bloody chooky cock-up was going to stop him.

'I don't care if you haven't seen them since Methuselah was a pup,' Nifty said. 'We need your arse back here. Now.'

Terry hung up and put the phone next to his esky. There was a text chime a few seconds later, but he didn't check it. Bugger him! Nifty could sort it out. If he couldn't handle a burn off he didn't deserve his job.

A few days before, Terry had told everyone concerned that his decision was final: the paddock the abandoned FJ sat in would have to be torched. Old Tom Heath had taken it in his stride.

'Yeah, nah, I understand Tezz. We've got to put safety first.'

Tom had put his pen down on the table. Everyone else in the porta office had shuffled their papers. But nobody had got up to leave.

'Look, I'm real sorry Tom...'

Terry had a soft spot for Tom. He was good at his job and his wife had finally passed the year before. He'd barely smiled since.

'Nah, look Tezz, you're doing what's right. No choice. Just how it is.'

And he'd got up and walked out. No more arguments. Suddenly the FJ's cremation was fine by him.

Terry was shocked. At every morning meeting, Tom had been first to arrive, navy CFA polo on, sharp grey hair and clean-shaven, and offering up a new way to save his dead father's FJ. And Terry had shot down all of them. Except one.

'We could try moving it,' Terry had told him.

It was an afternoon early in the piece when he was standing in the paddock with Tom and inspecting the car. Terry had no intention of moving it. And, as he'd hoped, Tom had shelved the idea for him.

'We can't mate. Thing'd fall to bits.'

It would have been a fine motor vehicle in its day. Now it was just a rust bucket with no glass in the front window frame and grass growing on the seats. But it still had a little bar above the bumper proper that looked like a moustache. In the '50s, that FJ would have pranced and winked up Bairnsdale's Main Street. It would have owned the joint.

'We'll have to find another way to protect it,' Tom had said to the wreck, and Terry had watched him join one of his sons for a smoke. As the pair of them had kicked gravel and mumbled, Terry had wondered why Tom didn't care about the shell of his grandfather's house. Flames might give it a going over as well if they weren't careful. He could have asked Tom about it all, but he didn't get around to it. Too much work on. Bengweeren was 150 square ks of shitfight. The only place in Victoria where Parks Vic, the chookies and the Department, the government boys who always thought they had rank but didn't, could have a say on how to manage the burn offs.

And didn't they all give it a go!

When Terry had turned up the first morning of the job, the chookies were already into it. In their yellow coats and hats, they flitted around like stained cabbage moths, reeling hoses off the trucks and slip-ons. Made themselves so busy it was like they expected a bloody fire to flare up all on its own.

Terry knew he shouldn't rib the chookies so much. Most of them did a pretty good job. Tom, for example, was pretty reasonable when you got him on his own. Knew his way around a long-term fire plan, too, not just the whooshing end of a hose. But blood's thicker than grass.

'Grandpa's old stretch,' Tom told Terry that first morning, barely waiting for Terry to buzz down the window of his Parks Vic ute. Flies scouted Tom's cap peak and there was a broken windmill off in the distance.

'Still got to sort it out, Tom.'

'Yeah... Lot of memories here though.'

The grass was high enough in his grandfather's front paddock to hide an infantry unit. It had to be flamed. Only then would the dirt beneath be able to keep everything safe for another couple of hundred hectares. Terry had taken his sunnies off and put them on the dashboard. He'd got out of the ute.

'Beautiful part of the world,' he'd said, shielding his eyes.

'My Grandpa used to say it was God's own country.'

They'd watched the gums and pines parading on the borders of hay-strewn paddocks. In the distance, it got greener and hillier. Further back, hidden waves bashed away at the coastline, trying for all money to carve it into a new shape. Blackfellas, whitefellas: everyone reckoned they owned that spread from the highway to the waves. And they liked the shape just fine.

Except for the long grass.

'Place needs a bit of hell to keep it in good nick,' Terry had said, and Tom had turned to the FJ. 'My old man bought it new in '56. Grandpa thought it was a piece of shit But Dad reckoned it ran on honey.'

Probably did back then. Or kero.

Terry had hauled his computer bag from the car and set up in the shitty porta office. All week he'd argued with the chooky big guns, Department knobs and anyone else who thought God's own country gave them a right as fat as the Bible to say how to manage it. He'd taken four days to get the plan sorted and now it was on. Cleared, dug and set. But Terry had told everyone he wouldn't be there to light the torch. The only fire he wanted to see was coming out of an AC/DC stage cannon. He'd walked from the porta-office, given a mock salute and whispered, 'I'm about to rock!'

He checked his sideburns in the rear-view. Nicely clipped. Bit of grey, but neat. He'd even shaved. What that was about he didn't know. It wasn't as if AC/DC needed him to be presentable. But, shit, it was a big occasion for him. Kind of like a wedding. Bigger, really, but he'd never tell Kerryn that. For obvious reasons.

She had to have a violinist on their wedding day. The kid had looked bug-eyed when he'd found out he had to play an instrumental version of 'Ride On'. That was Terry's compromise: she could have a violinist, sure, but he had to play AC/DC. He even compromised more: the kid could play a ballad. Kerryn had laughed under her veil as the poor bloke had dragged his bow across the strings.

Some people had religion, Terry had AC/DC. Missing that concert in '96 was as bad as when his dad had cancer. Not something he told too many people, but there it was. Terry went through a Nirvana stage, like everyone, but he came back to Acca Dacca. He had a room in his house dedicated to the band. Dolls of them playing guitars and drums, posters covering every wall, and AC/DC mirrors on the ceiling. He had all their CDs, DVDs and most of their vinyl stacked in milk crates in the shape of one of Angus Young's guitars. And it had taken him fourteen years to sew the cotton AC/DC emblem into the carpet.

It was his rosary, he reckoned. And every day he sewed, AC/DC blaring from a mini-hi-fi, he'd think of his father. He didn't know why. He'd turn up the volume, thread that carpet, and hum through gritted teeth.

The night before he left for the concert, Terry drove back to get his phone from where he'd left it in the porta office. Moonlight was like snow on the paddocks. Tom stood against the FJ and it spooked Terry to see him there. He supposed the old bloke was just saying his goodbyes. Tom sipped a stubby and waved Terry over.

'Nice unit in its day,' Terry told him for the hundredth time.

Tom handed him a beer. The stubby was icy. Terry cracked it and gulped. Tom smelt of cologne, something musky, and he drummed his fingers on the FJ's hood.

'I grew up in this car. Went everywhere in it. When Dad was a buck, they couldn't get him out of it either...'

Tom took a long look at the dark horizon. Then he let out a strangled laugh.

'Jesus, Terry, I don't know...it's...'

Then he shut up and Terry wanted to talk for him.

It makes you feel something real, Tom. It matters and you can't figure out why. It's way more than just your old man's ride, but you don't know what it is. Anymore than I do.

Terry had an Angus Young solo in his head, but then he realised it wasn't. He was making one up. Different notes, but Angus's style. He wanted to tell Tom, even hum it to him. But he just tapped the car.

'They don't make them like this...' he said and Tom finished for him.

'They don't make anything like this anymore.'

The old bloke's eyes looked liked sucked plums. Terry dropped his empty stubby into the esky.

'Gotta go, Tom.'

As Terry drove off, he watched the old bloke wave at him and touch the peak of his cap.

Terry's mobile rang, again. He turned up the car stereo and let it ring out.

Christ, Nifty, you're the boss.

They've got no idea, Terry thought. They don't know a steering wheel in your hands can feel like it's on a tall ship. They don't know it's a long way to anywhere worth going. Terry gunned it all the way to Melbourne, and by the time he came out of the stadium after the concert, covered in sweat and tossed beer, there was a stream of missed calls and voicemails waiting for him.

He's in the FJ. He won't get out. Fire's comin in. Keeps raising the shotty every time we get close.

The crowd left the stadium singing and whooping, but Terry sat on a kerb near a taxi rank and rang Nifty back. He heard all about the flames growing round Tom until everyone stopped screaming and looked away.

Terry was gutted. He could have saved Tom. Maybe. But he felt most gutted because, instead of Tom, he saw Ron in that FJ. Grinning like a chimp.

13. Joe, Penny, Molly and Lee Stevenson

They were the ones, Peter remembered, that the extended family had always whispered about. If a member of the Stevenson clan lost a job or lucked out with some illness or other, they'd soon be reminded that things could be worse. They could be one of the Nutter Stevensons. A knowing silence would descend on backyard family gatherings, and only the sound of sizzling barbecue meat would remain. One after the other, Stevensons would raise stubbies or wine glasses to their lips and wonder how one family, those religious nutters, could stuff their lives up so entirely.

'They take it too far,' was Jules Stevenson's pronouncement on Joe and Penny Stevenson's approach to religion. 'And involving the kids like that! It's a disgrace.'

For more than twenty years, Jules and the rest of the Stevensons had based their understanding of Joe, Penny and their two kids, Molly and Lee, on half-substantiated tales. Because that's all there was.

When Peter was in his mid-thirties, divorced and just moved into a flat on his own, he'd contracted an illness that doctors could neither diagnose nor treat. He'd taken a desperate punt and allowed an old school friend turned born again Christian to bring a scrappy looking grey-headed man to his hospital bed. That man had laid hands on Peter, shouted various incantations to the heavens, and healed him. That very hour. Doctors had put Peter's recovery down to a mixture of penicillin and bed rest, but he wasn't sure. His friend hadn't left any contact details and he hadn't been told his healer's name. It wasn't until several years later, when Peter saw the news story about the discovery of Joe's dead body, if that was the right term for what was found, that he realised his healing had been all in the family.

He managed to track down Lee Stevenson, living in Hoppers Crossing. What Peter thought would be an hour-long catch up, at best, became a friendship. And as much as Peter's idea for initiating contact had been to try to authenticate his healing, he couldn't push the issue. In fact, he forgot about it. Because he was dealing with a man who was still grieving deeply. With a hell of a story. Or a heaven of a story. Lee seemed never sure which. Or whether he loved or hated his father. Peter sat and nodded at that one.

He thought he'd moved around a lot as a kid, but Lee's family had, from his earliest years, moved from one house to another. They had been billeted by Christian families who'd wanted to support Joe and Penny's work. Which was nothing more than trying to emulate, as a married couple, the monk St Francis of Assisi and his female counterpart, the nun Clare of Assisi. Those two ancient saints had lived in voluntary poverty and cared for the poor as they'd roved around. Enjoying ecstatic nights of prayer and fasting. Preaching with actions, rather than words.

Lee told Peter that when he was a toddler, Joe and Penny had come across a relative, Nick Stevenson, living rough in

Melbourne's CBD. Always a caring couple, they'd tried to help Nick. But he wouldn't hear of it.

'I have to be about my Father's work,' he'd said, smiling like an idiot. 'I'll pray for you both. You're both so, so poor.'

They never saw him again. But within a few days of each other, Joe and Penny had religious conversions. That had involved nothing less than visions of spinning crosses lighting up the night sky. They had decided, quickly and simply, full of euphoria and, Lee told Peter, surely a dose of madness, to commit their lives to voluntary poverty. They would live as mendicants, helping the poor and preaching a Gospel without words. And doing it all regardless of the fact that they had children.

After all, didn't the Bible tell them that nothing should get in the way of sharing the Gospel with the world?

But after ten years of living at different people's houses, being billeted on the back of Christian charity was too cushy a lifestyle for Joe Stevenson. It took him several weeks to convince Penny that their logical next step was to live on the streets like those to whom they ministered. Eventally, she had given in.

'We can try it, okay? But we can always go back...'

'Of course we can,' Joe had said in the lean-to of a couple's house in Bentleigh. The Stevensons were sleeping together in the room, on mattresses their hosts had hauled from a large shed, and Lee had heard it all despite the sleeping bag hood with which he'd covered his head.

Joe's idea was to keep schooling the kids while living near railway stations. It would allow them, he thought, reasonably quick getaways if authorities poked their nose into the Stevensons' business. If they decided to put him and Penny away for not looking after their kids properly.

Later, Lee wished they'd been found. Perhaps his father would have lived.

They were living near West Footscray train station, just before the major upgrade that brought lifts and a covered walk bridge, when the Stevensons' lives changed. And to this day Lee can't decide if it was for better or worse.

He was twelve at the time and he was first to see the plans for the upgrade. Two blue and black promotional advertisements next to the ticket machine and it wouldn't be long before work started on their side of the tracks. Behind a partially demolished brick building and a collection of empty petrol drums were the two shopping trolleys, three tattered picnic blankets and several cardboard boxes that marked his family's territory. Not that anyone else would have wanted it.

'The Met will have the yellow earthmovers here soon,' Joe said.

Lee didn't know why he mentioned the colour; everyone knew what they looked like. But maybe the luminescence hurt Joe's eyes. He'd always said he should be wearing glasses.

'No home, no glasses,' he'd laughed once on a train to somewhere.

Joe brushed long grey hair from his eyes one night and gathered his family on the narrow and decaying walk-bridge.

In the late summer air's quiet he told everyone to prepare for another move. A regional train rushed past and lit them up for a moment. Lee's elder sister, Molly, played with one of the holes in her denim skirt and her mum told her to stop. Lee watched the city lights busy themselves. So he wouldn't start crying.

They'd been at West Footscray for a couple of months. It was a good station. No one bothered them. Not like Dandenong. Molly couldn't sleep after the sword gang had tried to rob them, before realising they had nothing. Then the gang had fled, cursing them and laughing at the Stevensons' stupidity. As they'd run, Joe had said, over and over, 'No one got cut.'

There were gangs around West Footscray, plenty. But it seemed they had better things to do than wave swords or fists at the Stevensons. Maybe there were more drugs to sell. They never saw a Human Services car either, not even a worker. Lee was allowed to cross the back road, hardly ever used, and watch the Western Bulldogs train. With an AFL team so close he'd started to understand football. He loved to watch the players run, especially Matty Boyd. He was tough as a jackhammer and just as consistent said the old men in faded scarves.

Dandenong had been a rodent zoo minus the cages, but there weren't as many rats at West Footscray. And it was a shorter ride to the station Joe would never let them name, in case they got caught riding for free. The station they'd all jump off at after they'd passed through Flinders. Then they'd walk back to the Clocks.

The city lights were a sparkling treasure behind Joe as he spruiked the Stevensons' next station. Wherever it was going to be.

'It's an adventure to move.'

He kept on with his talk: life was a movable feast; rolling stones and moss; Jews trooping the wilderness with Moses while Jehovah led the way in a puff of smoke. There was smoke on the horizon, out beyond the Dandenongs. Bushfires, maybe under control, maybe not. Hot there and hot here. West Footscray was much warmer than Dandenong. Because, according to Joe, the diesel fumes got trapped.

'When it's time, kids, you'll fold up the cardboard,' he said. 'Neatly please.'

He twisted hairs on his salt and pepper beard. Told them their mother would manage the cutlery and he'd load the garbage bags full of clothes and books, then pile them into the shopping carts. But before all that, he and Lee would have to find them a new station.

'Well, not a *new* station,' Joe smiled. 'They're useless.'

Too much surveillance, too open to the elements. And not enough long grass or nooks or crannies.

Lee told Peter about this time so vividly that Peter could picture it for himself. When everyone was asleep, Lee stripped off and stared at the greasy clouds. After the thick cardboard got damp beneath him, he put his shorts and t-shirt back on. It was the only way to get an okay night's sleep in summer. The cooler air passed over his sweaty clothes and train engines ground and shunted in the yards. He imagined their sounds were elephants crying on an African savannah. They were caring for their calves, keeping them cool by blowing water all over them.

Lee's father had read him plenty of books about Africa. Joe

had read him and Molly plenty of books about everything.

Lee's skin cooled and he watched hamburger wrappers and newspapers catch in the cyclone fence. They fluttered, a band of misfit angels, some of them floating onto the porch of the abandoned and boarded up station guardhouse.

Railway workers often came to the platform to smoke and waste the last few minutes of their shifts, but they never looked inside the guardhouse. If Joe had allowed it, the Stevensons could have made that paint peeling wreck into a three-bedroom house. It would have been prime real estate. Close, very close, to public transport. And, yes, ample city views.

But his father, on his life-on-the-street mission, wouldn't have considered it.

'The Son of Man had nowhere to lay his head!'

Beneath *their* heads every night were clothes bunched together to form makeshift pillows.

Lee stopped worrying about where their next station would be and allowed the rustle of papers in the wire fence to carry him off to sleep. He dreamt his family were still living at West Footscray, but had leather chairs to sit on, brown and squeaky. A giant TV was set up in the long grass at the back of the guard-house. An advertisement came on for a shampoo, and a man showered on the top floor of a house that didn't have any walls. Then Joe came on the screen, shouting, 'The Son of Man has no head!' A jagged knife flew towards the screen and Lee woke to the sound of a dawn train tearing the morning open.

It was another hot day and Molly and Lee wandered the edges of the storm drains until they came to the creek bend where Geelong Road met the Westgate Freeway. It was a Sunday and the traffic was quiet. They trod carefully down the steep embankment and sat at the creek's edge next to a supermarket trolley without any wheels. They stripped down to their underwear and hung their clothes on the trolley. The creek was still running from a recent storm, but when they paddled in to their waists the current wasn't strong enough to worry them. They splashed each other in the murky water, but after a while Lee didn't want to play. A heaviness sat in his chest.

'What is it?' Molly asked, shaking her wet hair on him.

'Nothing.'

'*Nothing?* Nothing's always something.'

'That's what Dad would say.'

'Shut up,' Molly groaned, and she splashed cool water onto his chest. It didn't shift the heaviness. She swam away and left Lee to his mood.

'I don't want to move, that's all.'

They were sitting on the creek bank and letting the sun dry them. Lee kicked a crushed soft drink can into the water. Then he rose and pulled it out again. Why make everything worse? He sat next to his sister.

'We'll move one day,' she said and touched him briefly on the shoulder.

'What do you mean? Of course we will. A new station, real soon.'

Molly looked away to the other side of the creek, its high

embankment and the top of a service station sign.

'I don't mean that. I mean really move.'

She dressed and shook her hair as dry as she could get it. Lee thought she looked beautiful. The last thing he'd tell her. They walked silently along the storm drain's edge and back to camp.

Peter was facinated to hear about Lee's life on the streets. Lee told him how he used to watch dinner broil in the pan and listen to the singing coming from the back of the Potter's Wheel Church. It was only a few roller doors away. The church's door had a huge cartoon of a red pot being shaped by a gust of wind. The music was full of busy drumming and off-key guitar, and the words, *My God is a great God, a mighty God is He.* Their songs never made any sense to Lee. If there was a God, which his father said there was, why did He need to be told He was great and mighty? Didn't He know that already?

'People like to praise God. And God likes it, too,' Joe said.

'Do you praise God?'

'Yes.'

'When?'

'All the time.'

'I don't hear you.'

His father laughed.

'You mustn't be listening.'

Joe stirred the tomato and beans. Penny and Molly mushed a dessert out of some fruit they'd found. His father threw a sprig of thyme into the pan. He'd asked a man in a tracksuit that afternoon if he could take some from his garden. The man had looked at Joe and his family suspiciously. Then, as if something strong had wrestled him, he'd handed Joe three branches.

'I've never heard you praise God.'

'Lee, you don't have to make a song and dance about praising God.'

His father told him again about the Great Nick Stevenson. Who'd marched through the Little Desert and survived when he shouldn't have. Who'd taught Joe more about God in a few minutes than a thousand churches could. Who was the reason Joe and his family lived the way he did. And blah and blah.

The church music stopped and applause started up.

'You *do* believe in God, don't you?' Lee asked.

Joe raised an eyebrow.

'Haven't I just been telling you—'

'—why don't you go to church? At least sometimes?'

'I do... I just don't go in the buildings.'

'What?'

Joe stirred the contents of the pan. Harder than he needed to. When he spoke again, he didn't seem to be addressing Lee.

'I'm worried about what would happen if I went to church. And, anyway, do you think church people would be happy to have us?'

His mother had dust all over her cut-off jeans. Molly's hair was sideways and her face was dirty. Lee didn't dare look at his own cut-off jeans, but he got a good whiff of them. Even in amongst the thyme, tomato and red kidney beans, he caught the smell. Like mouldy bread mixed with rotten apples. Washing day was tomorrow.

'There's enough God out here,' Joe smiled, waving at the starless sky. 'There's enough God in *you*, young man, to keep me busy thinking good thoughts for years!'

Lee waited for him to ruffle his hair, but he didn't. He just served beans onto the white plastic plate Lee was holding. The middle of the plate was warm where the food gathered. His mum and Molly took their servings, and Lee bent his head and sniffed. The smell of his jeans was gone. There was only the mighty aroma of vegetables and herbs. Joe gave thanks for it all and they sat in a circle and ate.

'This tastes good, Dad.'

'It's the same as always.'

'No, it's better.'

'If you say so.'

The hot sun clung to the horizon for a while then gave up and a V-Line train thundered its way to Ballarat. Lee often wished they could ride one and leave the city, but that night he didn't.

The sun had gone to bed angry and its mood hadn't improved. It was going to take it out on everyone, all day. The Stevensons sweated through a breakfast of dry bread and warm water. Joe read to Lee and Molly as usual; this time an essay by Orwell. Lee had loved *Animal Farm* when Joe had read it to them a few weeks before they'd give up their billeting. The morning's essay had an animal in it, too. An elephant. Orwell wrote about working as a policeman in Burma. He'd had to shoot an elephant that an Indian immigrant had owned. Orwell hadn't wanted to shoot it, but it was either that or the elephant would destroy a village.

So he did it. The shot flew, the elephant's face seemed to sag, and the beast's life disappeared into the humid air. Joe said Orwell had felt conflicted about the killing. He'd believed he'd done the right thing, but he hadn't felt right about doing the right thing.

Joe closed the book and stood.

'So that, my charges, is the way it was. Let's see how it is, and get on with today's business.'

He always let a story sit with them for a day before they discussed it. Now it was time to look for a new home.

Lee rode with his dad to their get-off-station and walked the kilometre and a half back to the Clocks. It was so hot even the Yarra seemed ready to fry. Today they were looking for a station, but normally they'd be amongst people like them. Sort of like them. The people they worked with were different. They seemed sad. Crushed. The Stevensons helped them get clothes and find food. But Joe wouldn't take their return offers of money or protection. From the time he'd consigned his family to life on the street he'd only accepted certain things: offers of food or clothing, used books from libraries, and whatever he could find in laneway bins. But he never took money.

Joe stood under the Flinders Street timetable screen as announcements blared in Indian accents. Lee thought of Orwell's elephant owner. It had been a sad day for him. He'd loved that animal. And it was a *working* elephant. That fact had made it even harder for Orwell to shoot it. Lee knew his father was going to ask him tonight if he'd have shot it. He wouldn't have.

Joe gave the timetable a final stare. Like this was its last chance to give an account of itself. He put his hand on Lee's shoulder.

'Werribee Line.'

They could have got off all the way back at Footscray to ride Werribee!

Lee got on the train with his dad and watched backyards pass, hills hoists draped with white sheets and underwear. Graffiti covered the severed iron fences. His father hated graffiti, but Lee didn't. It was lively. It was an expression of something, he didn't quite know what. But he liked it. *But it's illegal*, his father had said when they'd first discussed it. Then he'd smiled when Lee had reminded him their train rides were illegal too.

'Yes, but you know what I think about that.'

Homeless people should be able to register with the Housing Commission. And that registration, he said, should provide them with free public transport until they were no longer homeless.

'The fact is the Government won't do it. And it's not because the train companies can't afford it. It's because they don't want people like us on their trains. Tickets or not.'

They had been riding the Glen Waverley Line that day. A middle-aged couple had been trying hard not to stare at Joe and Lee. The man was wearing a tartan cap, and the woman a mint blazer. At Joe's pronouncement the man had stuck his nose back into his newspaper, but the woman had met Joe's eyes. Even attempted a smile.

'You can ride the train...' the woman said.

'And disembark near your house?'

Joe's voice had turned acid. He loved showing off his vocabulary when the occasion called for it. Whether it was the couple's stop or not, they'd got off at Kooyong.

Lee and his father disembarked now at Newport and got a drink from the public toilets. The sun's mood had turned from annoyed to vicious. Joe told him to put his ripped Bulldogs cap on and he did. Sweat ran into Lee's eyes and stung them. He wiped, but the sweat came on again like tears. He exhaled loudly when they got back on the air-conditioned train.

Could they *live* on a train? Air conditioning! Seats! Trains had it all. Even views. Soon it was Point Cook's outskirts; fields of grey steel-roofed houses pressed close together, surrounded by petrol stations and bright-painted signs on warehouses. Then the view shifted. It became the man on the seat opposite in tattered black track pants, holding his stomach and groaning. Joe was beside him like Orwell's bullet, his arm around his shoulder before the guy even threw up.

'Are you alright mate?'

Pale vomit on the guy's pants was the answer. He couldn't speak. He couldn't do anything because, as Lee had learnt from an early age, the man was full of heroin.

'Just hold on, buddy,' Joe told him. 'Someone alert the driver! And call triple zero.'

There wasn't exactly a rush to get it done. Suits shuffled,

handbags were hugged tighter, but a boy with a twisted baseball cap and white shiny track pants got busy following Joe's commands. He seemed proud. Joe was.

'Thanks kid. You're a credit to yourself.'

A stunning woman with high cheekbones called out from a seat at the other end of the train.

'You're a credit. You're an angel.'

Joe ignored her. The guy threw up again.

The train made a long stop at Aircraft station and staff hauled the sick guy from the carriage. Joe wanted to go with him, but the staff thanked him and ushered him and Lee back into the carriage. There was a scattered round of applause.

Joe said nothing, just took his seat. The attractive woman moved and sat across from them. Oblivious, it seemed, to the lingering smell of vomit.

'What's your name?' she asked. Lee couldn't stop looking at her teeth. So white and straight. Like a piano minus the ebony.

'Are you police?' Joe asked.

'No, I'm—'

'—a journalist?'

'I'm a church elder.'

Everyone in the train had been listening. Now they went back to newspapers, screens and earphones.

She didn't look old enough to be an elder. She looked young enough for Lee to think about doing the things he'd been thinking more and more about doing. Every time he saw a billboard with a Berlei bra ad. There was a lot to think about. A lot he'd like to do. He just didn't know what any of it was.

The woman's hair was blonde like on shampoo billboards. Like a collection of gold necklaces bunched together. She'd called Joe an angel. Wrong. Because she was. She even wore a short white dress that stuck to every bit of her. A sexy angel. Lee swallowed the thought. His father would kill him. At least tell him off and read the Bible at him for a day.

He looked at his father's lined face to see what he was thinking. There was a sparkle in his eyes.

'I'm a church elder too.'

'*Really?* What church?'

Joe smirked and looked at himself dramatically. His clothes had always seemed tatty, even to Lee, but never more than in that moment. There was a rip above the knee of his green King Gees. It showed the matted dark hair on his thigh. His round-necked, grey t-shirt was more grease than cotton. You'd have thought twice before cleaning up the vomit with it.

'I'm not really a church elder.'

'Where do you go to church?'

Joe looked out the window. The houses were almost identical now. Their roofs and doors staring at each other.

'Everywhere.'

'Well, come to mine sometime. Would you?'

'Why don't you stop talking to me?'

'I'm sorry,' she said. 'I don't mean to be pushy. It's just that I think you could teach our congregation a lot.'

His father had taught at small gatherings. For a long time. But never in a church.

'Thanks. I'm sure I could. But I'm not going to.'

Somehow she knew exactly how to respond.

'I can help you with food.'

Lee told Peter that he knew his father couldn't refuse. They were running low. And this could only be, in Joe's words, a blessing.

'I'll think about it.'

'Great. Here's my card.'

Joe studied it.

'I don't have a phone. Or a computer.'

'Where do you live?' she asked.

Joe shook his head, smiled and studied the newly cleaned floor.

'Where can I find you?' angel woman persisted.

'West Footscray station. Know where that is?'

'I'll come tomorrow. And we'll make arrangements.'

Joe nodded slowly. He surely wasn't going to make them move before then?

'Okay,' he said and put her card in his pants pocket.

He was *definitely* going to make them move. They'd be folding cardboard and packing shopping trolleys tonight.

'You'll love our church.'

'I doubt it.'

The train passed through a station under construction. Forget an upgrade, Walton's Landing hadn't got a grade at all. Orange tape sealed off stairwells and the spaces where escalators would go. Beyond the station were flat fields marked with tiny white flags; the blocks on which houses would soon rise. Other flags noted where roads would be paved. More cars would soon pump the sky, *the dying sky* as Joe called it, with more fumes in a day than every bird in history had swallowed.

'It's really an alive church,' she smiled. 'Full of life. Like you.'

'Really?' Joe scoffed.

'Yes! You helped that man quicker than, I don't know...'

A bullet could hit an elephant? There were graders the size of those animals in the paddocks now. Quiet and lazy. Workmen wandered around them.

'Look,' Joe took her card from his pocket, 'Della. I just do what I do. I've always done what I do. It makes me who I am.'

Sometimes Lee wanted to cry when his father spoke. From shame and love.

'You're an amazing man.'

'No, I'm...'

'No, no, of course you're not. You're just a man with God on his side.'

Joe pulled himself up taller in his seat.

'If that's God's choice.'

'Everything's God's choice.'

'*Is* it? Is it God's choice that all that land out there, all those houses when they pop up, will be occupied by people who keep this ridiculous system running? A system that keeps out people like me, who don't believe in it, who won't compete in it, who won't do the things it demands, who won't corrupt their souls, as well as those who literally can't do any of it, even if they wanted to, is it God's choice that...'

He moaned and berated and the angel woman watched, expressionless. Careful not to annoy him. Lee tuned out. He thought of last night's dinner. The beautiful smell of beans, thyme and tomato. And of his father seeing preciousness in him.

'You might be right, that's why—'

'—of course I'm right,' Joe snapped.

'Shut up mate. There's other people here. Who don't give a fuck.'

It was a big man who'd got on after Aircraft station. He hadn't seen Joe help the sick guy. The stranger's shoulders were round and hairy and his visibility vest was losing its shine.

'I'm sorry to bother you,' Joe said.

Della slipped Lee one of her cards too. Insurance, maybe. He took it.

'Should be sorry. Get a bloody job.'

Joe nodded. He knew when to keep quiet. And how to keep others quiet. It was the same when they got back to camp that night; Lee wanted to talk more about the train incident and his father said they would—after they'd talked about the Orwell story. Which would be after they'd packed up to move. They bent over their blankets and folded them. They'd barely started when Della showed up.

'Hi,' she said. There was a Samoan guy next to her in a tight and shiny grey suit. The pair had arrived so quietly the Stevensons had jolted. Except Joe.

'Hello,' he said and he rose to greet them. He shook their hands, but studied the stony ground. The silent Samoan guy smiled. Lee didn't know whether to be scared of him or climb on his shoulders for a ride. Della's hair glittered, Lee thought.

'Are you all off for a picnic?'

Joe didn't play the game.

'No. We're off to live somewhere else.'

'So I wouldn't have found you tomorrow?'

He shrugged. Lee and Molly kept at their packing.

'A good thing I came then?'

Her voice worried Lee. It was as if she owned their station. And every other station. His dad didn't seem concerned, but Lee's mum got to her feet. She studied Della and the Samoan guy calmly. Then addressed Della while positioning herself between her children and the strangers.

'Excuse me, who are you?'

Joe began to explain hesitantly, apologetically, but Della took over. She told Penny about the sick guy and Joe's work. Penny frowned.

'Why didn't you tell me, Joe?'

'Because...we were leaving. It didn't matter if—'

'—here's what we can offer you to come and talk at our church, sir.'

It was the Samoan super hero. He handed Joe a Coles gift card. Lee had seen them before. His father couldn't stop his bolt of surprise when he read the back.

'I can't accept it,' he said and thrust it back at the Samoan. But the big man kept his hands behind his back. Della smiled at Joe softly.

'Is that really true? You can't accept it?'

Joe was beaten.

'No.'

'This Sunday then?'

He nodded.

'We'll send a car.'

'No you won't.'

The Samoan guy flinched.

'We'll catch the train,' Joe groaned and the Samoan nodded.

'Coles near here?' the big man asked.

'Yes,' Penny nodded.

'Enjoy then,' he smiled.

Lee caught a look in his father's eyes he'd never seen. Like he was in the middle of throwing wet tissues on a factory fire. For a second he thought Joe would toss the gift card away. Della and her friend said their goodbyes and the look passed from Joe's face. He put the card in the pocket of his pants. Molly and Lee bombarded him with questions about what he was going to say in church, but he wouldn't answer. He left his kids to murmur at each other and climbed the walk bridge. He stopped at the top and gazed at the city lights. They knew to leave him. When sleep was ready to haul Lee in, his father was still holding the railing. The lights were winking at him but he was giving them nothing in return.

The inside of Hopper's Crossing's Wayfarer Church was twice the size of Flinders Street station's foyer.

'This way, up the front,' Della said, pointing to an empty row of padded seats. She wore black slacks and a white sleeveless shirt. Like a businesswoman ready for sport.

'No thanks,' Joe said and he led his family to the rows of plastic seats in the middle of the auditorium. A thousand or more people were going to fill this place. As the Stevensons shuffled towards some empty spaces, people smiled at them so brightly Lee got chills. The churchgoers wore beautiful clothes. Bright coloured suits, clean shirts, and pleated dresses. Pressed chino pants and freshly washed jeans were popular. Giant wafts of perfume and aftershave. Everyone said hello and shook their hands. Asked how they all were. And they responded. Even Joe, finally.

The crowd's warmth came at Lee like an arrow made of jelly. It landed in his chest then spread to his stomach and head. He reckoned his father copped an arrow, too; Joe smiled for a second before he remembered to put on the grumpy face he'd held throughout the morning's train journey.

A polished timber lectern stood beside a row of empty black chairs on the stage. A group of men in sharp suits filed from the wings and sat. A drum kit was suddenly occupied, and then the rest of a rock band pulled into position, plugging in guitars and testing keyboards. Backing singers performed warm-up scales in the hub-hub of people finding seats and greeting each other.

Della was the lead singer but she didn't warm up her voice. She adjusted her microphone stand and tapped the mike. A man in a Lakers' cap stuck up his thumb where he sat at a sound desk a few rows in front of the Stevensons. Della smiled and nodded. She said good morning and a thousand people said good morning back. Except Joe.

He hadn't changed his clothes for his day in church. He

wore the same filmy t-shirt and ripped King Gee pants. Penny had made sure Molly and Lee were in their best clothes; their jeans and the patterned t-shirts without holes or stains. Before they'd left, she'd smiled at them warmly. But their father was unimpressed.

'No need for them to look any different.'

He'd stalked off then and Penny had whispered for them to be on their best behaviour.

'This could be the start of something,' she said.

Lee noticed there was a lightness about his mother; she moved quickly as she went from, annoyingly, brushing his hair to smoothing down the pale blue cotton dress she was wearing. It was a pretty one Lee had never seen. This could be the start of what, he wanted to ask her, but he didn't bother. Because he knew, somehow. He had known it since Della had called out to Joe on the train.

When his family had reached the doors of the church that morning, Lee had winked at his mother. She'd tried to suppress a smile but she'd failed. Then she'd winked back.

Telling his story to Peter, Lee became animated when he recalled that first visit, how he had shifted in his plastic seat as Della had said a more rousing good morning. A thousand voices whooped and shouted. It spooked and excited Lee. Words appeared on the big screen as she sang.

He is our God today, tomorrow and evermore/We know His name and He knows ours...

Lee tried to catch the melody then stopped. The Bible said only God knew his own name. Yes, there was Jesus, but he was part man. And part God. Or something. But God, the starter God, the one who yelled and everything in the universe took off with a bang and a rumble, he had a name that no one knew. Lee wondered if his father had noticed this glitch in the lyrics, but Joe was looking at his shoes. Which were so floppy and disappointing that he may as well not have worn any at all. It was like he was trying to upset everyone by dressing as horribly as he could. It was embarrassing. He should have at least tried to look interested.

'Today, we will hear from one of the most fascinating men I have met...'

The singing, church news, Bible readings and prayers had finished. Time for the main event: Lee's father. Joe Stevenson. *Joe-looking-at-his-ugly-shoes Stevenson.* Lee wanted to shake him. Penny looked at Joe sharply and held his forearm. Her action said, *Sort yourself out!* but Joe loosed her grip.

Della told the congregation how Joe and his family lived. That they were poor, but had always cared for those poorer. What they would and wouldn't accept as payment. And her opinion on why. The congregation stormed its applause.

The Stevensons were Jesus' best buddies. Angels in the flesh!

Joe lumbered to the front of the church as more applause rained. He climbed the stage steps and stood behind the lectern. He didn't say anything until the auditorium was silent. A toddler wailed in the church crèche. Joe smiled in spite of himself. Or was he at last happy to be there?

'Jesus asks us upon what we will build the foundations for our houses. Will we build them upon sand, swept away by the power of a storm? Or will we build them on rock? Upon what, upon WHAT, will you build your foundation...?'

Nine and a half months after his first sermon, Joe disappeared. Or died.

As it turned out it was one and the same thing.

Lee told Peter that he had taken the blame for it. His father had taught him well enough to take responsibility for the things for which he was responsible.

Joe's sermons had turned Pentecostal businesspeople with mansions into overseas aid workers. His spit and fire-breathing message, his voice in the wilderness making the path crooked for the comfortable had made Pentecostal teenagers pull out their ear buds. Those happy-clappy, aren't-we-all-so-pretty-in-our-designer-jeans-and-Christian-rock-band-hoodies had opened a soup kitchen in downtown Hoppers Crossing. It fed thirty-five people every night. Some of the soupies wandered in from the paddocks. Like the Stevensons might have if they hadn't been receiving so many Coles vouchers. And that was a good thing. It had meant Lee didn't have to be around sweaty, grog-screwed old men in crunchy coats at Salvo refuges anymore.

The family changed. Joe didn't, of course. But the rest of them did.

A clan of reformed happy-clappy teenagers gave Molly some clothes. Beautiful dresses.

'She's never needed them before,' Joe had said, cooking stew on the burner. They'd moved to a new station, Lestona West. They could smell the sea at night. A shopping hub and car park were right across the road. They were closer to Wayfarers, which meant less travel. Joe was preaching every week.

'She's never had them before,' Penny had replied as she'd chopped strawberries and peaches, fresh, for dessert. She had a new breadboard to slice the fruit on. A gift from Della.

Molly had looked amazing. A pale lemon dress with thin straps, washes of white through it. Like a granita. Her shoulders were brown.

'And it's good she's never had them before.'

'You don't know anything Dad!' Molly had cried and she'd run along the semi-enclosed platform. There were still evening commuters around, dashing this way and that. Wondering what this girl with brown shoulders, a new dress and a pretty face was all about, shouting across the tracks to a man hunched over a burner.

'I don't know *anything*,' Joe had muttered. 'Yes, that's right. I don't know anything. I don't know a single thing about this crooked and—'

'—you don't have to preach tonight,' Lee's mum had said. 'It's Monday.'

Joe had scooped the beef and vegetables from the pot with a plastic ladle and thrown it on their plates.

'Every day is a good enough day to speak your mind.'

Penny had worked some stew into her mouth and chewed.

'They'll offer you a job soon,' she said hopefully.

'Who?'

'The Wayfarers.'

'They won't see me for the dust I'll wipe from my feet if they offer me a job.'

Lee's mum had groaned and they'd all eaten their stew.

The Wayfarers did offer Joe a job. Associate Pastor.

'Church council approved you in less than five minutes!'

Della's red lipstick looked pink under the church foyer lights.

'That's flattering,' he said. 'But I'm not taking it.'

Joe had preached twenty-six times at the Wayfarers. Morning and night services. After the night gatherings, he drank mugs of instant coffee in the church function room. The remnant, wide-eyed disciples sipped along with him. Mainly young men. In their polos and pale blue jeans, they cleaned the collection plates and put music players into docks before church services, pressing buttons and starting up love songs to Jesus. They stacked away chairs after services and washed dishes. They dusted. And as a reward, it seemed, Joe gave them extra preaching after his official duties.

He seemed, in fact, to only do the regular preaching to give him an excuse to talk to this wild-eyed bunch. Their clean cut and smiling faces gathered around the tables. Listening intently even if Joe was only saying he needed another coffee.

Lee sat bored in the corner. Reading the Kierkegaard he would be quizzed on afterwards while his father stalked the tables. Joe even lay down on the carpet between them sometimes. Shouted from down there. Banged his fists. Yelled about foundations and the system they were all trapped in. If they didn't get out in a hurry, it would swallow them whole. Like a snake gulps mice.

'...like quicksand rises to your ears before you even know if they're on your head to hear with...'

Joe tossed new parables into a gospel salad. A gospel Lee had heard his whole life. A gospel he was so sick of he could have pulled each hair from his forearms as he listened. Those forearm hairs were in greater abundance, he noticed. More hair everywhere now. Joe saw. And saw Lee blocking his father's gospel out. Lee thought Joe would get in his face about it, but he didn't. He just gave him more and more books to read and report on.

'This is Nietzsche. You need to understand the enemy, son. But don't imagine he's not brilliant...'

He was. But Lee liked the cover art more. A giant eating its own arm? He wasn't sure. But it blew him away. Along with the fact that Nietzsche, someone so smart, had gone mad and killed himself. That distressed and strangely encouraged him. Nietzsche was a man, wasn't he, like any other? He didn't deserve to go crazy and die, surely, regardless of saying God was mad and trying to kill Him off?

'He was a man like anyone. A man under orders.'

Lee knew his father meant the Devil. But Joe never named him.

'Resist him and he flees.'

He gave Lee a van Gogh biography. Maybe it was supposed to be an antidote to Nietzsche. He gave him several biographies of St Francis, a bunch of capitalist and socialist economics texts, and more Orwell.

'You need to know the system. The systems! And how to get out.'

In hindsight, Lee explained to Peter, it was easy to see that he wanted out, for sure. Out of all systems. Including his father's.

Joe must have been watching him all those times they rode the train to Wayfarers. That's what Lee liked to think. He wanted to think he was to blame. Because if he was, then his father wasn't. Or at least Joe had been a little less to blame. And if he was less to blame for what he did, then Lee could understand him better.

He wanted to think that Joe followed his son's eyes into the paddocks where the timber frames were growing. Because Lee wanted a house. With a video game console and his own room. A giant TV screen on the lounge room wall and maybe a spa in the backyard. Where he could take some of the girls from Wayfarers.

Joe must have read his thoughts. Or God had. And told Joe. Or someone at the Wayfarers had told him. Lee could never remember, but he must have told someone what he wanted. He'd had so many chats with Wayfarers after services. He'd drunk litres of hot chocolate and stared at all the white and perfect teeth. Lee thought if the Stevensons stayed around the Wayfarers, eventually they'd convince Joe to take one of the beautiful homes they offered. Wayfarers would cover the rent. Della said it once before Joe shushed Lee away.

The Stevensons visited Wayfarer homes. Without Joe. They were invited for lunch and coffee and Joe didn't stop them. They were free, it seemed. Foolish, but free to visit the likes of Veronica and her family. She met them at a huge door that had a gold knocker.

'Look, it's embarrassing, Penny,' she said, 'This house...after your husband's sermons. I just, well...'

Her black hair shone. She stood in a hallway of polished boards that the Stevensons could have slept, cooked, entertained and played mini-golf in. There was a set of golf clubs away up a hall that led to a giant kitchen and dining room. Veronica stared at her own clean white runners as if they'd brought her to the door without permission. Penny ushered Lee and Molly inside.

'Oh, Veronica, don't worry. Don't think about it.'

It was a Sunday afternoon. A strangely warm October day. Veronica's property developer husband was working. They had a late lunch in the backyard at a gun metal grey table. It was situated on the lawn and surrounded by twelve weatherproof chairs. Two-storey houses loomed over Veronica's three fences, and two bowls of roast chicken salad sat in the middle of the table, with sides of buttered green beans and potato wedges. With sour cream. They had fresh sliced coconut for dessert.

The table didn't attract or hold the afternoon heat. Lee touched next to his plate. Totally cool. Molly swished her fresh-combed hair from side to side for the pre-teen boy at the other end of the table. The boy's white baseball cap was leaning to one side. As if he were ghetto. The two of them kept looking at each other. Lee laughed.

'What is it?' his mum asked.

'Nothing. I'm, ah, it's just amazing the table's not hot.'

Veronica explained the technology. As if he cared. What he cared about was the pool. It was like something from a dream. If he could ever have a dream so brilliant. The fenced pool was rectangular with two ponds at each end surrounded by ferns. Water trickled down rocks into the pool. There was a spa at the far end, semi-enclosed by a bark hut.

They hadn't brought their swimming gear!

Because they didn't have any.

Veronica said she might be able to find some spare shorts of her husband's for Lee. But she wasn't sure how she could help Molly.

'Don't worry,' Penny said. 'They don't have to swim.'

Lee ate the last of his coconut and noticed Veronica's sunhat was ragged. Her black hair out the sides of it made her look like a goat. Everything else was shiny and beautiful. The manicured lawn. The hanging gardens of Babylon behind her, complete with mini-waterfalls. Her sunglasses were especially shiny. And bumble bee huge. He could see himself in them.

But that sunhat. Soft cotton, yet somehow grim. It was cream but had surely once been white.

Ghetto boy asked if he could go play Wii with Molly.

'Is that okay with you Penny?' Veronica asked. Molly pretended not to care either way.

'Yes, it's fine,' Penny said. Her green nylon dress, seams failing in places, looked better, Lee thought, than Veronica's hat.

His sister and ghetto boy left the table and something ticked over in Lee's brain. That's the way he thought of it years later, the way he told the story to Peter. Like his life had led to the decision he was about to make, a decision he took without it even seeming like one. As if it were made for him.

He stripped naked at the table and ran for the pool.

The water held him, caressed him, and took him in a cool embrace. He dived and, like a turtle looking for food, he scanned the blue paint down there. Then he realised, whoops, those times at the creek hadn't prepared him for this.

It was deep.

He felt closed in. Yet free. He forgot about his mum, Veronica, ghetto boy and Molly. Did he even have a father?

He came up for air and dog paddled to the pool's edge. His mum was crouched there, her face struck in horror. As if he'd pressed the button for the apocalypse. She couldn't even say his name. She gasped as if she'd been the one struggling in deep water. Veronica stayed at the table, her back firmly against her chair. She picked up her teacup and drank. She seemed to smile, but Lee couldn't be sure. His mum finally broke her silence.

'Lee! Get out!'

'It's nice in,' he heard himself say.

'Get out. And get dressed!'

Veronica arrived with a small towel on her arm.

'This might help?'

No hiding her smirk now. And was she trying to get a look through the water to see what she could see? Or did Lee just want her to? She handed the towel to Penny and walked back to the table. Penny clenched her teeth.

'Out!'

He wanted to care about his mum in that moment. He wanted

to behave well for her. Somewhere inside, he did want those things. But instead he laughed and dived under again. When he came up he looked past his mum to the upstairs window. Molly was kissing ghetto boy. And he had his hand, didn't he, under her skirt? Veronica saw. She wandered to the wide glass doors, stopping to pat her white Labrador's head on the way.

When his father disappeared, Penny within a week took up the Wayfarers' offer of somewhere to live. She must have been in shock, Lee thought.

'What about when Dad comes back?'

She shook her head.

'He won't be back.'

They got a house with two sinks. A kitchen with a walk-in pantry. Three bedrooms and an upstairs playroom with a view to Point Cook Beach; a narrow strip of sand and shallow ocean stretching away to nothing.

They didn't have a pool.

Molly and Lee had bedrooms on the second floor. Hers had a big single bed with a pink doona; Lee's doona had a Bulldogs emblem. He barracked for them now, definitely. Penny covered her red doona cover with a pattern of tears.

She called Lee into her bedroom one morning and told him she didn't blame him. She admitted Joe may not even have known about the pool incident. So she didn't blame him and she never would. His father, she said, had made his own decision.

'He's gone,' she said, 'and, now and forever, we have to live without him.' Had they been doing something else the last few weeks? Lee was worried his mum had caught Joe's preaching bug. He gave her breakfast on a tray; he'd learnt to boil eggs and make toast. They had always looked after each other and that hadn't changed now they had a house and no father.

'He'll come back,' Lee told her. 'He's just angry. Really angry. He'll be back.'

He tried to ignore the dark tear marks on the edge of her doona.

'He's never coming back, Lee. I know him. He won't be back.'

Penny was never wrong about anything. But neither was Joe. Maybe that's what they liked about each other. She brushed her sandy hair from her eyes.

'I'm angry with him though.'

She didn't look it. Her sad eyes were like planets wondering where the sun had gone.

'Thanks for the eggs. They look delicious.'

Eventually, Penny cooked all the time and the smile returned to her face. Like the one she'd had on the first day they'd entered Wayfarers' Church, only now she didn't try to hide it.

Lee learnt to live in a house. And he stayed close with the Wayfarers. He wasn't sure about their God, wasn't sure theirs was the same as his father's. And he wasn't sure what he thought of his father's God, either. Or his father.

Where the hell was he? Had he gone to some other church, in

some other country, preaching his gospel and rounding up disciples? Was he hiding out in a cave or a little hut like St Francis?

Lee got sick of wondering. He could have filled his days with it, but, strangely, what Joe had taught him wouldn't let him.

The Wayfarers felt they owed the Stevensons. And Lee took their pained offering: a free education at Westburne College. That education finished or destroyed, he was never sure which, the one his father had started. Lee was ahead of his peers academically but a stranger in a foreign land. Like Orwell in Burma and Catalonia. He'd tried to enlist Orwell to help him through the hostile lunchtimes when mop-top boys laughed at him and tormented him, tried to recall Orwell's words about who controlled the past, what the future could be if we understood it, and how telling the truth was an act of revolution in a society full of liars. But he couldn't.

And he got tired of Orwell's revolution. All revolution. Where did it lead? Where had it led his father? He wanted to survive on his own.

One afternoon he put Orwell's books into a garbage bag and threw it beneath the house. His mum found it a few weeks later. Lee looked down from his bedroom window as she emptied it into the recycle bin. The books fell like shot birds.

He got a university degree. Then a teaching post back at Westburne College.

And his own house in Hopper's Crossing.

It had an artful, low brick fence. Native grasses sprouted from carefully laid white stones. A sleek, grey rendered house sat behind those stones, with a wife inside and a baby in her arms. What a beautiful home, visitors said, what a beautiful family. And Lee nodded. But it was a house in which he daily felt the urge to take every electronic gadget that played a movie or song; every framed print, cereal packet or book, pile it in some garbage bags and grab his wife and child and say, Rachel, it's time for us to move on.

'I can't live here, but I do. That's what I kept telling myself, Peter.'

It was one of the first times Peter had hung out with Lee. In a god-awful bistro in Hopper's Crossing. Pokie machines clucking and beeping, and snotty toddlers screaming behind the glass of an indoor playground.

'You like it here? In Hoppers?'

'I couldn't live anywhere else.'

He sipped his lemon squash and told Peter that, a few years ago, it was as if something was holding him in the suburb.

'I mean, I knew it was my father. His memory. But it was somehow more.'

Before the news hit the media, his mum had come to his doorstep on a Sunday morning and told him about Joe. Lee had just nodded. And, strangely, had found himself smiling.

'I wanted to tell her I was proud of him,' he said, remembering that his mum had cried softly through the whole visit. 'I know it sounds nuts, but I wanted to beat my chest,' Lee said, demonstrating. 'Beat it in honour of my mad bastard of a father! Only he could have come up with something as crazy and perfect as what he did. On what will we build our foundations!'

He laughed but it caught in his throat.

'Mum told me about some strange guy in Point Cook who'd

pulled apart his house and left it there.'

It had been built on a crawl space foundation and the new owners couldn't figure out why the walls were cracking. Stumping problem was the usual diagnosis. Like all the other exploratory surgeons before him, one bloke delved into the crawl space to check the struts. All fine. But while he was down there, the halogen lamp exposed the outline of a skeleton on the cement base. It looked like graffiti, scratched in before the wood struts were laid.

'They decided to take a look, Peter, and cut it open...'

As Lee told the story, Peter could see the workers slicing into the concrete with powerful buzz saws. They had been careful not to dislodge the remains. They had worked in silence and been meticulous. They had been respectful of Joe Stevenson, apparently.

'I let mum cry on my shoulder.'

He told Peter he'd thought of a million things to say and a million reasons not to say them.

'I didn't ask her if the people's house was okay now. I knew it would be.'

14. Simon Stevenson

He made himself a deal: if the family walking the slipway approached his jetty, Simon would personally help them aboard. They'd be his last fare for the day. On '*Cruising Easy*'s Daintree Croc Tour'.

The family approached and he made good on his deal; he clomped his fat work boot onto the jetty and took the mother's hand. There was no harm in being generous. Plus, she was gorgeous. A natural beauty, holding her baby boy. Well, not really a baby. Simon was no judge but he reckoned the kid in tiny sneakers was about eighteen months old. The toddler's mum wore no make-up. There was no fancy hair-do or jewellery. Just smooth, tanned skin and deep-set eyes. And there was something South American about those full lips. Her chunk of a husband followed her, steering two older kids. Simon let go of the beauty's soft palm. She smiled, thanked him, and took hold of the boat's slim railing.

'Crocs can't get in, can they?'

'Nah, *Cruisin Easy*'s safe as houses.'

She carried her child to the bench seat. Her cream dress showed the faint outline of polka-dot underwear. Simon had been dog-tired before, useless as old gravy. Now the Daintree was glassy and the mangroves full of Grey Whistlers and Fantails, chirping and having a ball. Simon perched himself behind the boat's pirate ship-style wheel, and ran his hand through his wreck of hair. The family got organized, pulled sunscreen and water bottles from bags. The husband had a big nose. He was pale-skinned and younger than the beauty. And he'd seen too much city gym time. His brand new straw hat was too small. Despite his bulging shoulders, he had long, spindly fingers. He was probably one of those tech heads, Simon thought.

The bloke said he was a plumber.

'More management these days than anything.'

What a drone of a voice. From under his straw hat he peered for crocs through the onboard binoculars. Wanker. The boat was still tied to the jetty. The kids, the boy in a baseball cap and the girl in a lime dress, they weren't the mother's, no way. She was much too interested in the baby, playing with plastic drinking cups on the hull floor.

'Are you from up this way?' she asked Simon.

Her voice was caramel with a lick of dark chocolate. She adjusted her cotton hat and put on bumblebee sunglasses. Simon saw himself in them.

'No, from Mexico.'

She looked nonplussed.

'You know, from Victoria, *south of the border*?' he explained. 'I was in Gippsland, Westmore, few other places. Came up to Queensland, Rockhampton mainly. Fishing boats. Now I'm here. Just getting further north. Be off the end of Cape York next.'

She smiled as Simon took the ropes from the jetty knobs and coiled them on deck. The beauty put a floppy hat on the nappy-filler. The kid whined. She made sure the other kids put sunscreen on, too, and asked Straw Hat if he was wearing anyway.

'Yeah, I'm right,' he snapped at her.

She was only asking, you tool.

It wasn't that hot anyway. At least not for Simon. Heat was different in Queensland. It got into your bones, then it was your bones. Then your bones slowed down. Simon never thought his legs would get so brown or weathered. His dirty socks, wound down at the boot lip, were part of him. Thick wool hinted that trouble lurked nearby. Something might bite. They said Danger! to thong-wearing passengers. And that kept the women all ears for his onboard commentary.

He puttered the boat from the jetty and decided he'd better win the husband over.

'Had my ex-wife on the last tour before you blokes...'

He didn't add that Fiona came, under sufferance, just to show him his son, Ryan. Who was suddenly interested in him after God knows how many years.

'The boss suggested a few places I could drop her off...'

Straw Hat held the binoculars to his chest and couldn't hide a smirk. He looked away before the big kids saw him and he studied the sky. It was big, blue and open. Trees dropping the first frangipanis of the season into the river.

'Looks like a Balinese wedding,' Simon observed. The beauty tried to get her husband's attention, but he was all eyes through the binoculars, searching for crocs. Wondering if he'd get his money's worth. I'll give it to you, Simon thought, don't worry about that.

There's no other way to see a croc but in its natural habitat. It's a dead-eyed terrorist with a Neo Jurassic head, boogie boarding towards you. And everyone wants to see a croc on their Daintree cruise. If they don't, they tell their friends, *Hey, I went with* Cruisin Easy *and I saw diddlysquat. Don't go with them, go with the other mob,* Bottom Feeders.

The ones with 'croc cam' stuck to the arse of their boat.

That bloody camera. Simon wished the crocs would swallow it. But as Tony 'Bottom Feeder' Bourne kept telling him, 'They're not just killing machines, Simon. They're curious creatures.'

The bloody things only nudged at the camera with their snouts. Simon wondered how curious they'd be if someone accidentally pushed el suavo Bourne in the river.

Simon didn't get why southerners thought croc cam was a good deal. It was no way to see an evolutionary masterpiece, an animal that hadn't changed in two hundred million years because it hadn't needed to. It was a case of survival of the killer. A croc was stronger than ten blokes could ever get in a lifetime of pumping iron. A salty crunched its jaws through wild pigs, rabbits, possums, sheep—whatever—then thunder-crashed its way through still water and mangroves. If his catch was too big to swallow, he'd wrestle it into the undergrowth. Thrash it round until a limb snapped off. The way Simon wound off a chewed fingernail.

The Daintree knew no other royalty. There were mangroves, pink and white frangipanis and wide-winged water birds.

Spiders spun domed webs that sat like morning mist in the branches. But there was nothing like his royal highness, King Happy Jaws. He had no one to fear.

Simon brought the boat close to some frangipanis. The family touched them and smelt the petals. Then he shunted them to a few more spots along the banks. He let the motor idle and chatted about how the Daintree forest supported its snakes, insects, spiders and plants. All primed to snare the unthinking southerner. The kids whispered to Straw Hat and he yelled at them. God knows why. Surely not for talking while Simon was? That's what Simon's father had always done. Straw Hat's yell made the beauty jump, but she didn't dare cross her husband. She hugged her baby instead.

Simon took a good look at Straw Hat's pink shaving rash and his glum lips. Those frown lines and the red puffs on the tops of his high cheekbones. All good targets for a right cross or a left hook.

It was time for action. Simon motored the family to Scooter's hideaway.

Scooter was an insurance croc. It was right on change of season, which meant high tides and no crocs. The bastards, especially the bigger ones, were out of sight. Good for *Bottom Feeders*, no good for *Cruisin Easy*. So it was thank Christ for Scooter. He was a young, two-metre male whose favourite hiding spot left part of his leather above the waterline. And helped Simon pay his rent.

'Wow, look Dad! It's a croc. Look!'

Straw Hat joined his son at the railing. He pulled his camera out and started videoing. He got some nice close ups of Scooter trying to hide in the bushes, his long mouth fixed in a grin.

Scooter knew the drill.

Straw Hat managed a smile. He filmed his kids' wide-eyed reactions. He got some shots of his nervous wife at the railing.

'Wow! Isn't he amazing?' she gasped.

Simon explained he knew it was Scooter by the band of black markings on his right leg.

'He's only a pup, but he'll be a powerhouse one day,' Simon told her, pumping his chest out at the wheel. The beauty bent to pick up her baby. Her round arse was so peachy he couldn't help smiling and flapping his tongue out. Like she was an ice block and he'd been dry for days. It'd been months, actually. But he felt stupid for waving his tongue around. That was no way for a Skipper to behave. Besides, he'd promised he'd sort himself out. As far as he saw it, Fiona had kicked him out—and the court had banned him from his son—because of porn. Not because she was scared he'd hit her. And their kids.

When Fiona had put those prints of Tahitian chicks and their tits all around the house, Simon was as confused as a carrot-flavored lollypop. If she hated porn, why did she do that? Yes, she'd all of a sudden started thinking she was a painter, like Simon's brother, but that was no reason to porn up the house. And why tell him to nick off for good and he can't see his son, Ryan, and then bring the kid all the way to Queensland all of a sudden?

To fuck with his head. That's what it was.

His son had stared at him, his headphones on for the whole cruise. Said nothing. Now the family in his boat was staring at him because he was forgetting to do his job.

'Okay, Scooter's had his fifteen minutes of fame.'

Simon hit the throttle hard. He pulled himself together and told Scooter's story. The still air carried his voice.

'A bloke like Scooter, he does it hard. You see, crocs are territorial. Scooter's got to get himself some territory without pissing off, pardon my language, the big bloke down the river.'

The family was listening, but only the mother looked at him. After staring at her arse he couldn't meet her eyes. He checked out the mangroves. He thought of his son and then, strangely, his fibro porch and the view of the sugarcane. Miles and miles of it.

Straw Hat looked like Simon's dead father. That square jaw and big nose. That's what was really pissing Simon off about him. His father who had threatened to kill him, but couldn't even give him, really, a decent whack when the occasion called for it. His beltings never hurt. But he still knew how to hand out the pain: why make it Simon's duty to keep the whole family together after he died? Now Simon was on this tour of nowhere with a family, while his own was in bits and pieces all over the country.

'The old bloke's almost double Scooter's size,' Simon stammered on, shaken by the bullshit he was letting fester in his head. 'About four metres. That's more than half the size of this boat.'

Straw Hat bent and inspected the hull. Did the mental

arithmetic. Simon calmed himself. Got professional again and steadied his voice.

'He gets pretty annoyed if a croc like Scooter even looks like he's heading to his part of town. A bloke like Scooter, he'll find himself in more than a few scraps with the big one. And if he doesn't watch himself, it's all over...'

He explained that only ten per cent of male crocs made it to adulthood. 'Hardly any of the young ones have a hope against the old blokes. Most of them, in a situation like Scooter's, they head further up river and try to get away from grizzly old blokes. If they're really lucky, they find themselves a lady croc.'

Simon's mouth was even drier after his speech. He thought of Fiona, looking half-decent today. She'd lost weight. Not much, but some.

He went for his water bottle beneath the steering wheel. He wanted to look up and see the beauty smiling at him. But it was just another cruise and she was just another wife. So when he settled back behind the wheel and saw her smiling, he got a buzz in his groin. Her smile was probably for the baby, but her head was tilted in Simon's direction. The setting sun turned her face to choc-malt. He'd ignore a slab of beer to taste that flavour tonight.

The baby played with empty cups for the rest of the tour. The older kids slouched with headphones while the mother placed her hat on the seat beside her dopey husband and let her hair flow free.

Simon cruised up a tight inlet. On Fiona's cruise he'd seen a green tree snake hanging from a mangrove. He tacked the boat carefully around the overhanging trees, but the snake had gone. It made him sad and he didn't know why. He hated snakes; the slurping and sliding over branches. The boy reckoned he spotted a water snake flashing to stern, but Simon saw only the boat's tiny wake.

On the ride back to the jetty, Straw Hat checked every frame of his video footage. He nodded for a while. Then his face went stiffer than usual. He pointed at the screen, at Simon's tongue flapping no doubt, and he stared hard at the captain of the boat. But Simon ignored him. He sat back and enjoyed the warmth on his face, the glint from the water as the boat chopped towards the jetty. If you decide to send them all to the car and face off with me, Simon thought, that's fine. It's your duty. A man has to protect his family. You can have the first punch free. And maybe even the rest.

15. Ryan Stevenson

Ryan moved out of home as soon as he turned eighteen. His plan was to do what the rest of his family couldn't do. Get it right. What he meant was living. Just going about a day under Westmore's moody skies. Under them completely, come to think of it: his job was cracking open suburban footpaths to find and fix water pipes. He was happiest when he was down there. There was no one to tell him if he was connecting the PVC 300mm female joint correctly to the male joint. He just did it. Then moved to the next one. A square of light above him and, up there with it, his crew moving from van to hole to lower him, tools on a pulley. He got his work done right, every time. He was team leader. He knew stuff. His head was on straight, as straight as those pipes. But when he came up again for air at the end of the day, his stuff ups were right in front of his face. Like losing a girlfriend whose dad was made of money. And telling his old school friends at a reunion that he believed in UFOs and he wouldn't mind being abducted by aliens. His granddad had told him about the ones he'd seen as a kid.

You've got an excuse for stuffing up, his younger sister Alice always reminded him. *Your dad left when you were a teenager. Remember?*

But it was her dad who left too. Not that she ever seemed to care. She never wanted to see him or know him.

Simon Stevenson pissed off to Queensland. But it hadn't changed a thing in Ryan's life. It hadn't left any holes. It hadn't turned him into a statistic. It hadn't forced him to become anything.

Sometimes he wished he lived underground. Like at that opal mine town in the desert. But that was too far from Westmore and his grandma, Jules. He owed her for looking after him so much when his father left. Now it was time to help look after her. And he was doing that one afternoon, helping Jules out by taking a package of hers to the tiny post office on Grey Street, when Ryan met his wife-to-be, Sally.

She was coming out the door and her face was all sideways. Like someone had grabbed her cheek and pulled until it had got stuck. But she was good looking; she had her hair set nicely. It fell in brown waves. Her legs were all bent though, and she pegged along with a walking frame. But she took care of herself.

That's good, Ryan thought, for no reason that made sense.

Sally kept apologizing for being slow getting out the door. Her bum in her jeans was just fine; round and sweet and not at all disabled. Like the prints of Tahitian women his mum had stuck up on her wall.

Ryan held the door open for Sally.

'Don't worry,' she said.

'It's all right. I'm in no rush.'

He had nowhere to go, his shift was over. But suits were queuing behind him in that edgy way that suits get; straining their necks because they want to get past, but not wanting to be rude because, you know, the poor woman's disabled. If they'd pushed through him and Sally it would be admitting what heartless pricks they were for wanting to get on with their oh-so-important days. Making more money in an hour than Ryan probably made in a week.

Westmore had gone to shit.

Sally clomped to the post box. Ryan would have let her disappear but she dropped her letter. The envelope scampered down the street in the wind like a mouse going for a block of cheese. Ryan shot after it. He picked it up and gave it to her. She flicked him a loose-lipped smile and in a drawl like a Texan on downers said, 'Hey, thank you.'

'Ah, that's no worries. Do you want me to put it in the slot for you?'

He didn't even think how that sounded. But she gave him a smile and didn't answer. And, whoops, he felt a rush in his groin. What the hell am I doing? he thought. She's disabled. But then he remembered her bum.

He flipped her letter into the box and asked her out for coffee.

The last thing he would normally ask anybody to do.

They headed slowly to Drew's on the Corner. He hated that upmarket joint but couldn't think where else to take her. People looked up from their lattes when they walked in. Sally, all weird looking, and him wearing his orange safety vest.

Suck on your whatevers, Ryan thought. She's all right.

They found a table near the window. The waitress was wearing a dress like one of Ryan's grandma's outfits and she made a fuss of getting them seated.

'Now, what would you like?' Sally asked.

'A beer?'

She laughed.

'I don't think they sell them.'

'A chocolate milkshake then.'

Ryan found out Sally hadn't always been smashed to shit. It'd happened in a stack on her ex-boyfriend's Triumph. She'd come off at more than a hundred ks an hour.

'I'm lucky to be alive.'

Ryan thought she winked but it might have just been her face doing whatever it wanted on its own. She went on about the Epworth Hospital, the buzzers and lights. How people died in wards around her. And how her boyfriend became her ex.

'He didn't want to even look at me...'

Ryan zoned out and played with a sugar packet. He wanted to crack it open and gulp it. His mum, before she'd gone health mad, had always done that when she was nervous and thought no one was looking. Ryan stopped his sugar urge. He caught his reflection in the window; four-day growth and pimple pock marks that had hung around since TAFE. He took off his safety vest. He wouldn't have minded taking off and replacing his nose, too. It was bent from Lechie Freisa's fist in Year 11. That was the day Lechie said, 'Ryo, your dad fucked off because he didn't want to look at your head anymore.' Ryan threw a punch, it missed, and Lechie threw a better one.

Ryan asked Sally what she was up to for the rest of the day. She said she didn't know, maybe some study.

'I've hired *Alien*.'

For the tenth time, could have been eleventh.

Okay, it was getting onto more like fifty. And he hadn't bought a copy because he liked the look of the rental shop girl and her purple lipstick. Sally looked at Ryan now, like she was a culture vulture who went to the theatre. She probably did. She upped her eyebrows. A massive effort. But then she said, 'Yeah, great, let's go.'

It took them a long time to get the DVD into the player.

When she clomped into Ryan's flat, Sally got free of her walking frame and planted herself on his couch. She didn't seem to care about the cotton threads running loose or the empty chip packets. She asked what he did and he said, 'Whatever the hell I like.' That was a lie, but he loved saying it, always had. She laughed, as most people did, but hers turned to a gurgle.

Sally dived for his belt and flung the thing off. She pulled his work daks down before he had a chance to sit next to her.

It was a mighty effort getting Sally's clothes off. Even more of a struggle trying to get her legs apart. And it didn't really work. She tried hard, strained, and he tugged as gently as he could. But together they could only get her legs halfway open. She started crying. Just quiet tears she didn't bother wiping. He liked her then. A lot. He sat her up, no easy thing, and said, 'You know, we don't have to worry. Let's watch the movie.'

He was glad to have company. And only her body was stuffed. Chances are she thought he was the retarded one anyway. Ryan was pulling himself about that; he knew she thought he was retarded. But it seemed she didn't give a crap.

It all felt wrong, pretty quickly; Sally turned around and bent over as best she could in front of his couch. She rested her breasts and shoulders on the dirty seat cushion. Her legs were still basically locked together, and when Ryan rustled up behind her, there was only one option for what he could do. He didn't like the idea, but she understood the situation.

'Whatever,' she said, all breathy.

It felt weird and good and bad at the same time. And he couldn't tell if she was hurting or happy. Or sad. Maybe all three. He tried to give her little bloke in the boat some work, but she pulled his hand away and told him just to get on with it.

She hated it and so did he. They couldn't touch each other when they finished. Or talk. They got dressed and sorted and he stuck on *Alien*. The movie had been going an hour before they talked.

'I've never seen this the whole way through,' Sally said.

'I've seen it heaps.'

'Why?'

'Because I like it.'

Because watching it protected him from the aliens he knew were out there. If not out there, then underground. Where he protected the city's water supply from them. Nor was he going to tell her he thought his mum had been abducted by one a few years ago then returned. But the fucking alien had stayed in her body and taken her over. Changed her.

Sally asked lots of this and that about the plot and the alien and where the ship was going and how many sequels there'd been. She got cuddly. Ryan wanted her arms off his neck, her minty breath gone and back down the street. Because the sex had been bad and she was making him feel stupid and he liked her.

'Why do you love *Alien* so much, really, Ryan? I mean, I get that Sigourney Weaver's great, and the feminist narrative. But I thought you'd be more a *Terminator* man.'

He was not a *Terminator* man.

He was an *Alien* man.

That's how it was and always would be.

The movie finished and he told Sally he had to go and visit his grandmother. It was true, but Sally looked at him like the alien was shooting straight out from his head.

'Well, if you think you can just invite me back to your flat and use me you've got another think coming.'

After what they'd done, Ryan didn't know what that other thing might be.

'I catch up with her every month for dinner,' he said softly.

Because his granddad was long gone and Jules needed family around, what with her sons scattered across the state.

'Get fucked,' Sally told him.

'Oh, look, you know, we could hang out again some time...'

He wanted to. Maybe they could even become an item. Even if she'd probably drop him later because she thought he was stupid for believing in aliens. But Sally was in a major huff. She wobbled to her feet and got hold of her walking frame. She told him she'd thought he was different. He said I am different. She said not in that way. And he wanted to throw his hands in the air.

'I had a good time,' he said, meaning after the sex had finished.

Her face was even saggier now than when he'd first seen it.

'Do you know how rich I am?' she asked.

After he got over the shock of her saying something so weird, he replied, 'No, tell me.'

'I could buy your flat and the other six in this crappy block.'

'Great,' he said. It must have been a decent TAC payout.

'I hate you, Ryan,' she said.

'Well, you know, I don't hate you, Sally. I think you're a good sort of chick.' She laughed bitterly and went chick! chick! like she was scratching in a henhouse.

'I could get a better man than you in a raffle.'

'No one raffles blokes.'

That set her off. She said there would be no point raffling blokes like him. She dissed him, told him he was everything wrong under the sun. He didn't hear most of it because he 'zoned out. But when she finished she leant on her frame in front of his TV. He couldn't see the DVD symbol. He liked to watch it when it flicked from side to side after a movie. It settled him. Sometimes he watched it for half an hour or more, and afterwards he was so calm he felt like he'd smoked a joint.

He sat on the couch like a numb nuts.

'I have to go. I really do.'

'Fine,' she said, but didn't move. Ryan stood and hugged her round the waist and she let him. Then, oh no, it was pants off again.

He only had a quarter of an hour to get to his grandma's place. He wouldn't have time to shower. And he wanted to. Bad. But his grandma hated it when he was late because it meant the beef got dry in the oven.

'Sally, I've really got to head off.'

She nodded fiercely.

'Can you at least give me a lift?'

'Yeah, no trouble at all,' he said, knowing it would be. He'd be late for sure now.

'Well, it wouldn't want to be any trouble...'

Sally told him where she lived. In a lovely house with two bathrooms and a spa, and pity, really, that he wouldn't get to see it because he was such an arsehole. He asked her for her address. And stopped buttoning his shirt.

'No worries, it's on the way,' he stammered, trying not to let the shock get to him.

'I couldn't care less if it isn't on the way...'

'Okay. All right.'

Sally lived next-door to his grandma.

'What is it Ryan?'

'Nothing.'

He was breathing fast, he felt it. She leant on her frame and squinted at him like he was something squiggly under a microscope.

219

They drove under Porter Avenue's elms and past the rundown Scout Hall. Not far to go now.

Sally laughed and laughed. Maybe because she'd just got laid and it had been the first time since the crash. Ryan was sure it had been.

She laughed like a car alarm. Ha hee, ha hee.

Her laughing was slicing him up.

'Stop that or I'm kicking you out!'

She kept right on laughing. When he stopped the car and dragged her out of the front seat, she let him. But he got a fierce look from an old woman pushing a stroller.

Ryan left Sally next to a telephone pole. She was still laughing like a mad arse. He dragged her walking frame from the boot then drove away without even looking in his rear-vision mirror.

Yes, he did. Once. But he didn't feel bad. Not really.

He felt bloody terrible.

What kind of a bloke...

It had started to look like rain. Sally only had half a kilometre of the Avenue to walk. Not much more than that. Maybe he should go back. But she'd probably still be laughing at him and he couldn't bear it.

He hoped it wouldn't rain

Grandma Jules was pissed with him for showing up late. The little squint behind her glasses said it all. But she didn't stay miffed for long. She told him the beef was hardening up but not too bad.

'I've put on a vegie dish, too. In a wok. I invited a friend. Do you mind?'

Too bad now if he did. He looked at the three places set at her long pine table and just knew who it was coming to dinner. That's what all the laughing had been about, for sure.

'Need a shower, Gran. Been workin' hard.'

'That's fine. I'm not sure now what time Sally said she'd be here.'

She was at the dinner table when Ryan got out of the shower.

His hair was still a bit wet, but parted neatly because his gran liked it that way and why annoy her?

He didn't care how Sally liked it.

She'd stopped laughing now. Oh, yeah, butter wouldn't melt near her crooked lips.

'Ryan, this is Sally.'

'We met at the post office this morning. Sally was trying to post a letter.'

His gran gave him a scolding look.

Can't you tell she's disabled? Of course she'd struggle posting a letter!

Sally grinned from ear-to-ear on that crazy slant. Here we go, he thought.

'Ryan helped me get it in, didn't you, Ryan?'

'Yeah, yeah... I did my best.'

His grandma laid the beef on the table in a dish.

'I hope it's not too hard.'

'Sally quite likes hard meat... That's what you said at the butcher's this morning, didn't you?'

'Oh, yeah, that's true, Ryan. But I like the longer cuts. They're harder to find though.'

His gran was at the head of the table fussing vegetables out of the wok. Sally and Ryan sat across from each other. Ryan had a view out the dining room window of the neighbour's renovated weatherboard McMansion. Going purple in the stormy sunset. Like Ryan's face would if he didn't settle down.

Women! Always have a go about your size after the deed's done. Stuff this.

'But you said that sausage was good enough to eat.'

'Yeah, but, very, very cold, wasn't it? Almost frozen.'

His gran looked at him sternly. And knowingly.

'I thought you said you met at the Post Office.'

'Ryan took me down to the butchers in the IGA.'

Sally looked straight at him. 'I'd probably need to skip a few suburbs to get some decent meat.'

Ryan's grandma took off her glasses and laid them next to her bread plate. She knew something was up.

'Is this meat all right, Sally?'

'It's the best I've ever had, Julie. I could eat it all day.'

'Well, I got it from the butcher's near the post office. If you're interested.'

Jules looked at Ryan like she always did. Full of pride. It was why he kept coming over. Not just to look after her, but to get that chuffed feeling in his chest. Sally looked at him too. And got the tears on. She stared at Ryan like he was Brad Pitt in *Titanic*. Or whoever it was.

'You could be right, Julie. I'll have to see, won't I?'

'Yes. Yes you will.'

Ryan and Sally looked at each other, hostility dissipated.

'Dessert will be nice, too, I think you'll find.'

Ryan should have finished his main meal, excused himself and said, You two ladies have a lovely time. But, no, he stayed for the baked sultana pudding. He listened to the women talk about the fashions in the new boutique, the one with the head-less mannequins. Then he offered to walk Sally home—what, fifty metres?—and he went in and sucked champagne in her spa. He let her play with him and carry on and joke about how good the meat actually was around here. And he thought, *Sometimes I get things right.*

He could move out of his shithole flat and live next-door to his grandma. Right here. There were worse things in life. He knew that. His gran would soon need more looking after. She'd done a mighty job looking after him when he was a kid and his mum had been working hard at the hospital. These two, this Sally and his grandma, they'd need a lot of looking after.

He laughed and dunked Sally's head in her spa, let her bubble for a bit, then pulled her out.

'How'd you like that?' he asked as she spluttered. Then she started laughing her head off.

'Do it again!'

16. The Stevensons

Peter and Simon finished kicking the football around the overgrown park with their primary school-aged sons, Will and Ryan. The men had sweat on their brows and up the backs of their t-shirts. But even in their footy jumpers, the kids hadn't raised a sweat.

They all dodged footpath dogshit on their way back to Simon's house. Simon was as excited as the boys; he wanted to bounce the footy. He handed his stubby to Peter, and Simon's little son Ryan tried to steal the ball from his father.

'Too slow, fella.'

Peter tried to take an interest in his brother's complaints about his boss.

'He's a wanker, mate. A total fucking wanker. I tell you, one day I'll chuck it all in and head up north. Fishing boats or something, fuck it.'

Little Will smirked; he couldn't believe all the swearing he'd heard today. Peter decided not to talk to his son about it right then. He'd do it later. When the night was finally over and he'd driven him back to Melbourne and bed.

Peter gave the stubby back to its owner and Simon dragged open the wonky gates of his Westmore home. They all negotiated the parked cars; Peter's Subaru wagon and Simon's Holden work ute. Simon initiated a mock race and the boys rocketed up the patio steps behind him.

In the kitchen, Simon sculled the rest of his fifth stubby then headed to his bedroom to get dressed. Peter changed into a clean, white shirt and helped his mum set the dinner table. Simon's wife Fiona tried again to get Peter's attention. She wanted to talk to him about the prints she'd stuck on the corridor walls. He told her he'd have a look at them when he'd finished setting the table. But he had no intention of doing it.

They were prints. Not originals, for God's sake.

Framed wedding photos lined Fiona's buffet: Peter's from his first marriage to Jayne; Fiona and Simon's big day; and Terry and Kerryn's wedding in Nongo National Park. Peter picked up Simon's wedding photo. His penguin-suited brother had his arm around his bride as if she were a teammate in a footy photo.

Peter hadn't been to Simon and Fiona's house for years. Why were his and Terry's wedding photos on display? Then he realised that Jules had probably put them there, a collection she'd no doubt also established at Terry's place. She'd put them in Peter's apartment, too, if he gave her the chance. All without a thought for the irony that she'd divorced their father.

Do as I say, kids. Not as I do.

Peter put knives on placemats that featured a shiny Surfer's Paradise scene. He'd always had trouble making sense of what Jules said and did. More so every year since his father's death. Like this Dinner to Celebrate the Anniversary of Ron's Passing.

He laid the dessert spoons then brought glasses from the buffet.

He'd never been to one of these memorials. He'd always

found something else to put in his diary. But his son turning six this year made him think it was time to deepen his connection with his family. Go the whole hog.

Come on, son, he'd have said if the boy were older. *Let's go on the Ron Mausoleum Tour.*

Will was playing with his cousins. They stampeded into the dining room and shot each other with massive plastic guns dispensing foam balls. A red one hit Peter in the head and he wanted to laugh, but didn't. He knew his wife Celia would have, but he hadn't let her come. They'd eloped a year ago. Celia had met Terry, but no one else in the family. It was the way Peter wanted it. For now. Tonight, with everyone behaving civilly, he'd almost forgotten why.

He went to the kitchen to get the pepper and salt grinders and Simon was there in a fresh, black heavy metal t-shirt and red undies. The bottom of his t-shirt didn't quite reach the waistband of his undies, which meant his stomach was a white belt between the two tight articles of clothing. Peter said something. No one, not even Peter, could remember later what it was. But Simon told him to fuck off. Picked up another stubby. Cracked it. Drank from it in gulps that set his Adam's apple to tumbling.

'You're no bloody help,' he snapped at Peter.

'What do you mean? I'm setting the table.'

Simon scoffed.

'You know what I mean. You were no help with... I mean, you're... You're just fucked... You're up yourself and you always have been.'

The last dribble of stubby number six went down.

Hadn't Peter just gone to the park and had fun with Simon and his kid? What the hell was this?

'I'm out of here,' Peter told Jules. He slapped the salt and pepper grinders on the kitchen bench. 'Come on Will, we're going home.'

Once Will was safely in the car, Peter decided he should go back inside and say goodbye to the others properly. He shouldn't have come at all, that much was obvious. But he should tell them all exactly why he was leaving: because Simon, all these years on, was still angry with his dead father. And it was easier to take it out on Peter than to do a damn thing about his own problems.

Before Peter reached the patio steps on his way back inside, Simon was down them like a wild boar. He grabbed Peter and shoved him hard into the ute's side panel. Shit Peter thought, but didn't say. Will had the window open. It was enough that this was happening in front of him without his dad swearing as well.

Simon got into Peter's face and Peter held his brother's arms down. Terry made his way towards the commotion then stopped. He couldn't manhandle either of them without making everything worse. Kerryn and the other women were frozen on the patio and the kids, in their pyjamas, were holding their mothers' hands or gripping their legs.

Kerryn and Jules squealed, but Fiona couldn't get a sound out.

Can the whole of Westmore hear us? she wondered.

Neighbours across the road peered through venetian blinds. Some turned down their TVs to hear the Stevensons go at it.

'You're an arsehole, Pete... You fucken didn't give a shit about the old man.'

Drunk as Simon was, Peter still had to work hard to stop him from throwing a punch. He couldn't let this turn into a full-blown fight. He didn't want to look at Will, but he knew the kid would be shaking in fright. Maybe crying. Christ, if he fought his brother in front of Will he could sign away his access.

'Let go, Simon. All right?'

Peter had red marks on his arms where his brother's thumbs were digging in. Jules was crying now. Collapsed on the steps. Peter couldn't bear it. He roared, but it made Simon's grip tighter.

'Cut it out, fellas,' Terry said calmly.

'I'll let go when I fucken want!' Simon said through clenched teeth. And he heard Ron's voice mixed up with his own and that made him angrier.

Simon later blamed the whole shitfight on the books Fiona had read. She'd leave him to the TV once the kids were in bed, huddle herself next to that touch lamp she'd bought from Target. All the rage. She read big shiny books about art. Just like Peter probably did. He probably had his own touch lamp and cup of tea right next to his canvas or easel or whatever.

All that reading got right up Simon's nose.

Fiona was putting on too much weight, he thought. And she

was always in tracksuit pants, even though she'd stopped going to the gym. Then she started reading about that Tahitian bastard and stuck his prints on the corridor walls. That corridor was too tight for prints or anything else on the walls, hardly enough room to fart, Simon thought. But, no, apparently there was room for pictures. The painter, Fiona told him, had left his wife and kids and pissed off to Tahiti.

'His women are beautiful,' Fiona had told him.

She'd hung another print one afternoon. This time next to Simon's study slash office.

Slash porn computer room.

The print was the right kind for its location; a dark woman lay nude on her stomach on a bed. But in the background there was a little bloke with a green face and what looked like a cut-off black condom on his head. Maybe perving at the woman, maybe not.

'What's the bloke doing?'

'To me, he represents the effects of colonisation.'

Jesus, why didn't she just go and live with Peter?

All Simon knew of Tahiti was that TV ad in the '70s. There was a woman in a spa on a plane and she said, Tahiti looks nice, and her husband, with a hairy chest, called the pilot on a phone: *Simon, Tahiti!* and suddenly the spa tilted and they were all off and away. Pure irony that the pilot had the same name as him. Fiona's artist would have tripped along with them, don't worry. The whole lot of them, off to Tahiti because of a lump of soap. Simon couldn't even remember which brand.

Fiona stuck up another print. This time a white woman was

on a bed with a giant red flower in her hair. There was a black man coming at her with a whole bunch of the same flowers. Or maybe it was a scrunched up tea towel with a floral print.

'What's the flower in the hair all about?'

Simon didn't even know why he was asking. The marriage vow, he supposed. Better or worse. No prizes for guessing where they were now.

'It's a hibiscus,' she said. She pushed the framed print this way and that, trying to get it straight.

'Right. *So?*'

'It's got a meaning.'

'What?'

'Can't remember. I'll read up on it.'

Great. He'd be watching the Sunday night movie on his own again.

Simon smashed Peter against the ute.

'You're supposed to be my brother. Why didn't you help? We were all there. Helping Mum and Dad. But where were you?'

'I had reasons—'

Simon dug his fingernails into his brother's chest.

'I'll give you some fucken reasons,' he hissed and tried a punch at Peter but he was strong enough to hold it off. Just. But Peter best white shirt was ripped. That incensed him.

'I don't have to listen to this from you! Let me go, arsehole...'

He tried to escape, but his brother wriggled his bulk and held him. Simon's gut wobbled and his arse in his undies tightened up. Jules raised herself from the puddle she'd become. It was her idea to push hard and get Peter to come to this anniversary. All she'd wanted was to pull the family together before it became a beehive no-one wanted to go near. Just be normal for a change. Get on with caring for each other and being like families were supposed to be. Not that she'd known one like hers, but in lots of the novels she read things worked out fine and why couldn't they for the Stevensons?

Despite everything else, all the other upshots of the driveway stoush, one thing really got at Simon afterwards. Years before, Ron had expressly told him, over a half-dozen pots at the Westmore Hotel, that he wanted things to work out right for his boys.

Don't go on bickering and fighting and carrying on. You're bloody adults. Act like it.

Christ, he even wanted them to love each other.

If I have to say it, son, then, all right, I will.

He didn't say it, but Simon had known he'd meant it. That's all Ron had wanted before he'd carked it, his kids to get along. If anyone had bothered thinking about him. Thinking about something else, anyway, instead of carrying on with all the rubbish and bloody stupidity and arguing. It was beneath them, wasn't it? It should have been beneath the artist! The oh-so-mighty artist. But, no, Peter didn't even bother to call Simon anymore. Call and just see how he was. Arsehole! Look what it had taken to get him to come to the anniversary dinner: his mum on the phone daily for two weeks. Waste of money. Ringing his mobile.

For all his faults and fuck-ups, Ron hadn't raised them to be losers.

What do the Yanks call it? Trailer rubbish? I didn't raise you for that rubbish. And neither did Jules.

But she'd been there in the driveway that night, too. Caught in the bloody of middle of it.

Peter blamed Simon.

Simon blamed the Tahitian bloke.

Jules blamed herself.

But it was all about Ron.

It was all about what they had and hadn't done for him while he was busy dying in hospital. They were all guilty.

But Simon felt the guiltiest. Because Ron had sat him down in the Westmore Hotel.

He'd asked his father to speak up, get his voice above the beeping poker machines. Simon had wondered later if Ron had already known about his cancer that day. Regardless, the old bloke had laid down the law. Lazy bugger that Ron was when it came to his boys, he told him what had to happen as far as he was concerned. What would make him happy.

Dead or alive, it seemed.

But as his father had talked, swiveling in his bar chair, Simon could think of only one thing. Ron coming at him with a knife in the kitchen when he was a kid.

A memory that he didn't even trust.

He didn't know if it was real and it shook him up that he

didn't know.

He knew Ron had belted him plenty of times, but that hadn't hurt at all. Not like this fucking stupid arse memory that he wasn't even sure was one!

Whether the truth was that his dad had wanted to kill him, or Simon was just a kid that made up fairytales, either way he felt like a bogged car without a towrope. Going nowhere.

He could have asked his father about it then and there in the bar. But instead he just listened to the old man's orders and slugged down his beer.

You understand, son? You realise what's important in life?

'Can't you two see what you're doing?'

Terry turned to listen to his mum, but the other two were still a tangle of arms against the ute.

'Your father's memory...' she said.

That riled Peter.

'That's the problem! That's his problem, anyway.'

'What the fuck are you on about?' Simon shouted in Peter's face.

'Cut out the language and the yelling! I don't care what sort of father he was. It doesn't matter anymore. He's gone. And we've just got to get on with things and not worry too much about it. For goodness sake boys, I wasn't even married to him anymore.'

It was too much for Peter.

'So why the bloody Memorial Dinner?'

Jules gave an angry sigh.

'What I'm saying, Peter, is that I'd moved on...'

'Well, good on you... Brilliant.'

She puffed up her cheeks and blew out the air. Like it was full of fumes.

'Peter, just grow up.'

'Yeah, arsehole,' Simon said and bang he got a fist into Peter's ear.

Terry stepped in. He had to now or he'd get the blame for not sorting out the mess. He was the youngest, still his mum's little helper. He got between his brothers and grappled with the rams. Peter headed to his car, got it started, put the stereo on and he was off, down the street and onto Fawkner's Road.

'Well done, Simon,' Jules said, her sarcasm dripping like fat from her hotplate. 'We get him here, we finally might sort a few things out for everyone, but you go and belt him!'

'What? You said we should all move on!'

'Yes, but...it's hard. I didn't say it'd been easy.'

Simon looked to Terry but his brother gave him nothing. Simon, still in his undies. With a crumpled black heavy metal t-shirt and hair at all angles.

'Nothing's bloody easy, Mum. You weren't there... He belted us.'

'I was there, Simon, and I know. And I'm sorry about that. Why do you think I left him? And wouldn't let him see you much?'

Simon looked towards the highway.

'And he threatened to kill us.'

'Who? Peter?'

'Ron.'

'Your father?'

'Who do you think?'

'I don't know what you're talking about,' Jules said softly.

'Well, you should know.'

Simon looked again for Terry to back him up but his brother turned his palms to the pale orange Westmore night sky.

'You should know about it, Mum.'

Jules knew her son could be telling the truth. Still, she'd threatened to kill them too. Doesn't everyone do that at times when it gets too hard? It's just an empty threat.

But it probably wasn't the best thing to do. Ron used to be a scary man.

She didn't know the half of what she should about Ron. He'd had more secrets than the KGB and the FBI combined. Now she was stuck with them and her thoughts, halfway between the porch and the ute. Going nowhere.

Kerryn and Fiona were still on the porch. Kerryn rubbed at her short blonde hair as if the fight was caught there, knitted to her scalp. But she took the risk and stepped into family business. Into the shit.

'Haven't you scared the kids enough now?' she said, pointing at her youngest son in pyjamas at her knees. Her fierce eyes were on Terry, but he could tell she wanted to give Simon and Jules a rocket. Terry tried his hands-in-the-air tactic again.

'I was trying to sort it out!'

He climbed the steps to her, but she stepped back. He didn't know what to do. Luckily, one of his kids hugged him.

'It's all right mate. It's all okay.'

Simon reached through the window of his ute for a pack of cigarettes. He tapped one out and lit it. Fiona had her two kids, Ryan and Alice, in pjs wrapped to her legs. She couldn't move. Or wouldn't. Jules hugged her, but Fiona just stared. Not at Simon or the ute where he and his brother had fought. Not even at the chalky moon clouding up. She might have been looking at something on another planet. No one had a clue.

Jules let go, but kept a hand on her shoulder.

'You all right?'

She was stock-still. Eyes wide.

She's a worry, Simon thought.

She's in a trance, Terry thought. He followed the line of her stare. She was looking over the lower part of her paling fence and into her neighbour's yard at a hibiscus bush.

'Just let her be,' Simon said.

He finished his cigarette and flicked the butt to the ground. He didn't want to stamp on it in bare feet so he left it to smoulder. He walked past his wife and back inside. Ryan squawked up at her.

'What's wrong Mum? What is it?'

She didn't respond. She looked right through him at the flowers until the boy fell away.

Nothing worked. Fiona stayed on the porch until Terry, Kerryn and Jules shunted her onto the couch in the lean-to. Simon headed off in his ute. The rest of them tried to talk to Fiona but she was silent. She just kept up her staring, at the door now. It was shut, she couldn't see through it, but she was trying her best.

The rest of them got the kids to bed. It took an hour. They had to settle them all down. Especially Ryan. Alice was too young to care. She thought it was all a big laugh.

'Why were Daddy and Uncle Peter playing wrestles?'

Once the kids were down, Jules made hot chocolate. She took one to the couch and Fiona, but her daughter-in-law was asleep. Not for long. Once everyone was in bed, she went outside, straight to the neighbour's yard. She picked one of the hibiscuses from the bush and stuck it behind her ear.

Terry got up in the night for a piss. He looked out the kitchen window to see if Simon's ute was back. No such luck. But he saw Fiona on the patio, sitting on a white iron chair. She was twirling the hibiscus and staring at the bush like it was a long-lost lover.

Peter could have told them what it was all about. Or tried. He knew about Gauguin and his symbolism. But that wouldn't have helped him make sense of Fiona. Nor would it have helped anyone at Simon's place that night. They'd have laughed and said Fiona was already married.

Terry held her hand and took her to her room. He settled her beneath her doona.

'You all right, Fee?'

She didn't answer. He tried to pull the hibiscus away, but she clamped it hard to her ear.

Fiona didn't say anything to Simon for two weeks. Then she finally spoke one night. They were sitting in front of the TV. She had another red hibiscus in her hair and she gave him just one word.

'Leave.'

He'd been waiting for it.

'Why?'

A Coles ad. Crunchy carrots. Simon shook his head.

'Cos of Peter? Cos I belted him on the ear? Come on, you said yourself he never helped out with Ron...'

The show they'd been watching came back on. Two spooks on a dark street. Miami or New York. It didn't matter.

'Is it cos of the porn...? I can cut back...cut it out...'

The spooks sorted something. Planted a bug in a bus stop.

'I said I'd never scare you again and I haven't, remember? I haven't touched you.'

He had, he just didn't remember. Too drunk at the time.

The spooks were back at HQ. They had a serious talk with the big boss man in his glass office.

'Well, stuff you. I'm goin'.'

And he went. That night. North, a long way. And she stayed on the couch.

She didn't cry. Not until Ryan was in his teens and she woke one night to the neighbours yelling. She went out and the old couple were in their dressing gowns in their front yard. They were hollering at Ryan. He was in a black singlet and trying to dig up their hibiscus bush. They screamed at him to stop, but he wouldn't. The old man tried to pull the shovel out of his hands and Ryan pushed him to the ground. The old bloke hauled himself up, swearing, but Ryan pushed him down again. The police arrived and Ryan kept trying to dig the plant out. The police wrapped him in a full Nelson hold and began to drag him from the yard. He swore at the hibiscus and saw his mum coming towards him in her dressing gown. She was crying. She was coming to stop the police from taking him away. Or maybe she was going to hug him. Or whack him? He got ready for anything. But his mum walked straight past him to the hibiscus bush, knelt beside it and made sure it was safe in the ground.

17. Trevor Randall and Simon Stevenson

At daybreak old Trevor Randall pulled on his blue overalls, fitted his earmuffs and took to his house with a jackhammer. He crashed it into the wall beside the lounge room window. Cement rendering and plywood panels shattered. Neighbours showed up on the footpath in their dressing gowns. A silver-haired bloke holding a tea towel scowled at the racket, and a woman in black three-quarter pants muttered. A couple of other men came to investigate: a stay-at-home dad called Foster, carrying his toddler son, and Simon Stevenson, back from living in Queensland, and wearing his wharfie jacket.

'What the hell's going on?' Simon shouted.

Trevor turned off the hammer and put it down. He stepped carefully around the building waste and hung his earmuffs around his neck.

'Reno-varting.'

Simon shook his head at Trevor's odd way of talking. He had no idea who Trevor Randall was beyond him being a weird-arsed neighbor—who'd just this morning become a lot weirder.

Foster put his toddler on the footpath and the boy made to cross Trevor's unfenced lawn. His father pulled him back by the hood of his raincoat. Simon had to get to work.

'A bit early for all this, Trevor?' he asked, adding you wanker under his breath.

'Sorry. Finjun at four.'

Trevor flipped the muffs back on his ears and fired up his jackhammer.

Years ago, Human Services had moved Trevor Randall all the way to his house in Point Cook. It was before the suburb grew. A paper pusher had thought Trevor would be better off; closer to the warehouse job they'd given him in Laverton, and not too far from Werribee's specialist hospital. He had to go there every week for a check-up.

Trevor had got a good price for his run down three-bedroom house in the centre of Westmore. He'd lived there twenty-six years and the place had got trendy around him. Cafes instead of coffee lounges. Yoga had taken over one of the pubs. Not that Trevor had cared much about what happened in Westmore after his boy had died.

After Trevor had seen him get hit by a car.

There were six lanes of traffic out his second-storey Point Cook window, and he saw the Holden Calais that had hit his son in every stream that flowed up and down. He could have chosen for his bedroom the one that faced the sea, but he'd told the removalists to put his double bed in the one that faced the road.

The night before he'd started jackhammering, he'd watched the traffic carefully. Peak hour cars were crawling, there was a lot to analyse. A driver switched on his headlights. Laser beams, Trevor thought, and the driver blasted the car in front of him.

Away in the distance, giant power poles in the paddocks threw lines to each other in the long grass. The poles ended at the start of the McMansions. Those houses were giving birth daily and their babies were crawling across the paddocks. They'd soon make it all the way to the highway noise barrier and nuzzle up to it. For now, they were far off, the last blobs of sunset reflecting in their windows. But Trevor wasn't fooled. They were coming. New foundations were growing in cement mixers somewhere. Men in orange safety vests and hard hats were holding electronic gadgets and inspecting the timber to make frames. They were putting in orders for 150 x 38 unseasoned hardwood. Trevor thought the timber would be shaking with excitement.

The long grass out there was peaceful in the breeze. But it would soon be home to hundreds of wooden skeletons. They'd get wrapped in plaster, topped with maroon helmets and ringed by tight beige fences. There would be no trees to shade the tiny rockeries and ponds, and none of the plants would be real. Just plastic because you don't have to water plastic. And the wiring would be underground, so no more poles.

Nothing would grow out there anymore except houses.

Trevor had opened his window and his empty bedroom walls had hummed with the sound of grumbling engines. He'd tapped his hanging fern, a gift from his late son, and it had started to swing. A light had flashed on in the window of a house way off and Trevor had stared at it for a long time. Then he'd turned off his own bedside lamp and headed for the garage.

He'd fished in a milk crate full of spanners, wrenches and

screwdrivers, and found his hammer. He'd blown dust off the rubber handle and taken it to the front footpath. Under the streetlight, he'd gazed at his house; the two front bedroom windows and the lounge window above them; the dark roller door and the study window above it; his solid timber front door guarded by square pillars and two fruit trees in pots beside them. The gold '17' on his letterbox looked sturdy and stuck there for life. But Trevor had taken the claw end of his hammer and flipped off both the numbers easily. They had clanged on the footpath and he'd looked up and down the street as if he'd committed a crime. But he was safe; there were only parked cars in driveways and at the curbs. The blue glow of next-door's television and no one on the footpaths, not even the first after-dinner dog walkers. He had kicked the numbers into the drain and grinned.

Drizzle mixed with Trevor's sweat all day as he jackhammered holes in his house. By four o'clock he was cold and soaked. His canary yellow rain jacket and rubber boots hadn't helped much.

He folded up his aluminum ladder and carried the jackhammer to the porch before wandering back onto his soggy lawn. He inspected his work; apart from the windows, the entire lower part of the front wall was gone. He could see his furniture through the timber frame. The royal blue lounge suite and the entertainment unit. Beyond that, the fridge, the kitchen bench and the cupboards.

A smaller crowd than the morning's was on the footpath.

'You'll be cold tonight,' Foster laughed, pushing back his rain-flecked hair, and Trevor nodded. Simon threw his cigarette on the footpath. He crushed it out and shook his head. Everyone left for dinners and television.

Trevor started work at six the next morning and kept at it until seven at night. He turned the house into a timber skeleton. Apart from the furniture, only the charcoal roof and the carpet were left. Everyone could see Trevor's large photos of his son, leaning against the lounge's timber frame. A toy lamb from when the boy was little sat on a single bed in the spare room.

Trevor put on his work beanie and a Bluey jacket. He cooked himself scrambled eggs with fried tomatoes and, like a zoo exhibit, ate them at his dinner table. The neighbours were out the front.

'We should call the cops,' Simon said.

'And say what?' Foster asked. 'Our neighbour's chopped his house down? It's not against the law. I don't think.'

'It's pretty bloody stupid,' Simon glared.

'I agree,' said a woman called Izobel, scratching at the sleeve of her red puffer jacket. An African woman, Samanya, nodded along.

'What will the children think?'

That silenced everyone. What kind of example was Trevor setting? He was in his upstairs bedroom now, stripping off his overalls and jacket. And turning on his shower. The neighbours covered their kids' eyes and shouted at Trevor. Steam fogged the glass walls of his shower recess and the neighbours dispersed.

Trevor got home from work and found a divvy van parked at the front of his house. He got out of his mini and met the police on his lawn. The policewoman stared at what was left of 17 Doveton Close.

'Trevor Randall?'

He nodded.

'We've had a report of indecent exposure. Would it be possible...'

She shook her head and couldn't finish. Her partner chipped in.

'...to cover up in the shower mate?'

Trevor nodded. The cops didn't move. The policeman craned his head at the ensuite toilet, then looked at the bathroom under the stairs.

'Cover up everywhere, all right?'

The cops told Trevor they'd be back.

'You can't do this, mate. You've got to get a permit.'

Later, Trevor sat on his couch and kicked off his boots. He turned on his television. He showered as usual, poured shampoo on his hand and rubbed it through his hair.

From where they'd gathered in Foster's lounge room, his neighbours watched The Trevor Show. Simon closed the blinds.

'So. Cops did nothing.'

Simon sat at the table with the others.

'*We've* got to do something.'

He pointed at Izobel's two pyjamed boys watching *Who Wants to be a Millionaire?* in the lounge.

'They shouldn't be exposed to this kind of thing. We're not

living in bloody Fitzroy.'

That got heads nodding. Samanya finished sipping her herbal tea.

'Someone must speak to him,' she said.

'Not me, he's nuts,' Izobel laughed.

'I'll talk to him,' Foster said, but Simon wouldn't have it.

'Forget it. I'll do it.'

He offered Foster a plate of his own chocolate biscuits, but Foster waved them away.

'I'll do it, Simon. I'll talk to him. I live the closest.'

'Mate, we don't know what he'll do. I'll handle it.'

Simon sat at his computer monitor, drinking mineral water. He still couldn't find anything in any real estate document about dismantling houses. He went to his study window. He waited for Trevor Randall's mini to pass but it didn't.

'Might be at the pub,' he told the huge Darth Vader doll on his desk.

Simon decided to take a stroll to Trevor's, just in case his neighbor had been off work sick. Which would be no surprise, given the cold.

He found a group of kids in Trevor's house and wanted to shoo them out. Cheeky bastards; Trevor might be a nuff nuff but that's no reason to invade a man's privacy. When he got closer he saw the kids were riding skateboards and BMXs through an empty house.

There was nothing. No couches, beds, TVs or furniture to get in their way. Even the lounge and hall carpet was gone. And no Trevor Randall. The only thing left was the fern, hanging from the wood frame at the back beside a window with no glass in it.

Simon watched the kids. They did their tricks and cackled, slouched in corners and smoked. There were more kids than he'd ever seen in the neighbourhood. Might've been a gang. And the crazy thing about them was, apart from the rub of their bike tyres and the rattle of their skateboard wheels, they were quiet. Even, you'd have to say it, well behaved.

Simon heard Foster's door open and he headed for home.

He could never say what it was that had made him get out of bed later that night. He thought he'd had a dream. But when he looked back, he wasn't sure if he woke at all.

Simon's father was still alive. Standing over him in the kitchen at their house in Corumbul. Simon had never left the breakfast table. He was a man, not a kid. But Ron's yelling was still scaring him. He could smell his father. Fresh showered with a whiff of apple shampoo. Roaring and disappearing now into the bedroom wall of Simon's Point Cook house until he was just a speck.

Simon put on his red dressing gown and black slippers. But he didn't own any. He dragged himself to the front door. By the time he got to Trevor's front lawn he was asking himself what the hell he was doing: it was bloody freezing! He wouldn't have been surprised to see snow on the ground. There was a strange whiteness to the night. The moon, he thought, sprinkling leftovers for the sheep. But he couldn't see the moon and there were no sheep. He was thinking of Corumbul. Acres of green hills.

He wished he'd never left. And that he'd never fought with his brother in his driveway and never left his wife. He wanted to collapse on the lawn in sadness, but he kept on. He crept around Trevor's empty house. The gang of kids was gone, but there were three caps, a large, a medium and a small, lying on the concrete. They made him smile then cry. Over and over, his mouth going up and down. He couldn't stop it.

Upstairs, all his neighbours were in Trevor's bedroom. Everyone nodding at each other and talking about the cold. No one asked anyone else what they were doing there. Foster swung Trevor's fern back and forward like a metronome. They all watched it tick. Then they turned and looked at hundreds of shapes in the paddock across the highway.

'House frames?' Simon asked, but Foster shook his head. Simon looked closer and shivered like a baby in a cold bath. There were skeletons with faces out there.

All of them Ron's.

'Don't worry son,' he heard his father say. But it didn't do any good. Simon shivered until his skin fell from his bones.

18. Sheree Stevenson

She is sparkling in her ruin. She is a dirty diamond. She's the dirt floor in the kitchen of her family's Wimmera farmhouse. They grew up there, she and Ron and Stan and Ken. For a while. Until the orphanages.

She's a baked custard tart, then and now, that's been stepped on. She still tastes good.

Don't imagine any different!

What the rest of them don't know won't hurt them. And they don't know how to be anything. So it doesn't matter what they think, does it?

Not really.

But she knows her redeemer lives. The handsome bloke looked her in the eye. Someone big and bright looked at her. She's not the same. Something hovered then lit up in her. Dead or gone or alive or here.

She was a bit different.

She can say that. She can say what she wants now.

They're praying for her and bringing her casseroles. All the church people. Good souls. One wearing a long, white dress. Washing Sheree's dishes. She can see her from the lounge. The woman with the dishes has got everything but the halo.

The woman in the white dress.

Sheree's dress is driving her crazy. She wants to fling it up and run round the lounge with it over her head. Like a halo, that'd be funny!

She loves casserole.

And look, out the lounge room window: her nephews. The sweet little things. The three of them on the swing she made. Those cotton shorts they're wearing, the scoops in the sides. And their hair, cut straight across.

Ron took Peter to the barber. The boy told her. Ron scared the poor little soul! He put a plastic ear in his hand and said, 'It's mine! The barber missed my hair and cut me instead!'

The barber in his white apron that glowed blue from the sterilizer.

He cut off Ron's ear! Snip, just like that.

No, he didn't.

But Ron's got ears, hasn't he? He's got ears to hear. Ha, ha, ha. Who's the mad one? Cross your heart and hope you died.

She knows her redeemer lives. There's a puddle of blood someone left behind on the kitchen floor, shaped like a flower.

It's not Ron's fault, really. He couldn't speak when he needed to. Say what he needed to say to be a man.

You're just a bunch of silly women, he'd say.

But he couldn't be a man like Sheree's a woman.

One thing or another. Here or there, up or down, alive or dead.

Her little nephews. Swing, swing, back and forth. Now Peter's on the see-saw, by himself, up and down, lifting it with his legs, up and down.

Is he crying?

See-saw, Marjorie Door. That's it, isn't it? That's what you say, that's what you sing?

Sheree's dancing under her bed covers. Grey blankets. Nurses watching. White uniforms. No casseroles. Where's her beanbag? Where is the woman doing her dishes? Where's Jules? Come here, someone. The tie-dye angel in the morning light is freezing.

She can't stop dancing. Or the flowers from becoming her skin. Oh, the sweet music of voices that must be planets and stars humming the news of the universe being born. She knows her redeemer lives. Someone lives. Someone nearby. Red and green lights.

And all that stink and crying.

All the urine running down the sides of the mountain. Or was that the Promised Land, gone off like stale milk? She doesn't know, but something keeps her, and keeps her safe.

There's Ron. On a see-saw, Marjorie Door, the cat's got his tongue. Up and down, round and round he goes. Little Ronnie. His father's son.

There are no play things where they live with the dirt floor and the custard tarts, but Ron's on a see-saw. At the farm at Laharum. Sheree's in the kitchen. Where she always was. Sitting in her highchair. She's never left. And there's Ron, sitting in his chair at the kitchen table. Like he always did. He's not moving and Sheree can smell him.

Her brother.

How old is he, seven? He's pissed his pants.

He's sitting in his chair. He can't move.

He never has. He's always sat there, his whole life.

But he's outside on the see-saw. Up, down, turn around, Marjorie door, and the dish ran away with the spoons. And the knives. And Ron and Sheree's father.

The floor's dirt. But there's no custard tart, just cabbage all over the kitchen. And blood. In Sheree's hair and on Ron's face. It came pelting out of the bowl when their mother flew across the table. Cabbage and blood.

A baby emu came in the house once. They can't fly.

They had a baby emu, but they never had a see-saw. She's as sure of that as she is that her redeemer lives. Sheree's eyes have seen the glory of the Big Daddy O and he's coming down with a grin and a tongue made of swords and fists made of fire. And he loves her. Shut up, he does.

She is the dust in her own eye. She is the mountain that has pulled itself out of the sea. She is the snake eating itself inside an apple. She is the rainbow that's had its colours spat onto her skirt. She is the living God's cousin, nephew and niece.

She is Ron's sister. *Sister Sheree?* Get her to a nunnery? Get her to an asylum!?

He can't hear her, can he? He doesn't even know where tomorrow or Sheree is. She could laugh all night now that it's day and he doesn't know where the screaming's coming from.

But don't worry. She'll put in a good word for Ron. She can see the truth. And the truth has fangs.

Ron put her here. But she's not anymore. She was there, in Tonvale, but she never, *ever* was.

They played tennis against the back wall while their father roared at their mother. Their father's voice sizzled and spat, but that was the barbecue, wasn't it? Their father said he was sorry? Sheree can't see the sun anymore; it's so bright here. So many lights, so much buzzing.

Look at the table, their mum lying on it: her nose bleeding, her face disappearing. The blood on her, the blood on Ron and Sheree. Their father's fist, flying; free of the house, free of his children. Their father, running down the dirt road, trees bending to watch; they're screaming, he's screaming; he's killed his wife.

He's killed her, Ron.

He didn't mean it. But he did.

She didn't mean to go.

They can't bring her round. There was no ambulance. The neighbours can't bring her round, Ron. She's gone.

Sheree's stuck in her high chair, how can she help?

Ron could have helped before the neighbours came. But Ron couldn't move.

He was a knife without a blade. Useless.

Can't cut it. Ha, ha.

Ron's no good now. No good for anything. Alive or dead.

What your daddy did to you, Ronny boy, no one will find out. No one will ever know because you won't tell and neither will I.

I won't tell, if you won't tell, your daddy said too.

And now that's all we know.

Stop running, Ron. Marjorie Door will get you! Stop running, stop flying, stop screaming, stop buzzing. Get out of here and get away.

Love your boys. Even now, dead as you are, hover, Ron, and love them.

Sheree loves you Ron, you hateful bastard. You put her here and now she's never coming out but she knows her redeemer lives because he's flying the sky in a cross-shaped ship.

And he loves her. Someone loves her.

Can you hear the whizz and roar of motors made of muscle? Can you see the clouds breaking and the sky turning to fire?

Sheree can see it all, Ron.

She can see everything and darkness. She can see you.

19. Peter Stevenson

Tomorrow night Peter will finally take Celia, his wife of three years, who is now pregnant, to meet his mother and the rest of his family. But tonight he'll go fishing. By himself. A stupid idea, really. He's never been fishing by himself. He doesn't know what to do. He checks another angling app on his phone.

'Looking up places to go for dinner?'

'I'm going fishing.'

They're staying in a country cottage not far from Westmore. Peter's idea. A relaxing break before the family introduction stroke reunion stroke God knows what else. There's a river five minutes walk across a paddock. Short grass, ornamental. No cows or sheep or dung. Farm tourism.

'Going by yourself, honey? I'll come.'

'No, I need a bit of time out.'

'But we've just had a lot of time out...'

Three months ago Peter had read her diary and discovered past lovers he'd known nothing about. That he shouldn't have cared about. But he did care about them. He got obsessed and pissed off. Daily.

They had separated. Celia had wanted some time apart to see if that arrangement needed to become permanent.

My diary's not your business, Peter. Why did you do it? Things were going so well. Why do you have to start fights? You undermine us. You do it all the time. And, God, you talk about your brothers having bad tempers! Why do you do things like this?

Because, Peter's hastily acquired relationship counselor told him, he was a self-sabotager.

'When things are going well, you can't trust them to keep going well.'

His counselor was plump and she smiled a lot. Her room smelt of sandalwood essence.

'Your family relationships, your moving towns, your first marriage—whenever things were going well they fell to pieces, didn't they? So this marriage to Celia, the best relationship you've had, you say, will fall to pieces too? Won't it? That's what you think.'

Peter nodded. But he wasn't sure. She went on.

'So you have to get in first, don't you? Peter, you have to stop getting in first.'

'How?'

'You have to recognise what you're doing.'

Peter was picking the couch threads. He stopped.

'You have to capture the moment,' she smiled, 'when you're about to do something like pick up Celia's diary or start an argument. See the problem. Freeze it. Change it.'

See it, freeze it?

'How?'

The counselor leant forward. Her gold watch was too bulky. And she didn't have a single motivational poster in her room.

'By self-soothing. You'll lose your anxiety. I think meditation can help.'

Peter understood that he had to pull it together quickly or Celia would leave him for good. Cold prickles emerged on his forehead.

'How can I sort through...all the reasons... I'd be here for years...'

But he wasn't. Celia had come back soon after that session. His email had convinced her. He was okay, he'd written, about having a baby with her; the son they'd watched roll and squiggle in an ultrasound image a few weeks before. And he was okay, too, about introducing her to his family. So Peter had ended the counselling sessions, against the counsellor's advice.

He put his phone away now and its diagrams of paternoster rigs.

'It's okay,' he told Celia. 'I just want to go fishing. Nothing else. No stress. I'll meditate, too. I promise.'

'All right. I'll go and buy some pasta or something. Eat later?'

She kissed his head where his hair was thinning.

'We'll eat fish,' he said.

She laughed.

'We'll eat pasta!'

Peter carried his fishing rod, bucket and eco shopping bag of tackle across the paddock. The sun was low. The gum trees and banksia bushes hiding the river were mauve, and the grass leading towards them was a carpet. He should stop this ridiculous fishing mission, take his paints from the cottage and set up his easel. All very van Gogh. Then he remembered the Dutchman's demise. And pressed on.

The river was idyllic; the water shone and the dragonflies

were industrious. The reeds on the opposite bank were golden in the lazy sun. There came a *twip-twip* of birds he hadn't heard since he was a kid. They sounded fresh. Just made. He wanted to shout for joy across the river. What a world!

But he didn't. Because he didn't believe in the world. Not exactly.

There was something else.

He didn't know what it was, but this river and its birds and perfect dragonflies weren't everything. There was more, and it shone behind the shine of things.

He'd once believed in UFOs. Now he believed in things he understood even less.

His dead father had been closer by his side this past year than when he was alive. Ron had shushed him, even helped him freeze those moments when he was all set to self-sabotage. Peter wouldn't have believed it was his father's voice unless he'd heard it. In his head and in his gut, somehow. Peter felt like his dead father had become his teacher. Helping him to settle, helping him to, it had to be said, feel loved. But his old man had never been that smart or bold or compassionate. So maybe it was just Peter's own voice in his head.

Whomever it was sounded like the best version of his father combined with the best version of himself. And that would do for an explanation.

Peter hauled his meandering mind back to its surroundings. The actual world. The river was beautiful. It flowed regardless of rocks and fallen trees trying to block it. Tonight, the river and its smooth banks were enough of everything that was good.

Peter took the rod in his hands and skimmed his phone screen for instructions. The paternoster took a lot of work; he had to create two dropper knots for the hooks then seal them off so that the sinker was below them. He wasn't sure if he got it right. And he wondered if it would be worth it. If there were fish in this river, wouldn't there also be empty stubbies, abandoned fishing line and floaters all over the banks?

He threaded worms on both hooks. A memory or a voice, he didn't care which, reminded him how to do it. His life was now all about getting things done. And he would soon know enough about fishing to take his next child with him. If not, he would at least make sure he got started with his new boy or girl better than he had with his seven-year-old, Will. Peter could already sense his first child might regard him as useless. Like Simon's boy Ryan considered his old man. He felt for Simon, wondered where he was. Peter remembered his last phone chat with his mum.

'You boys!' she'd said. 'You find trouble wherever you can. And if you can't, you make it up!'

Then, as usual, she'd gone on about all the other Stevenson blokes. Peter reckoned she talked about all the others because she'd never been able to get a bloody thing out of her husband. What made him tick. Or turn off. Whatever it was that she couldn't find out, that's what made her obsess about her family. Why hadn't he understood that before?

Because you were too far buried up your own arse.

Peter laughed as he cast his line with a plop into the gentle creek.

Tell me that wasn't *Ron's voice!* he thought.

All those wedding photos in his mum's house and everyone else's. All that time framing and staring at what she considered her boys' best days. Despite her own divorce. And now she had a new daughter-in-law and another grandson on the way, a fresh start for her stories.

Peter looked along the banks for a stick to rest his fishing rod in. Maybe he shouldn't go and visit Jules tomorrow. Maybe he'd be best to sit here and fish. Let the family take care of itself.

He found a vee-shaped stick and shoved it into the moist earth. He rested his rod in it then sat on a smooth rock that seemed set there for him. A perfect distance from the river. His line stretched straight into the water and the birds talked business. The river lapped the banks while reeds swayed in the gentlest of breezes. A pair of swallows skimmed the surface of the river and scattered the dragonflies. Peter wound his line in. Part of it had tangled behind the reel. He freed it and recast. The line pulled a little as it sailed through the air and plonked. He wound it straight but more line tangled again behind the reel.

Shit.

Since he and Celia had reunited, Peter had felt the need to start an argument every hour. Because things were so good between them. And he knew he'd want to start an argument when he got back to the cottage tonight. He'd have to hang on and listen to his father or himself and try to freeze another whole bunch of moments.

When the hell was it going to stop?

He had to go back to the counselor. But then Celia would

worry, wouldn't she? And they'd argue anyway.

His line was taut. But there were no bites. There were no fish here. Never would be.

He could be here for years. On these banks. Fishing and trying to sort out the mess he was in before he made a mess of his marriage. Another one.

Again and again. Casting and re-casting.

There was a rustle in the trees behind him. He ignored it for as long as he could. But it kept coming. He gave up pretending it wasn't happening and hunted in the trees for whatever it was. But the noise stopped. He'd almost known it would. On his way out, he jagged his leg on a protruding branch. It hurt. He lashed out at the tree with his boot.

No one in the trees. Nothing to see, anyway.

He sat back on his rock with his line. There was another rustle but he didn't turn around. A fish jumped from the river. A flash and it was gone.

'Wow.'

A trout. It had to be. Did they jump? Peter knew how hard they were to catch. He'd heard his father talk them up. He knew he had no chance. And he liked it that way. Still, he thought, it was time to check his bait.

He wound his line in. It was a mighty effort. It had become entangled, he was sure, beneath a submerged log. A fish had probably pulled it there. That jumping fish, for sure. When he finally retrieved his line, the paternoster he'd created so pains-takingly was a circle of hell. There was fishing line looped over the empty hooks, and sinkers and swivels were tangled and embroiled in the mess. It looked like the busy part of a cyclone.

He picked at the tangle, but every pull on the line tightened it. There was no sign of a fish. No sign of anything. The birds were going home and the river was darkening.

He couldn't untangle his rig. Celia would be back by now, probably already cooking. He gave another pull on the line and the knot firmed even more. The sun was giving its last wink to the day. There surely wasn't enough time, for a man of his skill level, to build a new rig and start fishing again before nightfall. By then the trout would be gone and the eels would have arrived.

But Peter took a fishing knife from his bag and cut his line. He let the whirlwind fall to the moist riverbank. He let out a cry. And, by the light from his phone, he relaxed into the slow and careful work of building a new paternoster.

20. Peter, Simon, Terry and Ron Stevenson

His father would have called it a turn up for the books. Because it was Peter who rang his brothers and got them organised to go on The Famous Fishing Trip.

It had taken Peter years to pick up the phone, but only seconds to put it down.

'Simon?'

'Yeah?'

'It's Peter.'

Silence. 'What do you want?'

'To stop all the crap.'

'What crap?'

'You know.'

Long silence. 'Yeah, well...'

More silence. Too much for Peter to deal with. He spat out his idea.

'Let's go on Ron's Famous Fishing Trip.'

Silence of another, deeper kind. Years' worth. Then laughter.

'All right!'

Peter rang Terry.

'Do you want to go on the old man's Famous Fishing Trip? With me and Simon?'

Short silence. Younger sibling length.

'Sounds a plan. Count me in.'

Ron would have loved it. His boys. Being no nonsense men.

Well, knock me over with a feather and whip me stupid with it!

'You sure you're okay to go on this trip, Tangles?'

They were in Simon's garage at Point Cook, packing up the fishing gear. Ron had given Peter the nickname Tangles when he was young. Because that's all he could do with his rod and reel.

'I've been practicing. I'll catch more than both of you.'

Simon had just told Peter that he'd worked fishing boats the length of the east coast. His brother must be joking. Terry thought so.

'If we were trying to catch paint, you'd be fine,' he said.

Simon put the last of the stubbies into the esky.

'Ron's Famous Fishing Trip, hey? Who'd have thought?'

His sons had named the trip years ago. When they saw him for Christmas, Ron would always promise to take them on a fishing trip. But he never got organised. Simon called him a gunner.

'Gunna go here, gunna go there, Ron.'

But their father did pack the gear once, even if he didn't make the phone calls. That was a few days before he was diagnosed with cancer. He was gunna take them before that, too. When Peter finished his degree and Simon got into trade school. Ron had been saying he was gunna take them since Terry left high school. Got booted out, actually; Terry had dropped his shorts on the diving board in the middle of the swimming sports carnival. A gold medal performance, Ron had called it. Then he'd cut his youngest son's pocket money for six months. But it was all beside the point: Ron never took them.

But now they were going.

They carried gear to Peter's silver Subaru wagon parked in the driveway. Peter had organized the trip so he thought it was only right to take his car.

'It's for lezzos,' Simon whispered, and Peter said, 'Don't start'. Terry told them both to take it easy.

'We haven't even got in the car yet!' he said and plonked the esky in the backseat. He hopped in with it, Simon climbed in the passenger seat and Peter got them quick smart up the road. Before any of them could change their minds.

Peter had planned out weeks before where they were going to camp: up at Ron's home patch. Laharum way. Lake Wartook near McKenzie Falls. Where the family and all its ghosts had lived.

In the middle of the night, Peter's feet were cold. He was standing on the concrete out front of the Wartook Fisherman's Campground toilet block. He could have just pissed near the tent, but he didn't want to risk waking his brothers. He wanted everything to go smoothly and waking them up would only cause trouble. Or they'd poke their heads out of the tent and start up talk of dick sizes or something stupid. Peter watched his penis now, doing what it had to do, and saw again why he hated them raising the topic.

Outside the loos, the array of stars he never saw from his Melbourne apartment rooted him to the spot. He never grew tired of the depths of the sky. He remembered the doco he'd watched just days before, all about the insane distances between stars. Still, he decided to get as close as he could to them; he walked past the shadow of the new Lake Wartook map sign and found himself on the concrete walkway. He wandered near the gushing gullet slipway where the water drained in and out of the lake. Where Ron was fishing.

Best time for eels.

Peter crept towards him.

'Dad?'

'Don't look so bloody surprised.'

Peter's breath came in gasps and he stepped back.

'Don't bugger off, son. Look, I'm sick of this bullshit I don't know where I am. Or what I'm doing.'

Peter tried to convince himself he was dreaming, despite the sheer physicality of his surroundings; the chill on his skin and his steamy breath in the cold air. There was no steam coming out of his father's mouth.

'I wasn't that useless. I don't deserve this, do I? What was I supposed to do? You can only work with what you've got. And now, mate, I want whatever's coming to me. Because it's got to be better than this. Even if it's worse!'

Ron laughed and Peter smiled.

It's one of those waking dreams, Peter told himself. It has to be.

Ron put his rod down. He held out his hand for Peter to shake and his son did, surprised that Ron's hand felt solid and warm.

'I want to go, son.' He wanted out of wherever he was, but he couldn't move, let alone disappear. Peter saw something above his father's head. A glow. He pointed, but Ron couldn't turn to look, no matter how hard he tried.

Then Peter was in the tent, on top of his sleeping bag and wide awake.

The next night, they were in their sleeping bags and Terry was already snoring when Simon decided he wanted to chat.

'Pete?'

'Yeah?'

'You awake?'

They'd eaten the brown trout Simon and Terry had caught. Peter's agent had once taken him to two of Australia's best seafood restaurants, but tonight's trout was the best fish Peter had ever eaten. He hadn't told his brothers. He knew he should have.

'No, I'm not awake Simon.'

Simon shuffled in his sleeping bag.

'You remember when the old man used to belt us?'

'Of course,' Peter said impatiently.

The pair went silent for a while. Peter wondered if he might take the risk and tell Simon about his waking dream.

I belted you, heaps, yeah, and it was stupid. But I'd never have hurt you blokes with that knife! Never. And, anyway, there you are! Not stabbed or killed. Farting and breathing! The Famous Fishing Trip, hey?

Peter shut his father up by thinking of Dostoyevsky. When the author was a prisoner and a firing squad was ready to execute him. How Dostoyevsky had been taken off death row at the last second. But that firing squad had followed him throughout his life. The deep and painful echo of shots that hadn't been fired.

'Pete?'

'What?'

'Sorry about the punch-up.'

'Which one?'

'You know.'

'Yep. So am I.'

Peter thought he should definitely tell Simon about his waking dream. But his brother let off a huge fart.

'Classy.'

'Fuck off. Better out than in.'

'I need to sleep. I'll cook eggs in the morning,' Peter yawned.

'I'll flop my cock in for the sausage.'

Silence. Simon thought, *Fuck, he's gunna get all shitty. This fishing trip's a fuck up. And I can't get anything right.*

'That'll be useless,' Peter said. 'We've got to feed the three of us.'

Terry found himself the next afternoon walking around in circles. They'd finished fishing in their tinny and dragged it back to shore. There was mud all up the sides of it and Peter washed it down. Simon was impressed.

'Nice job.'

'Want me to do your bum?'

He and Simon got the campfire sorted and Terry went off on a bush walk. He clomped into the scrubby forest, the smell of wattle and eucalyptus making him think of work. He walked faster. He walked and half jogged, then walked again. Around and around, thinking about Tom, the bloke who'd got flamed in his dad's abandoned FJ. Terry had set up the planned burn, he'd included the car on his ledger, but not its rightful owner. Terry couldn't have saved him. No way. All the Parks Vic staff and CFA members said, *Tez, he'd have listened to you,* but Terry didn't think they knew him very well. Because Tom's death was on his own hands and Terry wasn't having any of it. But at home in bed next to his wife's gentle breathing, he couldn't stop thinking that FJ on fire. And now it was getting into his days, his days off, and even his fishing trips.

He walked around and around.

Terry thought of Ron. And how he had never got the chance to take away even a bit of his old man's pain. That useless joint he'd rolled for him. But at least, Dad, he thought, I stopped your other sons from bashing each other to death! Surely that's a good effort?

Terry walked in tighter and tighter circles. In the long grass, into a clearing. He marched around until the sky went orange then violet. By the time he'd finished and headed back to the campsite, he'd left a pattern in the grass. If he'd turned to look from his vantage point, he'd have seen it looked like a poorly formed crop circle. If Simon had seen it, say from the top of a tree, he might have called it some kind of Pete-style art. If Peter had been in the same tree, he'd have held on tight to stop from falling in shock at the sight of the old man fishing.

On the last night of the Famous Fishing Trip, the brothers sat around a bonfire and had a cook up. Peter read a book on education. He'd decided to increase his teaching load. A little less painting, a little more secure income. That was being a better dad, wasn't it? Simon piss-farted around, putting a stick in the fire that was grilling the sausages. Terry made sure the tin-foiled spuds got plenty of coals on them and baked up properly. Like Ron had n't taught him but should have. He flipped one with some tongs, felt the potato's guts, but it was still hard.

Remember when? Simon thought, but that's where he stopped. Peter had said on the first night that they should try to forget the past. That sounded easy. And Simon had tried. He'd done his best. So he kept quiet now and watched the end of his twig burn.

At the start of the trip, Terry had wanted to tell Peter to stop acting like a big brother. Just for once. Just be a bloke, you know, like you should. The punch-up was ages ago and, one way or another, it probably needed to happen. But Peter had quickly laid off the big brother routine and they'd all been on their best behavior. So Terry hadn't needed to keep the peace because they already had it. Which had left him alone with his thoughts and he was sick of them.

Peter smelt the sausages. Another good meal. Every bit of food had tasted delicious on this trip. He felt almost ready now to tell his brothers he'd seen Ron the other night. In a waking dream or whatever it was. But he checked himself. He'd sound like an idiot. He didn't know, anyway, what seeing Ron was all about. All he knew was his hand still felt strangely warm from his father's touch.

Peter thought of primary school and flowers down a laneway. His father's hand on his all the way to school. One morning. One beautiful morning. He remembered Ron and Jules in the kitchen on other mornings, holding each other tight in their dressing gowns. Before their fighting started up and everything became what it was. Then Peter saw a light on the other side of the lake.

'What's that?'

Simon looked up from his burning stick.

'Car?'

'Don't think so. Too bright.'

'Might be a roo spotty,' Terry said. His brothers nodded. Then the light hovered above the tree line. None of them joked. They sat still and the light shimmered. It looked like a kid's night lamp. Blue then soft pink then blue again. Like it didn't know if it was for a boy or a girl.

'Let's go and check it out,' Peter almost whispered.

Simon hissed through his teeth and shook his head.

'Fuck off, Pete. Could be an army probe thing.'

'Well, who's the hard man?'

'Fuck off.'

'You said that already.'

'You got the keys?' Terry asked.

'Quicker in the boat.'

'Fuck. Right. *Off!* What if it shoots at us? We'll drown.'

'What do you think it is, Simon? An alien? It's probably a weather balloon or something,' Peter said, but hoped it wasn't.

It was Simon's boat but he refused to skipper; he didn't want to be the one who led them into trouble. Peter and Terry's wives—not to mention Jules—would give him hell for getting his idiot brothers into the shit. So Peter shunted the tinny steadily across the glassy lake. Until the engine stopped.

'Thank Christ,' Simon said. 'Now let's go back.'

'What did I do to it?' Peter said, embarrassed. Terry flipped the cap and looked inside the motor.

'Plenty of juice,' Terry said. He checked around the rest of the engine. 'Nothing wrong with it.'

Simon took off his beanie.

'It's that fucken light, that's what did it! Now we're all fucked.'

The light disappeared and the brothers shivered even though it hadn't got any colder. There was no wind, not a breath. They were all quiet and Ron wanted to scream at them.

I'm in the boat with you, idiots! Look, here I am!

Ron pulled at the coat or whatever it was he was wearing. But his sons just sat and looked at each other.

Terry thought suddenly of a night he'd dreamt Ron was hanging on a cross. Simon thought about how he'd seen skeleton bodies in a paddock, all with Ron's head on them. And with his cold hand, Peter felt his warm one.

But none of them said a word.

And then it came up in all of them, Ron included, it came up like wind that gets a bonfire's flames roaring. They were three little boys at a kitchen table and Ron looking out from a pink and blue mist. The lake was a massive tear drop that their tinny was floating in. Ron could see all the eels and trout beneath it, bright as day. His boys had no idea the goldmine they were sitting on in the dark. The pink and blue light on the tree line darted so quickly Simon fell back in surprise. Into the water, and he dragged Terry down with him. The boat rocked, Peter fell in too and the eels and trout scattered.

'We're drowning,' Simon spluttered as they panicked and tangled up in each others' limbs. Then they realised they were in three-feet of water.

'What a bunch of idiots,' Simon laughed.

They all stood and laughed together. Big and hearty, across the lake, into the bush, all through the district. Laughed loud enough to wake the dead and get them up and dancing.

Their laughter was an almighty howl in Ron's ears. And he was gone, out of there and out of the mist, thank Christ or the Devil or Mars. He didn't see his three soaking sons push their boat ashore and give each other the quickest of embraces. But they did it. Ron didn't see it, but he felt it with them. Like a bite. Like a bite on the end of a great fishing line being reeled in forever.

Acknowledgements

A family of sorts has come together to make this book a reality. I want to thank Anna Solding and MidnightSun Publishing for having the courage to bring it into the world, Tony Birch for barracking for me and my work for many years, and Jo Bowers, Hannah, Hugo and Ryland Mitchell for living with me through the writing of this book, and so much more. A big thanks to Carol and Bob too.

Many other people have believed in me and my work, and helped me get this project into book form. Thanks to my PhD supervisors over the journey: Lucy Sussex, Damien Barlow, David Tacey and Catherine Padmore. Thank you Helen Garner for your indefatigable support and encouragement, and to Chris Flynn for your early enthusiasm for what *We. Are. Family.* could be. Thanks Kevin Brophy for being a stalwart in defence, and Paul Wiegard for sailing all kinds of choppy waters (especially those off Fairhaven Beach). Thanks to Chris Grierson for comments on an early draft, and Harriet McKnight and Lynette Washington for your careful editing of separate drafts of this manuscript. A big thanks to Rebekah Clarkson for being a cheer squad leader for works of fiction that refuse easy definition and challenge comfortable sensibilities.

Thanks also to my students of the past decade, many of whom have been my teachers.

Sections of *We. Are. Family.* have been published, in different forms, as stories in the following journals:

1. The Stevensons—published as 'A Mansion on the Hill', *New Australian Stories 2006* (Scribe) and short-listed in the 2007 Hal Porter Short Story Prize;

6. Peter and Ron Stevenson—as 'Sighting' in *The Sleepers Almanac* No. 8, 2013;

7. Terry Stevenson—as 'Stick With What You Know' in *Meanjin*, No. 2, Winter, 2009;

9. Trevor Randall—as 'The Guard' in *Readings and Writings: Forty Years in Books* (Readings Books), 2009 and winner of the 2005 Eastern Regional Libraries National Short Story Competition as 'Safety Agenda Item 3A'; and

12. Terry Stevenson—as 'The Long Way' in *Overland* 203, Winter, 2011.

Thanks to all the editors and judges.

Photo: Virginia Cummins

Paul Mitchell's wry and moving considerations of society's undercurrents chronicle an unsettlingly recognisable Australia. His three poetry collections have received national prizes and wide acclaim, and his short story collection *Dodging the Bull* was included in the 2008 *The Age* Summer Read program. He is also a playwright, screenwriter and essayist. Mitchell's varied oeuvre explores the beauty in the seemingly mundane, the troubled history of Australian masculinity, and finds spirituality in the murky depths of life. He has continued this exploration with his sensitive and rugged first novel, *We. Are. Family.*

MidnightSun Publishing

We are a small, independent publisher based in Adelaide, South Australia. Since publishing our first novel, Anna Solding's *The Hum of Concrete* in 2012, MidnightSun has gone from strength to strength.

We create books that are beautifully produced, unusual, sexy, funny and poignant. Books that challenge, excite, enrage and overwhelm. When readers tell us they have lost themselves in our stories, we rejoice in a job well done.

MidnightSun Publishing aims to reach new readers every year by consistently publishing excellent books. Welcome to the family!

midnightsunpublishing.com

MidnightSun *Publishing Brilliance*

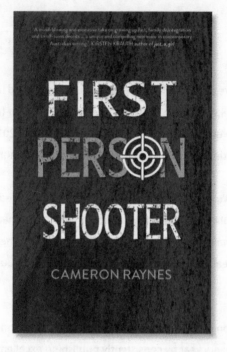

Also available from MidnightSun Publishing

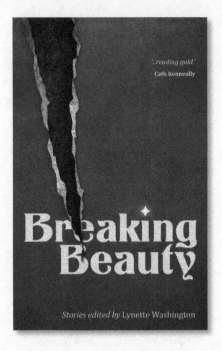

'The best of the writers in this collection take us outside our comfortable selves, to let us experience the world through sensibilities that are strange to us, even alien.'

J.M. Coetzee, Nobel laureate

MidnightSun

www.midnightsunpublishing.com

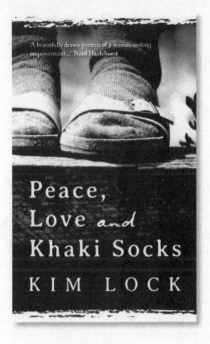

Also available from MidnightSun Publishing

MidnightSun

www.midnightsunpublishing.com